# Guardian Angels

## Guardian Series, Book 1

Andrew P. Weston

**Pagan Writers Press**

Houston, Texas

Library of Congress Catalog Number: 2012947549

ISBN: 978-1-938397-29-5

Published by Pagan Writers Press, Houston


Edited by Rosa Sophia
Cover by Christie A. C. Gucker
Typeset by Angelique Mroczka


Printed in the United States of America

# Guardian Angel

*A guardian spirit—a person who
performs an act of kindness in crucial times*

*One who protects and safeguards*

# Contents

# Acknowledgements

With this, my first major release, I must take the opportunity to mention a number of very special people.

I formulated the Guardian concept over many years spent in the military and the police service, witnessing first-hand the tragedy and suffering that can so easily intrude into our everyday lives. Sadly, because of the hectic pace of life this involved, I never had the time to do anything about it.

However, following an accident that brought an early end to my career, my wife encouraged me to seize the opportunity the extra time presented to actually do something positive with the story in my head.

So, I must say a heartfelt "thank you" to my wife, Annette, who not only encouraged me in those early stages, but who sacrificed precious time with me over the following months as the project began to come together.

Thank you to Karen, Dave, and the gang who acted as early proof readers and who gave me further ideas that helped tweak the storyline into what it is now.

I must also mention Marty and Sharon in the USA, who passed the word to the Brothers and Sisters, raising the profile of what I hope will become a major series of books.

Of course, that couldn't happen without someone actually taking a chance on me, an unknown writer. So, a special mention must go to Angie, at Pagan Writers Press. She was brave enough to take that chance and was a major contributor in helping me turn the dream into a reality.

Included within that special mention are the wonderful team at Pagan Writers Press itself. To my fellow authors who supported and encouraged me—to my editor, Rosa—who took the raw diamond and helped cut and polish it into something special—and to Christie, who worked her magic on the cover in such a way that will help it shine and stand out from others on the shelves.

Finally, I must say a special "thank you" to YOU, my former colleagues in the emergency services. Your unceasing efforts are the major inspiration behind the creation of something we all wish we could be part of.

So, although this book highlights the adventures of a group of superheroes, it is dedicated to the real life heroes out there who still face danger each and every single working day in an effort to make our communities a safer place to live.

—Andrew P. Weston

# Prologue

Looking out of the coffee shop window, twenty-two year old Samantha Drake was musing on her day.

It had started like any other day, woken again at dawn by her four-year-old son, Joshua. He was a hyperactive black hole who sucked in the time, energy, and attention of everyone around him at the cost of their patience and sanity.

He had bounced with unceasing energy on the end of her bed shouting, "Mommy, what are these for? Mommy, why do you keep those in there, why can't I have one?"

She knew he would have gone on and on until his curiosity was satisfied, so she had responded quickly. She was used to that; she wanted to quiet Joshua as soon as possible so that he didn't anger her useless excuse of a boyfriend while he slept beside her.

Yes, he was Joshua's father, but no one would have known that from his total lack of response to his son. Samantha had learned very quickly never to hope that he would drag his sorry ass out of bed to help, preferring instead to let her do virtually everything "messy" and difficult, especially if it was inconvenient for him to be a parent at those times.

It was the same old routine with Joshua, day after day; "What's this, what's that? Give me this, get me that. No, I don't want to get dressed, I don't want to eat Chocó Pops for breakfast, I want pancakes."

But at least today was better.

After an unexpected call from her best friend, Sophie, they had met in Exeter for coffee later that morning, and of course, Sophie would be as fresh as a daisy. And in her shoes, who wouldn't be?

Sophie's four-year-old, Chloe, born only two days after Joshua, was the complete opposite of her own little demon. Quiet and contented, she was the perfect child. She had delighted her parents by sleeping through the night from about two-weeks old, much to the envy of Samantha, who had forgotten what it was like to sleep and who had contemplated strangulation on more than one occasion.

But at least she was savoring the delight of this brief respite.

Josh had worked himself into an exhausted frenzy chasing the seagulls and pigeons that infested the city centre, and he now lay in a sweaty little heap, almost comatose in his stroller, dead to the world. If only she could get him to do that every night from eleven to seven, life would be so much better.

Still, at least she had these few minutes to herself, dissecting the latest gossip with Sophie.

After half an hour, Sophie stood and began edging in between the chairs. "Watch Chloe for me, I need to use the bathroom."

"Yeah, sure, no problem," replied Sam, knowing full well that where Chloe was concerned, there wouldn't be anything to do, especially since both children were fast asleep. "Do you want more coffee before we go?"

"Just a small one, otherwise we'll be going from bathroom to bathroom instead of shopping," Sophie warned.

Smirking at the truth of the remark, Sam checked the children in their strollers to make sure they were still asleep and went over to the short queue to order the drinks.

As she waited, the unforgettable chorus to "Mr. Lover, Lover" announced to everyone in the café that Sam's boyfriend was calling, causing quite a few to titter and shake their heads as she tried to answer her cell phone as quickly as she could.

"Babe, where are you?" he asked sleepily.

"I'm in town with Sophie. Ryan, are you still in bed?"

"*Yuh*, just getting up now, wondered where you were."

A voice cut in. "Excuse me."

"I said I'm in town. Sophie and I should be another hour or two yet, why?"

"An hour or two, but I'm out of beer and Dave's coming round soon to watch some sports on Sky, what will we do?"

"Well go and get it yourself. I'm not going to rush."

"Excuse me, young lady." The same voice repeated, louder this time.

"Hang on a minute, Ry." Sam turned to find an anxious looking middle-aged woman tugging on her arm. "Yeah, what do you want?"

Turning back toward where they had been sitting, Sam saw Sophie returning from the bathroom and nearing the table. The older lady pointed and said, "Is that your little boy who's just gone outside?"

Immediately, Sam's eyes zeroed in on Joshua's empty stroller, and a spark of alarm shot along her spine. Looking toward the doors, which were wedged open for the fresh air, she caught sight of a mop of blond hair bobbing along outside the window, and a squeal of delight as the first of a group of pigeons began to flee from their latest tormenter.

"Josh!" shouted Sam, in the vain hope that for the first time in his short life, he would actually take notice of his mother. "Josh, wait!" she screamed, louder this time, causing the whole coffee shop to fall silent. Everyone turned, searching for the cause of alarm.

"Oh no!" someone near the window gasped.

Sam's skin turned cold as she fought her way to the door among the crowded tables. She had a clearer view now, and saw Joshua momentarily stop, raising her hopes that he had actually listened for once, before she saw the object of his interest, the only small group of pigeons left in the near vicinity. The birds were strutting on the curb next to the busy road. They didn't seem bothered by the elderly lady who stood nearby.

His face twisting in glee, Joshua sucked in air, and, shrieking at the top of his little lungs, charged at the intruders who had dared not to fly away with the others.

Unaware for a moment that they were the focus of the charge, the pigeons continued in their own little world, hopping on and off the curb and into the road, hoping to snatch a discarded crumb before the next vehicle got too close and caused them to abandon their endless quest for food.

"JOSHUA, NO!" roared Sam, hoping the use of his full name might carry more weight.

But of course it didn't and, with his full attention on the birds, he ran and jumped toward them, arms flapping wildly, totally oblivious to the fact he was nearing the edge of the curb, and totally unaware of the truck, now only fifty yards away. The driver, absorbed in the stock manifest of his next delivery, was also unaware of the existence of the little boy about to step out in front of him.

What happened next varied depending upon who you spoke to.

The driver didn't realize anything was amiss until the last moment, when he glanced up from the manifest and actually looked at the road.

And there he was, a little boy only yards away, right in front of him.

It was too late to do anything except realize that there was a child where there shouldn't be one. It was too late to brake—too late to do anything except shut his eyes and wait for the inevitable impact.

The sound of crushing metal filled his ears and the front of the truck dipped sharply, lifting the rear completely off the ground, throwing parcels and equipment forward and all around the driver. *How on earth could a little boy do this to a truck? He must be dead, oh my God; I've killed a little boy!*

Broken glass and stock flew around his head in the confined cabin area, and he caught his breath as the vehicle seemed to pause, suspended for a moment, and balanced on its nose, before crashing back down to the earth with an almighty bang and the sound of grinding, protesting metal.

The windscreen had shattered and whatever glass was left in the frame tinkled lightly to the ground, accentuating the silence outside as the aftermath of the collision began to register.

Joshua had been completely unaware of what was about to happen. His whole world had been full of flapping wings, and squeals of delight, and his sense of triumph as the last bird flew up into the air beyond his reach. Suddenly, he was where he shouldn't be.

*Where is mommy?*

*Why am I in the road?*

The only sound he managed to utter was a sudden sharp intake of breath at the last moment as he realized something big, something hard, something travelling so very fast that blocked out the sunshine, was about to hit him.

There was no time to move, no time to even scream as an irresistible force slammed into him, throwing him backward, knocking the air from his lungs, and rendering him instantly unconscious.

\* \* \*

Several bystanders to the incident were unable to fully comprehend what had happened right in front of their eyes. It wasn't the fact that the little boy had run out into the road without looking that bothered them. It wasn't the fact that there was the inevitable gut wrenching sound of an impact, because after all, that's what you would expect in these circumstances.

None of these things surprised them, upsetting and unexpected as they were. Something just didn't add up.

When witnesses were interviewed by police, they all agreed on the initial events.

Yes, the boy did run out without looking. Yes, the truck was travelling quickly, but didn't really appear to be speeding. No, there wasn't a thing the driver could have done to avoid the boy.

All these things corroborated the events and what common sense suggested.

In each and every case, witnesses were adamant that the truck did not actually reach the child. It hadn't seemed to hit him, which was impossible, because they all heard the impact; they all saw the truck stop dead with its whole front crushed out of shape.

They saw the boy sailing through the air, surely dead.

People swarmed over the little boy, making it hard for his screaming mother to get to him.

\* \* \*

Samantha had watched in terror as the inevitable happened. No squeal of breaks, just a sickening crunch as her son was thrown into the air.

The utter twisting helplessness she felt as her son's small body flew through the air to land in some manicured flowerbeds twenty yards away was a feeling she would never forget.

Samantha didn't register the truck. It might as well never have existed. She just wanted to get to her boy and see with her own eyes the inevitable results of such an accident. But after the initial impact and momentary silence that followed, where everyone seemed frozen to the spot, (except for some cold hearted bastard on the other side of the road in a black fleece who was already walking rapidly away as if nothing of significance had taken place), she found she couldn't move.

A huge clamor broke out as some onlookers crowded round the truck, and far, far more began pushing and shoving to get to the boy, snapping Samantha back to the cruel reality of what she now faced.

"Joshua, Joshua," she cried over and over again as she began elbowing her way through the barrier of people separating her from her son. She made little headway as the press was so great, and so many people were shouting and demanding things all at once.

"Call the police."

"Get an ambulance."

"Does anyone know first aid?"

"What's the point? Poor little guy won't have survived that."

Tears began to flow uncontrollably down her face as those nearest her began to realize who she was, and what it would mean.

Slowly the press of people began to give way and they made space for her to get through.

Then, sudden alarm seemed to run through the entire crowd like an electric shock and one of them gasped, "No fucking way, he's alive!"

This was followed by several other exclamations.

"Don't be stupid, he can't be."

"Look, he's waking up."

"Where's the blood?"

"Josh, Josh!" Samantha shouted as she fought her way through the last few people.

"Mommy!" he screamed in reply, as he suddenly opened his eyes, and spotted his mother through the threatening press of people, sitting bolt upright, arms outstretched for comfort, the terror of the vehicle still at the forefront of his mind.

"Don't move him," someone pleaded as Samantha scooped her son into her arms. He clung to her so tightly and so strongly, the warning just didn't register, especially when he started bawling his eyes out, and buried his head in her shoulder.

*He's alive, he's alright,* was all she could think, over and over as she peeled him away from her to look him up and down.

Incredulously at first, then with mounting confusion, she checked him again. Then again, as she refused to believe what she saw.

Sirens could be heard in the distance now, the multi-tone warble announcing to the world that emergency services were at last responding.

But Sam didn't care, she just could not believe her son was in her arms, and somehow, there was not the slightest scratch on him.

No bruises, no swelling, no blood. How was that possible?

She turned, holding his sobbing little body tightly in her arms again, and wandered back through the crowd toward the truck, still there in the middle of the road.

An ashen-faced middle-aged man was in the road rooted to the spot like a tree, staring repeatedly from the truck and back to himself. His head shook from side to side and his jaw hung open as he muttered under his breath, as if he was arguing with someone and couldn't accept what he was hearing, obviously in shock.

As she drew closer, Sam immediately recognized why he was so shocked. He was obviously the driver and the front of his vehicle was crushed out of recognition back into the cab area. He should not have been able to walk away from the accident.

Sam could see it in his eyes, as he began looking to her, to Josh, to the truck, over and over, shaking his head in disbelief.

"Are you alright?" she asked, suddenly full of concern for him.

"I'm so sorry, I'm so sorry, I . . . he just stepped out, I didn't have. . . ."

"It's okay. He's fine. Look." She held out her son, who had now turned his attention to the source of the sirens.

"Mommy, mommy, is it a fire engine, is it a fire engine, is it a police car?"

Both of them looked Joshua up and down with blank unregistering faces, and the driver shook his head more firmly. "But he shouldn't be. Look at my truck. How could that much damage be caused without putting a scratch on him . . . Or me?" he added quietly, as he looked at his ruined vehicle again, at Joshua, and then himself, before his eyes rolled up and he folded slowly to the pavement, the shock finally getting the better of him.

\* \* \*

Police attending the scene were reportedly confused by conflicting accounts of the incident.

Multiple eyewitnesses were able to state the basics: a little boy ran in front of a vehicle, and there had been a horrendous impact. Both the boy and the driver of the vehicle had survived the accident with no injuries.

Authorities requested if anyone had information relating to the incident, that they please come forward, assuring such help and any information they had to offer would be treated in the strictest confidence. Police were keen to find a proper and satisfactory explanation to the events that day, which they felt might be related to other strange occurrences around the world.

The public request, and the assurance of confidentiality, is what spurred eighty-six year old May Randle to come forward.

May was a fiercely practical and independent God-fearing lady, who had served people all her life. She had been a nurse for over forty years when she had retired, and happily married to a doctor for over sixty years. After her husband's heart attack, she had been left as the matriarch to their three children, eight grandchildren, and four great-grandchildren. Everyone she knew was always amazed at how sharp she was for her age.

Yes, her hearing wasn't what it used to be, but she was very proud of the fact that she never had to wear glasses; it was always one of the first things she announced to people when she met them.

And thankfully for the police, it was her hearing problem that helped piece together the real events of the day.

May was supposed to use a hearing aid, but she often refused to use it unless family and friends were about, or unless she had to actually converse with someone.

She usually went about her business with the hearing aid turned off. This meant that May was very observant of what was going on around her.

Therefore, on that day, now two weeks in the past, May saw exactly what had happened without the distraction of sound. She saw it clearly and precisely, from only ten feet away, and it still didn't make sense to her. She was afraid that people would think she had lost it, and put her in a home for the mentally fragile. This fear had prevented her from stepping forward on the day of the accident, and caused her sleepless nights for two weeks since then.

Just before the accident, May had left her favorite shop, Marks & Spencer's, with her evening meal tucked safely in her bag. She had paused at the curb, to ensure her change was in her purse, that the purse was at the bottom of her shopping bag, and that the bag alarm she habitually used was switched on, the cord attached to her thumb.

*Pity anyone who picks on me just because I'm old*, she thought. She patted her bag and looked up and down the road before crossing, being careful not to upset a small flock of pigeons feeding right next to her.

May had seen the truck coming from over thirty yards away to her right and decided to wait for it to pass before she began crossing. She glanced across the road opposite, and immediately noticed the young man with a shaven head on the other side of the street, (although most people were young to her), dressed in one of those black fleece jackets that were so popular these days.

She noticed him, because after forty years of working with people, she was an excellent judge of bearing and character, and the man opposite, although appearing to be in his late thirties, perhaps his forties, seemed to radiate the confidence and authority of someone much older.

Not only that, but even at her age, she could see that he had the most magnetic grey eyes she had ever seen. Eyes that briefly flicked over all those around him, herself included, instantly taking in a wealth of information. Eyes that frowned at the CCTV camera's positioned only thirty yards away, before focusing intently on someone or something just to her right.

Puzzled, May glanced to her right, noticing almost immediately that the truck was drawing closer, and, somewhat startled by that same flock of pigeons that began flying into the air all around her, she looked more intently, and realized they were fleeing from a little boy who was so focused on the birds, he obviously wasn't watching where he was going.

He was running so fast, she knew in an instant that he would be unable to stop in time.

She glanced at the truck, back at the boy, and behind him to a young woman, most likely the boy's mother, who appeared terrified and was obviously shouting something to him.

*Oh dear*, she thought, knowing with dreadful certainty what was about to happen.

The last of the pigeons took to the air, just missing May's face, and causing her to duck and look away, back across the street to the striking young man in the black fleece.

In all her years of experience, she had never seen eyes that seemed to flash so brightly, as if they had an inner light, eyes that again flicked to her before one last glance at the CCTV cameras, causing him to grimace, almost as if in distaste at being forced to act in public.

Then he did the strangest of things.

Instead of reacting, or beginning to react like the people around her to the accident about to happen, the man stepped forward into what she would describe was a fighting stance, with both hands raised, at the exact moment the little boy came to a frozen halt in the road in front of her. By now, the truck was almost upon the boy, only a foot away, and because of the shock, time seemed to slow down.

May clearly saw the man's left hand suddenly shoot out; his palm and fingers opened like a policeman directing traffic to stop. Incredibly, the truck slammed to an instantaneous stop, as if an invisible wall had been placed in front of it, causing the front end to crush in on itself, and the back end to lift from the pavement.

With his other hand, the man made a sweeping motion, as if he were giving an imaginary opponent a back-handed slap to the face, and the little boy was swept away from the vehicle with inches to spare, flying past her at incredible speed.

May found it hard to tear her eyes away from the man as his hands continued to move so fast, that even in slow motion, they became a blur.

Because it was in front of her, she could see glass and other fragments from the truck fanning away from the point of impact, but instead of showering bystanders, including herself in debris, they seemed to pause momentarily in midair before dropping vertically straight down onto the ground.

The driver of the truck also seemed to be held in position, shock on his face, eyes tightly shut, despite the fact his vehicle was now so far up in the air it was almost on its nose, its contents spilling forward, remaining motionless for just a moment before beginning its descent.

She was aware the young man was still gesturing, now reaching out with his right hand upturned, as if he were about to grasp a light bulb, and looking back towards the boy. She was amazed to see his flight through the air altered away from the hard concrete of the road, and into the raised flowerbeds outside the bookstore twenty yards away.

As the child and vehicle came to rest, the man looked intently at them both in turn for a few moments, squinting as if he were reading small print, before nodding and giving a satisfied grin. People's attention were still diverted, and so, without ceremony he glanced around once more, focused again on the CCTV cameras with a look of concentration on his face, and began to turn to walk away.

May couldn't help but think at the young man, *Hang on. You clearly did something to help and you're just going to leave?*

Amazingly, the young man immediately checked his stride as if he had heard what she thought. He stopped, turned around and looked back at her smiling.

His thought came to her. *One day the world will see how special that little boy is, May, what he'll become. We can't have him messing things up before he's had a chance to shine, now can we?*

Then he turned again, and was lost from sight in moments, leaving May quite unnerved, and looking wide-eyed at the mother of the young boy who now stood next to her. She didn't seem to realize that May was there, and was staring in anger at the back of the young man's receding jacket, before jumping as if startled into remembering where she was.

Turning, the young lady shouted something and began fighting her way through the crowd toward her son, leaving a bemused May standing alone at the curb, wondering what on earth to do.

May was unnerved. What bothered her was the fact that the young man had heard what she'd thought; somehow, he even knew her name. And even though her hearing aid was switched off, she heard him speak to her across a crowded street without moving his lips. How on earth had he managed that?

*I think I'd better go home,* she thought, *otherwise people will put me in a home if I start telling them I've seen a guardian angel.*

# 1

# Revelations

You might not believe it, but May Randle's statement and the ancillary information she supplied was very well received. And it's no surprise, because she provided the answers to a lot of questions the police were keen to have solved.

Questions such as, why Joshua Drake not only survived that day, but also why he was able to walk away without a scratch.

Why was the truck was so badly damaged, (when it simply should not have been), and why did the driver escape from such a badly damaged vehicle without a mark on him?

Another reason May's statement was so welcomed, and why she was thanked so profusely by those involved, is that her account answered another very important mystery.

Most cities are now extensively covered by CCTV. They are in car parks, on the streets, within shopping malls, as well as the shops themselves. When major incidents occur, and answers need to be found or assistance is needed to discover the identity of witnesses or persons suspected of crime, it is invariably the CCTV system that is turned to for help.

And Exeter has excellent CCTV coverage.

And of course, this incident, which understandably received a lot of coverage in the media and press, was such an incident where police immediately requested the CCTV footage covering the area outside the coffee shop to assist them in the investigation.

However, on this occasion, the system initially raised more questions than it answered. A subsequent diagnostic check confirmed the system was working perfectly, both before and after the accident, but, for some unknown reason, the cameras at that location did not record anything. They just froze.

For ten seconds, they simply stopped working. That is why May Randle's statement was so very welcome. By adding in the details she provided, and cross-referencing them with other statements, and by checking CCTV in the surrounding area, the police were able to confirm the details she had provided were truthful and exactly correct.

CCTV footage in the surrounding area confirmed the route taken by the delivery truck prior to the accident. It clearly showed Joshua Drake running out from the shop and into the road chasing pigeons. It showed May herself, ambling away from Marks & Spencer's, and fiddling about in her bag just before the accident. It was also able to confirm the approach of a man wearing a black fleece jacket, who stopped on the corner opposite May and Joshua seconds before the accident, and who was seen staring directly at the camera just before it froze.

Ten seconds later that same man was seen walking back the way he had come. He paused and turned for a moment as if he was about to talk to someone, and then continued on his way toward the library.

After scouring CCTV records, the police were able to see the times, and the means by which May Randle, Samantha, and Joshua Drake arrived in Exeter that day, and left. Each and every single witness could clearly be seen, as their movements had been accurately recorded by various cameras.

Despite this, the man in black proved to be quite a mystery, because no matter how many records were checked, he could not be seen arriving or leaving.

It was as if he simply did not exist until about a minute before the accident, suddenly appearing out of the men's public rest room by the library, walking casually to the corner where the accident occurred, and where the CCTV then failed to work.

When they did start again, he was seen walking away, pausing momentarily before carrying on back to the rest room, from which he never emerged.

Before disappearing, he was seen looking at CCTV positions further down the road, one behind Lloyd's TSB Bank, and the other opposite, close to the library, as if checking to ensure that on this occasion, they were recording his movements.

The man then removed something from his coat pocket, something that looked like a silver ball. He stood still with it in his right hand by the entrance to the rest room, and waited for over a minute with his head bowed as if in prayer.

Then he looked pointedly at the cameras before suddenly throwing the ball up into the air, over his shoulder, where it landed on the roof, bouncing twice before coming to rest.

Once he had done this, he entered the rest room and never reemerged.

The police thoroughly checked the rest rooms, inside and out, and the floors, walls and ceiling were solid and sound. There were no hidden doorways, windows or trapdoors, no secret way in or out. And sure enough, when the rooftop was checked, they found the ball.

It was transparent, made of a solid resin type material, and contained a silver colored metallic wafer, set into the resin.

The wafer had a simple message clearly engraved on it:

*"AND SO IT BEGINS."*

The message caused quite a stir. By the time it was recovered, other startling incidents had begun occurring around the world, all of which were very public, very well covered by the media, and putting the authorities to shame in one country after another.

\* \* \*

*Sichuan, China.*

Two days after the Joshua Drake incident, a group of miners in Sichuan Provence, China, were wondering if they would ever see the light of day again.

They had entered their colliery at 7:00 a.m. for their shift as usual, and the day had started like every other day. The long descent into cold darkness, the trek to the workface, the exhausting, cramped, claustrophobic conditions, as they worked like ants with millions of tons or rock pressing down on them.

The brief pauses while fresh charges were laid, and the moments of anxiety following each shudder, waiting for the earth to stop shaking and the dust to settle before the inevitable trudge back to the new mounds of rubble, to start extracting yet more of the coal that provided over ninety percent of their country's energy needs.

When a seam was exhausted, they would retreat along the side tunnel toward the main artery, removing the pillars as they went.

Sometimes the coal roof would remain intact, slowly sinking down to the floor. Sometimes it began collapsing as the pillars were removed, trapping and crushing friends and workmates to death in an instant.

Although this mine was fully licensed by the State, it lacked much of the modern equipment other legally funded mines were blessed with, and instead of a bank of machines stripping rock and rubble away from the coal rich seams running through the area, the miners did it by hand, in grueling twelve-hour shifts. This reinforced the fact that this was one of the filthiest, hardest jobs in existence, in one of the most dangerous mines in the world.

When the explosion came four hours into the shift, it took all forty-three workers by surprise. Instead of being safely huddled together in the arterial corridor while a fresh seam was broken up in a side tunnel, they were still hard at work in the newest seam, having only just finished cutting the face and reinforcing the walls and roof prior to extraction charges being placed.

The explosion had originated behind them in the main corridor where the charges were kept. All five workers in that area had been incinerated, sending a wall of compressed roiling flames toward the survivors, and back up the lift shaft, to vent its fury out into the bright sunny morning above their heads over a mile away.

The force of the explosion caused buildings to shake, and blew away the machinery covering the shaft head. In the panic that followed, surface workers fled for their lives thinking they were in the middle of an earthquake before realizing what had happened and sending for emergency rescue services.

The pressure had nowhere to go except along the main corridor and into the few side tunnels still open. Of the thirty-eight survivors of the initial blast, over half died in the fireball that followed.

Of the fifteen or so who survived, most had been working in the side corridors, and avoided the worst of the ruptured eardrums, burst capillaries, and burns that eschewed.

All were thrown to the ground amid a cloud of choking, suffocating dust and rock, that together with the shredded supports, only added to their confusion and terror. The weight of the gut rock above them began to overwhelm the weakened integrity of the main tunnel, and the few who remained conscious listened to the groaning, snapping timbers, waiting for the final "snap" that would signal their doom.

Their helmet lamps were unable to cut through the thick dust that not only covered each survivor from head to foot, but also seemed to saturate the very air they breathed. They knew that death was inevitable, especially since the remaining air was rapidly thinning.

Cheung Xian, a veteran of over twenty years' service in six different mines, was doing his best to gather the surviving men together to assess their situation, and keep them busy and focused. But he was failing miserably.

In those twenty years, he had faced over a dozen different crises, including a tunnel collapse, wherein he had been confined below ground for over a week before being rescued. But he had never faced anything like this.

Of those surviving, most were unconscious, slowly dying from the carnage inside their ruined bodies, or writhing in agony with injuries received from the blast, increasing the panic of those who could hear them.

His own injuries were making him feel sick and dizzy, and all he wanted to do was lie down and quietly go to sleep and wake up in his next life. He sincerely hoped his sacrifice here meant it would be a better one.

To give Xian credit, he exerted heroic self-control, managing to calm those nearest him, despite the fact that now only three others were conscious, and they were clearly struggling to breathe.

Then, as he too started to submit to the effects of slow asphyxiation more fully, he smiled to himself, because he was obviously beginning to hallucinate, and his hallucination was so pleasant it was sure to make his passing that much easier.

He was reassuring the youngest of his co-workers, a lad of only nineteen years whose name he didn't even know yet. Suddenly, a painfully bright light washed over everyone, causing the few who remained conscious to avert their eyes.

He turned, squinting, too shocked to say a word, to see a young woman silhouetted by the light behind her, casually walking toward him along the tunnel and casting an almost ethereal glow about her as she walked.

As she drew closer, it looked as if bands of coruscating energy, almost like static discharges, flowed up and down her body, softly fading as she drew nearer.

He watched mutely as she strolled up to him, held out her hand and said, "Hello Xian, I think you'd better come with me. It's quite a strain keeping these tunnels up, and it would be a shame to get caught when it all comes down."

Xian didn't mean to be rude. He was just too stunned to react as courteously as he would have liked.

The young woman had the most stunning, electrifying eyes he had ever seen, and it took him a moment or two to tear his gaze away and gesture to his colleagues. "Err . . . thank you. But what about my comrades? They're badly hurt and need help, too."

"Don't worry about them, they're our concern now." She gestured casually behind her.

Xian realized other people were stepping down out of the vortex of bright light that filled the end of the corridor, a corridor that should have been a blank wall, dressed in similar dark coveralls. They began quietly, but efficiently, tending to the injured men close by, and appeared to be initiating a search for the others, too.

Somehow, they seemed totally unaffected by the conditions.

The young lady gently but firmly took his hand, and led him toward the light.

"Am I dead, are you of the Devas?" murmured Xian apprehensively, thinking he was looking at a deity come to life.

Giving his hand a gentle squeeze, and smiling warmly, the young woman replied, "Far from it, my friend . . . you'll find out. We want you to deliver something for us."

They stepped into the light.

It was the last thing Xian remembered until early afternoon, when he woke up in the West China Hospital, Sichuan University, Chengdu, along with all fifteen of his fellow workers who had survived.

At first, Xian thought he was at home, because he'd had the most pleasant dream about a stunning woman with beautiful eyes. As his awareness returned, he realized he was in a hospital ward and wearing crisp new cotton pajamas.

Sitting up, he saw the ward was full of sleeping men. It took him a few moments before he recognized the men on either side of him.

Gingerly, he swung his legs out of bed, and found he wasn't in the least bit sore or tired. In fact, he felt more refreshed and healthier than he had for many years. He walked up and down the ward, slowly going from bed to bed, amazed again and again to find his fellow workers, many whom he thought had died or were badly injured, sound asleep and looking as peaceful as babies. Most appeared unharmed, and they were all wearing new pajamas.

Xian looked himself up and down, noting his pajamas were the same cut and color, and then realized there was something hard in the chest pocket of his jacket.

Puzzled, he removed a thin wafer of odd material, inside of which was a silver colored piece of what he took to be metal, with writing on it.

Reading it, he smiled and thought. *Aah, the thing they wanted me to deliver.*

Placing it back in his pocket, he began walking toward the main doors. When they opened, a shocked nurse came in.

"What are you doing here?" she demanded.

"I'm sorry, I don't know," Xian admitted.

"Who are you, where are you from?"

Bowing, he replied, "I am Cheung Xian, a supervisor from the Neijiang Mine and . . . ."

"What?"

"We were working. There was an explosion, we were trapped."

"You were at the mine this morning when it exploded?" she gasped.

"Yes, we were underground. We thought we were going to die. Where are we?"

"You were underground. But how did you get here to Chengdu? You're in Sichuan Hospital. I'm only beginning to gather supplies for the doctors who are going to help in the rescue. What you're saying is impossible!"

Taking a deep breath, Xian began explaining the miraculous events of that day, only to discover that he was required to repeat those details again and again. First, he spoke with the doctors, then the Hospital Administrator, then to officials from the Works Safety Bureau who arrived later that day and finally to Government Officials the following morning.

Disbelief turned to suspicion, and suspicion to amazement, as one by one, Xian's fellow workers awoke, free from injury. They confirmed his story.

Those who had remained conscious at the time of the rescue verified the incredible manner that they had been plucked from the depths of the mine by people some had initially thought were deities, only to awaken in a new wing to the hospital that was not due to open for over two months.

Party officials were also very keen to examine the message Xian passed to investigators. A small sliver of metal sandwiched in resin bore the words:

*"WE ARE HERE TO ASSIST ALL THOSE IN NEED."*

The Chinese official Xinhug News Agency were uncharacteristically robust in reporting the exceptional events at the mine that day, as they initially believed the mysterious benefactors were there solely to help the Chinese people.

They were only partly right. Whoever the mysterious benefactors were, the following weeks revealed they would extend that help to *everyone* in dire need, no matter where they were from, or who they were.

The huge coverage given to the miraculous rescue in China helped other countries to become aware of other amazing rescues.

It soon became apparent that whoever these people were, they had access to incredible resources, and were in a position to respond globally, with great speed and efficiency.

\* \* \*

*Gold Coast Australia (Four days later)*

Although small, the Tallebudgera Gazette got quite a scoop several days after the events in China. One of their reporters, Marie Chandler, was on hand to witness what she described as a "Miraculous Rescue" in Coolangatta, when a family was plucked from certain death.

The article read as follows:

"Sunday started like any other family day out for the Stevens family from Brisbane. A morning enjoying the tranquility of Tallebodgera Creek Conservation, followed by a trip out in the small boat the family own off the point at Coolangatta, was just what the family needed.

However, what the Stevens family did not know, was that their day would have ended in tragedy, were it not for the prompt actions of two mysterious passers-by who stepped in to save the day.

Pete Stevens, the thirty-two year old father of Jamie, six, and Callum, four, and husband to Kristy, twenty-nine, had just steered their boat out into the bay, when they were struck full on, by a seven meter high performance power boat, stolen only minutes before from Jack Evans Boat Harbor Park, by two local men who are well known to the police.

The collision instantly destroyed the Stevens' boat and threw the family into the water. As I phoned the emergency services, I must confess, I was shocked at what happened next!

A young couple that had been strolling along Marine Parade only two yards in front of me immediately stripped down to their underwear, vaulted onto the sand and dived into the water. They disappeared beneath the waves, only to reappear–impossibly–moments later fifty yards offshore in the middle of the Stevens family. Then, the family and their mystery rescuers simply vanished!

Imagine my surprise when, I then received an unlisted call on my personal mobile phone only one minute later from a woman who identified herself as one of the rescuers.

She informed me the Stevens family would be found sleeping on the beach off Snapper Rocks road, (just off the end of Marine Parade), and that those responsible would also be found at that location along with a message.

After informing the authorities, I immediately went to that location to discover the Stevens family was indeed fit and well. They were completely dry and had just woken up and were unaware as to how they had got there. The thieves, Tom McAllister and Mike Thompson–both twenty-four from St George–were found just a few short yards away, still unconscious, and with their hands and feet in plastic restraints.

The unknown protectors left a message for me and for you, the readers, inside a plastic prism among the Stevens' belongings. The message said:

"SOON, THOSE WHO DISREGARD THE LAW AND HARM OTHERS WILL HAVE NOWHERE TO HIDE."

Who they are, we may never know, but Pete and Kristy Stevens have asked me to pass on their deepest, heartfelt thanks to the rescuers they are calling their Guardian Angels, for saving their lives, the lives of their children, and for preventing further tragedy from occurring that day.

Anyone with further information regarding this incident should contact me at the Tallebudgera Gazette."

The report was published with a photo of the Stevens family, taken on Marie Chandler's mobile phone at the scene, standing on the beach off Snapper Rocks road, smiling and in obvious good health, with Jamie and Callum holding the mysterious message in their hands.

Tom McAllister and Mike Thompson were comatose for almost two days before waking up. They were extremely eager to confess their crimes, many of which the police were unaware they were connected to. And those crimes proved to be rather revealing.

\* \* \*

*Addu Atoll—Maldives (two days later)*

The Maldives consist of about twelve thousand islands separated into a series of coral atolls just north of the equator in the Indian Ocean. Of those islands, only two hundred are inhabited, but all are at the mercy of any rise in sea level.

Addu Atoll lies just south of the equator, and is a ninety minute flight from the capital Male'. Of the twenty-three islands in that group, only six are inhabited.

Brian and Beth Cooper, from South Africa, were in their late forties. They had been married for twenty-five years, having met while diving nearly thirty years ago. They had decided to spend their anniversary here, doing what they both loved.

Until recently, they had been in the best of health. The past year had proved very stressful for Brian, as his import/export business had been strongly influenced by the global recession.

Still, his clinical and methodical approach to problem solving had proved a great boon to avoiding bankruptcy, and they had successfully managed to weather the storm, making cuts and adjustments where needed, and managing to stay in the black this last financial year.

They had been hoping their anniversary holiday would ease the headaches and cramps Brian had been blighted with in recent months.

Now four days into their holiday, the Coopers decided to dive the wreck of an old WWII submarine, about a mile offshore, close to the reef.

Reaching their destination in a locally hired Atlantic Rib inflatable speedboat, they were unable to resist the opportunity. Finding themselves alone in the middle of the ocean, they made love for almost an hour before eventually kitting up, and beginning the slow decent toward the broken encrusted remains, eighty feet below.

At this depth, they would only have fifteen minutes to have a look around, but it would be worth it, as evidently, the huge hole blown into the hull seventy years before by torpedoes, made one of the most surreal sights a diver would encounter in these waters. It had been described by other enthusiasts as entering a cave into the abyss.

The Coopers were so enthralled that they took numerous photos by flash and torchlight.

The interior of the submarine proved impressive, and the many upside-down compartments and long narrow corridors, now eerily filled with all manner of aquatic life, kept their enthusiasm and interest running high. As quickly as it had begun, the dive was over, and Beth indicated they should be making their way out of the craft, and back to the surface.

They began to retrace their route back through the corridors, following the twine they had lain out behind them as a matter of habit, as an extra safety precaution.

Beth led the way, hand over hand along the cord, smiling as she felt Brian's familiar fingers tracing lightly from her backside, down her legs and onto her fins, where he began flicking every few yards or so, reminding her he was there, (and truth be told, probably staring at her ass as well and imagining what they would do again as soon as they got back in the boat).

Yes, today had been a good day!

A few minutes later, as Beth approached the hole blown into the submarine's side, something inside her made her feel apprehensive.

Pausing, she looked behind to see Brian's wrist light jerking to and fro in the water six yards behind her, right in the doorway to the main corridor. Brian himself seemed to be writhing, as if wracked with pain.

*Brian!* She screamed at the top of her mind, already moving, already responding to danger, her professionalism kicking in. They were a mile out to sea, ten minutes from the hotel once on shore, ninety minutes by plane from the nearest hospital.

*Shit!*

As she began kicking strongly back toward him, fighting the rising panic, his body suddenly went limp, sending an electric charge down her spine, and spurring her to move faster.

What neither Beth, nor Brian, had realized was the stress of the past year had taken its toll. He had become a walking time bomb, with a stroke just waiting to happen.

Brian had been following his wife, studying her backside. She had kept herself in shape, and was the love of his life. It always made him smile when he realized just how much he still desired her, and wanted to be with her after all these years together. He had been planning all sorts of wickedness once they had returned to the surface.

And then—?

He was suddenly wracked in agony, and his whole body felt as if it was impaled on a spike of fire piercing his head. Wave after wave of nausea struck him, causing him to completely bite through his mouth piece just as his wife was coming to his aid.

His lungs filled with water, and his world went black.

Beth failed to notice the sudden arrival of something large; something moving at incredible speed.

It wasn't until she was swept out of the way and up against the inner hull, sending shadows cast by the beam of her torch dancing erratically about, that she realized she was not alone. Something was focused on her husband.

At blinding speed, something seized him around the chest and exploded upwards, taking him up through the hull as if it were made of paper.

Beth was sent careening out of control, deeper into the bowels of the wreck, before something else, with a grip like a vice, fastened itself around her waist, stopping her instantly, while her orientation continued to spiral like a corkscrew.

What looked like a human arm had wrapped around her waist, then another around her chest. She too was propelled upwards.

With her chin buried tight to her chest, Beth was able to look along the length of her body, over the arms that welded her in place, and back down toward the rapidly receding wreck. She watched uncomprehendingly as chunks of rusted steel, coral, and other debris arced away from the new hole that had somehow been blasted into the side of the submarine, mere yards from another new hole, where her husband had exited.

Like a rag doll, Beth felt herself pulled along helplessly. Strong hands lifted her upright, and then held her steady while her own reeling senses fought to catch up and regain their fragile equilibrium.

Gasping for breath as if she had just run a marathon, Beth realized she was waist deep in water, and that two arms were on her shoulders. Endlessly deep green eyes, belonging to a well-muscled middle-aged man were boring into her.

*Are you alright, Beth?*

"Why . . . yes," she stuttered in reply. "My husband, oh my God, Brian, he . . . ."

A soothing voice echoed in her mind. *Don't worry, Beth. He had a stroke, but fortunately we heard your scream and were able to get there in time, before our friends, in fact. He's going to be fine in just a few moments.*

Tearing her eyes away from the man in front of her, Beth looked over his shoulder to see her husband lying on the beach with a slightly younger looking woman kneeling behind him and a number of other guests beginning to congregate around them.

Her hands were held above him, one above his head, and the other above his chest. A look of rapt concentration was on her face, and her eyes were open as if she were focusing on some unseen picture. Her eyes glowed brightly as her hands moved over Brian, who was lying so quiet, so still.

Where her hands passed, faint whirls of color hung in the air for a few moments before fading.

"What are you doing to him, who are you?"

The man beside her spoke again, sending words into her mind. *Like yourself, we're here on holiday, although fortunately for you, we have a very particular set of skills that came in handy today.*

"What?" Beth whispered. She suddenly realized that he was speaking without moving his lips.

She noticed two other men, dressed in what looked like dark coveralls with hooded capes thrown back standing on the beach.

One was staring out to sea, hand stretched toward her boat, which was speeding across the water, empty, and engine off. That it was responding to some unseen force generated by the man was obvious and without question.

The other was looking up into the sky with a serene look on his face. He suddenly smiled, shrugged, and turned to the man next to her before shrugging again. He then waved to them both and vanished, followed moments later by the other one, who by now had secured her boat to the jetty.

Beth ignored the gasps of astonishment from the growing crowd, because some form of communication had obviously passed between them, and the man next to her.

Chuckling, he turned and confirmed her suspicions.

*They're just annoyed we beat them to it. They're on duty and should have gotten here first, but we were already here, sunbathing along the beach, and couldn't ignore such a cry for help. You're very lucky we were staying on the same island.*

"What are you talking about, and why can I hear you when you're not talking?"

*I'm very sorry. This is all very new, for both of us actually. You're still in shock, and we're not used to doing things so . . . openly yet . . . and . . . aaah?*

He suddenly turned toward the woman and spoke out loud. "It looks like your husband's just about done now."

Looking across to the young woman, Beth watched as her eyes came back into focus and with a satisfied look on her face, she flexed her fingers towards Brian's body.

A miniature streak of lightning left her hand and struck him in the chest, at which point his body convulsed once, before he gave a long, loud sigh and lay still, apparently sleeping.

The growing crowd was now murmuring amongst themselves. Some were on mobile phones jabbering away frantically, while a few others were recording with cameras. Glancing toward them, the woman walked briskly over to Beth and wordlessly spoke.

*Sorry I was so long, but you have to be careful with brain damage, as you can permanently screw things up if you're not careful, and I had to ensure his lungs were free of water.*

Beth gasped. "What do you mean, is he . . . ?"

*No, no, no! Don't worry, that's all sorted and he's fine now. What with the ingestion of water too, I just had to be careful and take my time with his brain. Just let him rest for a day or two to be sure, keep the reporters away, and he'll make a full recovery.*

"Oh." Beth was too stunned to say anything more.

With a hint of irony, the man nodded at the growing crowd. "At least you get to finish your holiday, I think we'd cause quite a stir if we stayed, eh?"

Giving Beth a friendly squeeze on the shoulder, he handed her a clear plastic triangular paperweight.

"Here, my friends gave me this for you." He dropped it into her cupped hands.

Beth found it surprisingly light, and before she could look at it closely, the woman gave her a very big hug, and said, "I'm so happy we could help today. We all are. And I hope you don't mind me saying, but when I was healing your husband I was able to see deeply into his mind. You're a very lucky woman because he loves you more than you know."

"Oh, I *do* know," Beth replied with utter conviction.

Looking deeply into Beth's eyes, the woman concentrated for a moment. Then she smiled, stepped back, and said, "Yes, I believe you do."

Giving Beth's hand one last squeeze, she went to join the man who had moved a few yards away. Looking closely at their body language, Beth suddenly thought, *Oh, they're a couple too!*

As the woman took her companion's hand in hers, she looked back over her shoulder and mentally replied, *Yup, and this one's all mine.*

They casually strolled along the beach toward the water villas, ignoring the crowd staring at them.

Looking down, Beth was examined the paperweight more closely, and was amazed to find what looked like a silver colored wafer inside, on which were etched the following words:

*"WHEN WE CAN, WE WILL BE THERE TO HELP THOSE IN NEED."*

Then she braced herself as the approaching crowds descended upon her, and their questions began.

When the rooms were checked, "Mr. & Mrs. Black" from New Zealand, who had paid up front in cash, were nowhere to be seen.

The many witnesses made for interesting press coverage, causing people in both "high and low places" to take note.

\* \* \*

*Fairbanks International Airport, Alaska (three days later)*

*Delta Airlines Flight FA157*

On her final run before retirement, Chief Purser Connie Radcliffe had prayed for a quiet, uneventful flight. And the Gods had answered her prayers.

Although the flight from Gatwick, London, had been full, all four-hundred and three passengers on board had behaved impeccably and her flight crew of fourteen members had handled everything smoothly and efficiently. They had even managed to throw a surprise party for her halfway into the nine-hour flight, which the passengers had taken to with vigorous support.

Yes, she had to suffer the embarrassment of mincing up and down the cabins of both decks to receive the congratulations of just about everyone on board, but she suffered that with graceful patience, knowing her team was genuinely fond of her.

Captain Chris Lye, one of the best pilots she had ever worked with, and someone she had known personally for over fourteen years, had called her forward to the flight deck. He presented her with a pair of very tasteful gold and diamond pilot wings and a bottle of champagne, which he jokingly reminded her, was not to be opened until they were groundside. She had sauntered back to her station to yet more loud applause, and congratulations from everyone present.

It had been one of her best flights ever, due in part to the very relaxed atmosphere on board, and indeed on all flights over the past few days. News was spreading about a mysterious group, being dubbed Guardian Angels, (or Jedi Knights by the kids on You Tube), who seemed to be a real life Thunderbirds outfit, turning up out of nowhere around the world, and saving people in the nick of time. In one case, they had even apprehended a gang of armed robbers in South Africa who had taken seventeen people hostage in a bank.

While some of the newspaper reports were hard to believe, she had to admit the video footage captured around the world was very convincing. The sense of safety and security people had begun to feel was clearly evident in the much more relaxed attitudes of those travelling by air.

Just four hours later, they had begun their decent toward Fairbanks International Airport, the passengers were in their seats, the team was squaring things away, and Connie was looking forward to the meal she had planned later that evening with her husband, and that bottle of champagne.

She had lived in Fairbanks all her life, and it felt good to be coming home knowing she could at last begin to feel settled.

Although her team was efficient and well drilled, they knew Connie liked to complete a check herself of all stations in person. She had just begun her final rounds when she felt an unfamiliar shudder run through the plane, causing her to stumble slightly.

She only had time to frown, when the shudder came again, this time more aggressively, causing some of the overhead lockers to pop open and spill items to the floor.

All chatter abruptly ceased, and passengers began gripping their seats, conversations forgotten. Some were staring wide-eyed out of the windows or at each other, while others began looking up and down the aisles as if they would discover the cause of the problem in front of them.

A moment later, a muffled bang was heard, followed by a prolonged grinding sound that caused the plane to lurch violently. Within seconds some of the passengers were on their mobile phones, speaking to their loved ones, just in case.

Captain Lye's voice cut in over the noise. "Would all passengers not seated, please return to them. We appear to be experiencing some unexpected turbulence, and request that for your safety, you are seated with seatbelts securely fastened. Please ensure all electronic devices are switched off now. Thank you."

A little boy seated with his family in the centre seats just outside the mid galley area, was putting on a show of being brave. Turning to his mother, he said gravely, "Don't worry, Mommy, if anything happens, the Jedi people will save us."

The mother didn't appear at all convinced by her son's brave attempt to ease her fears, as yet another violent shudder ran along the length of the plane, causing the oxygen masks to drop, lights to flicker on and off, and bringing loud shouts of surprise and fear from more of the passengers.

The plane continued shaking violently and seemed to roll over toward its port wing, the back end swinging round alarmingly. The engine pitch changed, as the crew began to battle to maintain control. As the shouts and sounds of panic grew, Connie had to struggle to calm her own fears and let her training kick in.

She fought to maintain her footing as the rotation gained speed. She began moving toward the mid galley and rest room area, intending to use the intercom phone to contact her staff at their stations.

Despite the Captain's request, Connie could see quite a few passengers screaming down their mobile phones, sure that this was their last chance to say their goodbyes before the end.

The plane was spinning so rapidly, Connie could barely stand, let alone remind them to stop the calls. She wished she had a chance to call her husband before it was too late.

The little boy was still trying to reassure his mother, who was now openly crying, and even though his father was trying to quiet him down, he persisted in his efforts and began shouting out loud, "Save us, we know you can, please save us, my mommy is frightened, don't let us die!"

A voice out of nowhere cut through the clamor, ringing loudly in everyone's minds. *Don't worry, little man, we're here now!*

A blinding flash announced the arrival of five striking individuals radiating power, dressed similarly in dark coveralls. They stood as if rooted to the floor.

The man in the middle appeared to lead them. His uniform was distinguished by a silver band at the end of each sleeve, and he was the only one who had a hooded cape.

Despite the gravity of the situation, Connie had to laugh to herself as she immediately recognized why You Tube was so full of Jedi references.

Their arrival was met by utter silence, as every passenger on board was struck mute in shock.

The man in the centre nodded left and right. The two younger men to his right immediately went forward, one ascending the stairs to the Upper Elite Lounge, while the young man and woman on his left went toward the rear.

Once in position, they faced inward with their heads bowed and eyes shut in concentration. Each one raised a hand toward the older man, who was waiting for some unseen signal with his hands out to his side, almost in a crucifix position, palms turned upwards.

It was the most surreal sight Connie had ever seen. Even though the plane was rapidly losing height and was bucking furiously as the speed of the spin increased, each of the rescuers stood as if frozen in position, like statues unaffected by gravity or motion.

Moments later, the oldest man's head snapped up, and waves of energy began pulsing from his hands, fanning outward in rippling halos with a faint sizzling sound.

The plane immediately began to stabilize, and the rate of spin began to slow, as they regained control of the stricken aircraft.

A pulse at a different pitch radiated from the Guardian's hands, and the laboring engines cut off moments later, causing the shuddering to cease completely. Instead of plunging toward the ground far, the plane appeared to remain stable. The spinning continued to slow, and the actual descent was now very similar to that experienced when an aircraft lands normally, albeit faster.

Within minutes, their rate of decent had slowed even more, and tensions among the passengers melted away. They began looking in wonder out of the windows, and at the miraculous saviors standing within touching distance. Soon, almost everyone had their mobile phones out, and conversations to various friends and families resumed along with rampant photo taking.

To hear about them on the news was one thing, to actually see them face to face was like a dream. The passengers feared they would wake up from what might have been a strange hallucination.

Looking out the window, Connie was surprised at how low they already were, and could clearly see landmarks she knew well.

They were passing State Highway Two, and swooping down over Creamers Field State Game reserve, the college and campus following less than a minute later.

As they crossed Robert Mitchell Expressway, the plane suddenly banked sharp left, bringing shouts of alarm from many of the passengers.

A calm voice suddenly sounded inside everyone's heads. *My apologies, ladies and gentlemen, but we won't be landing at Fairbanks International Airport and are making a little diversion to a nearby airfield to ensure you aren't all swamped by the massing media as you disembark.*

*That will be at the military base,* Connie thought.

And sure enough, a few minutes later, the plane swooped gracefully down toward the ground, gradually and gently slowing to a stop, before hovering over Ladd Army Airfield, Fairbanks.

Of all her landings, this would be the most memorable.

The huge two-hundred and thirty-two foot long hulk of metal, weighing in at just under nine-hundred thousand pounds, with a two-hundred and eleven foot wingspan, simply glided to a halt in the air, pierced by multiple arc lights from the base, just ten feet above the ground, before descending slowly, where it remained perfectly balanced as passengers disembarked in an orderly fashion.

In fact, it was difficult to get people to leave, so intent were they to file past their rescuers to thank them, some touching them to ensure they were not figments of the imagination.

The little boy gazed up in wonder at the personification of his hero made flesh as he walked past. He paused, tugged on the leader's leg, and said, "I knew you wouldn't let us die."

His savior looked down at him, ruffled his hair, and smiled. He then winked at him and replied, "That's no problem, little man, we can't have you being afraid to fly, now can we, especially after you were so brave?"

Outside, Connie could see the airbases reaction to the unannounced landing, as red and blue lights heralded the approach of a military response to a perceived threat. Typical!

Captain Lye was one of the last to leave along with Connie. As they walked past the leader toward the wing exit, he said, "One moment, please."

They turned, and he continued, "I'd like you to give this to the appropriate authorities if you would."

He handed Connie a large piece of clear plastic. Inside was a brief message inscribed into a metallic substance which read:

> "WHILE WE RESPECT THE SOVEREIGNTY OF EVERY COUNTRY, PLEASE BE AWARE THAT OUR PRIORITY IS, AND ALWAYS WILL BE, THE PRESERVATION OF HUMAN LIFE.
>
> IN THESE EARLY DAYS, WE WILL ALWAYS ENDEAVOUR TO RESPECT YOUR LAWS, BUT THERE MAY BE OCCASIONS WHEN EXTREME CIRCUMSTANCES REQUIRE AN IMMEDIATE RESPONSE TO SAVE LIFE.
>
> YOUR PATIENCE WILL BE MUCH APPRECIATED AT THOSE TIMES.
>
> WHEN THE TIME IS RIGHT, WE WILL APPROACH YOUR LEADERS TO OPEN A DIALOGUE."

As the last of the passengers and crew left the plane, it tilted slowly onto its starboard wing, rocked momentarily, and came to rest.

When the MP's and other military personnel entered brandishing their statutory firearms, no-one was left inside to be impressed by the abundance of testosterone filling the air.

# 2

# Consequences

*Old District—Tokyo*

The gentleman chairing this extraordinary meeting of the Council took a deep breath, pushed back his chair, and stood up. Although seventy-two years of age, Lei Yeung was still a strong and agile man, still able to display the formal bearing of one accustomed to a lifetime of hard work, focus, and discipline. Unfortunately for his enemies, he also had an incredible mind that matched his physical prowess.

Although he lacked a formal education, his quick mind and "gifts" had more than made up for it over the years.

He had the uncanny ability to know when people were lying to him; he was able to sense their motives.

If that were not impressive enough, Yeung also had the capability to insert a particular line of thought or an idea into another person's consciousness, which made them act on it as if it were their own.

Those abilities, together with that sharp, analytical mind and fearsome nose for business had guaranteed his meteoric rise to power within the White Tiger crime syndicate operating out of the Old District in Tokyo during the sixties.

As a teenager, he had seen the sense of consolidating power through the wise selection of loyal friends and business acquaintances, and had always managed to acquire such friends in the right places at the right time, ensuring his favors were reciprocated with all sorts of information that proved very useful to those he served.

He was noticed by those in power very quickly.

As he rose through the ranks, he was careful to build an honorable reputation, ensuring that his word was his bond. He would go to great lengths to keep any promises made, and ensured dissention and failure were ruthlessly answered. He was very skillful at finding traitors, always seeming to know who could and who couldn't be trusted.

That made him a favorite of those in power, leading to his speedy rise through the ranks.

Poignantly, his skills also ensured he had a broad and lethal power base, so that when he was only forty-five years old, he was perfectly placed to strike with clinical efficiency, and in a short time, either disposed of or blackmailed all opposition into submission.

His trusted puppets were then installed in positions of power and influence, while he melted into the background, seeking a "quieter" life.

Openly, the White Tigers thrived under their new father and ruling family, but that was never achieved by their own doing. The true mastermind and kingpin worked hard behind the scenes to ensure they were in the right places at the right times to build a sophisticated crime network, and a number of businesses that encompassed prostitution, drugs, gambling, smuggling, counterfeit goods, cash, and cyber-crime.

Employing the same strategy as before, he built the network by manipulating the minds of others so that, although they and their assets were his to use as he wished, none of them could in any way be connected to him.

Additionally, he realized from an early age that it was highly unlikely he was unique, and so he had kept a careful watch over the years for individuals like himself who were possessed of "unusual" talents.

And he had found them, some directly, others through much more dubious means.

Initially, they were invited into a secret world of crime, and using their talents extensively allowed him to consolidate his already considerable power base even more thoroughly. This began in Japan, and then as his influence grew, spread to other countries.

As time passed, he realized there was a safer, more lucrative way of making money, a way that meant he wouldn't have to dispose of those gifted ones so quickly, who were less inclined to resort to criminal activities.

He merely separated his assets.

Some, he used extensively to steal thoughts and ideas, thus paving the way for a fledgling "Yeung Technologies" to forge ahead in the world of scientific discovery.

So successful was he in his early endeavors that now his company was a world leader in "legitimate" technological advancement in all areas of science and medicine.

It was simple, it was elegant, and totally risk free, allowing him to maintain the front of one of the world's most respected business men, while gaining control of an enterprise that brought him increasing wealth and influence with each passing year.

Those with temperaments better suited to "darker" pursuits, he used to head "The Council", a fellowship of uniquely gifted criminal minds. He used their business links and partnerships with other crime syndicates in Japan and throughout the world to forge another empire based on knowledge.

The Council gained a great deal of influence over others because of what they knew. Information was knowledge, and knowledge was power, a power they could wield in tandem with their abilities.

It was thought that criminally, nothing of consequence happened anywhere without "The Council" knowing about it, as they had members secreted within the most influential crime families of the world.

So it was with eager expectation that the "Apostles" of The Council, representing the twelve most gifted individuals of syndicates from both Northern and Southern America, Europe, Asia, Africa, Russia, and Oceania, had convened the previous evening, keen to discuss the implications of recent events which had caused just about everyone in their line of business to panic and wonder if this was the end of criminal life as they knew it.

This past week had hit them hard, as the Guardian Angels had not only been busying themselves playing God at the scenes of the usual accidents and disasters that were being so well reported, but had also made their unwelcome presence felt at Sochi International Port, Russia, one of The Council's main operating bases. They had rescued over two-hundred drugged women recently procured by the minions of The Council, who were destined for brothels in Poland, Romania, and Japan.

Somehow, the Guardians had discovered which containers the women were being transported in. They had appeared at each one within the port only minutes ahead of local law enforcement officers, who swarmed over everything in an effort to apprehend their handlers.

The residual fallout from that fiasco had led to the capture of seventeen of their employees, the confiscation of nearly five-hundred kilograms of heroin, and the abandonment of several skin factories.

The loss in profits and potential income hadn't been properly calculated yet and the meeting that had been scheduled to end around midnight was still grinding on, as the Apostles vacillated over the best course of action.

Some wanted a speedy response, others were urging caution.

Leaning forward, Lei Yeung slowly moved his gaze across each face around the table, looking into the eyes of each Apostle present to ensure they were aware he acknowledged their concerns. He cleared his throat before speaking.

"Ladies and Gentlemen, I must confess, I feel recent events may have overwhelmed us a little and caused us to lose proper focus. If we do not address this problem calmly and simply, with clear heads and minds, it may be the tip of an iceberg which, if we are not cautious, will sink us all."

"So what do you propose we 'calmly and simply' do?" interrupted a bull-necked younger man. He was clearly aggravated, causing smoke to rise from the table in front of him where his hands touched the desk. This was evidence of the fiery elemental gift he possessed, a gift he was struggling to control.

Turning to him, Yeung acknowledged the newest member of The Council, the son of an old friend who had stepped down due to declining health in his old age. The younger man's inability to control his anger made it clear that he hadn't been ready to take his father's place.

Ignoring the damage to the table Yeung commanded, "Member Espasito, do you have something constructive to say?"

Refusing to be intimidated, Espasito replied, "Damned right I do! How are we going to answer this insult?"

"You appear to be taking this rather too personally. Why?" asked Yeung.

"Because those assholes cost me personally," retorted the younger man.

He referred to the heroin on the manifests in front of them. "Half of that shipment was due for my market in the United States. Those bastards have caused me to lose face on more than one occasion. Replacing this batch will cost me more than just dollars."

"You are worried about cost and favors?" asked Yeung, clearly annoyed.

"Of course I am! I thought that'd be something you'd understand. I recently promised three of our business associates in Romania, Georgia, and the Ukraine a consignment of luxury yachts and speed boats for their Black Sea resorts as a sweetener for future proposals I would like to make in that area. They accepted after I promised delivery of some new toys for their VIP harems over there within the next two weeks. My main source for merchandise in Australia was squeezed by these interfering morons! Not only did I lose face on that occasion, I lost future revenue on the new smuggling contacts I wanted for my counterfeit designer labels. Just imagine how hard it will be to restore confidence in my credibility now, especially when everyone gets wind of this latest fiasco. I might as well be blowing crap out my ass."

Looking him directly in the eye, Yeung whispered, "You are not the only one who has lost face on this occasion, young man. What affects one of us, affects us all. We have a reputation to maintain and the reason this Council exists is to ensure that reputation is upheld and the impact of such set backs are minimized."

"That's all well and good in theory, but how are we going to actually make them pay?" Espasito blustered, slamming his fist onto the desk. Sparks flew from his hand.

The outburst caused quite a number of the Apostles to bristle with indignation at the affront the young man was causing. A number of intimate thoughts began flying between those individuals blessed with that ability, some aimed at Yeung himself, insisting he discipline the upstart before he went too far.

Taking a deep breath to maintain his composure, Yeung replied, "I don't know how we will make them pay—yet! But what I can say is the matter is in hand, and it will not be rushed. It is vital we do not act rashly.

"It has only been a matter of weeks, so we do not know our enemy well enough to act. Can they be recruited? Time will tell. Are they easy to kill? I would imagine not. Can we embarrass them publicly? Possibly, but in any event we must gain the intelligence we need before making a decision.

"Personal affront takes second place to the welfare of The Council, understood?"

Yeung maintained eye contact with the younger man until he was forced to agree by an almost imperceptible nod of his head.

Turning to another older, pockmarked-faced man at the table, Yeung continued, "Member Belikov, I understand the men we have lost were part of your syndicate, yes?"

"Yes, Sir, they were," replied Belikov, a man in his late fifties who had made his name in the Russian Mafia as an enforcer who was very hard to kill, due mainly to his amazing ability to recover quickly from injuries.

"They were responsible for the initial round up of the latest girls from around Europe and for their onward transportation to the cattle ranches before placement in the pleasure clubs."

"How many of those men were in a privileged position?" asked Yeung.

"There were two of them, Sir, Dorogi and Koslov. Both can be trusted to remain silent and serve time rather than open their mouths. They know the consequences too well."

Yeung nodded. "Excellent, excellent, at least there is that. Please make sure their families are looked after while they are away from home. We must set an example of unity and support in this matter."

Belikov inclined his head respectfully, acknowledging it would be done.

Yeung began to walk slowly around the table, studying each of the men and women in turn. "These Guardian Angels or whatever they are, clearly represent a danger to our continued operations. In hindsight, our gifts have caused us to become complacent over the years, caused us to think we are untouchable, and that is obviously no longer the case.

"We must exercise caution, assess their capabilities, see if we can indeed make inroads into their organization and exploit it to our advantage. We will survive this difficult period, of that I have no doubt. But I also have no doubt of the fact that we must adapt to ensure our survival."

He paused to stand opposite Espasito, and looked him directly in the eye. "What we must NOT do is take matters into our own hands. We have seen what these people are capable of, and I am sure I am not alone when I say they are probably capable of much more. We see how the world is reacting. Is it any wonder they would work counter to our goals and designs when the opportunity presented itself?"

All heads around the table nodded in agreement, except for Espasito's, who was clearly unhappy at continuing to be singled out.

Seeing this, Yeung decided a short break might be appropriate before continuing. After resuming his place at the head of the table he announced, "Ladies and Gentlemen, much can be accomplished by a clear and focused mind. Please, let's enjoy a short recess and perhaps collect our thoughts before resuming in say, thirty minutes, when we will be in a better position to determine the wisest course to follow to avoid the iceberg that threatens us."

All but one agreed, and gradually left the conference room for the waiting refreshments next door.

Yeung concentrated on the newest Apostle to the Council as he left the room, and plainly saw the defiance and deceit that radiated from him as he walked out, tingeing his natural aura with deep blooms of scarlet, black, and neon red.

And something else that aroused suspicion.

*That one's going to be a problem if I don't do something,* he mused.

"Madam Papadakos, a moment?" called Yeung as the group left the room.

A voluptuous Greek woman in her mid-thirties checked her stride and walked quietly back to her seat, dark eyes flashing with every step.

An Apostle of The Council's European drug smuggling operations, her looks were very deceiving. She was telepathic and had the ability to remote-view an area up to a mile from her vicinity. She was also capable of draining the very life essence from a person just by touching them.

Smiling, she waited for the others to leave before asking, "Sir?"

"Angelika, I feel I may have need of your particular talents in the very near future. How are you with small aircraft, high rise buildings, and flammable substances?"

"It depends. Why, what do you have in mind?"

Yeung reached behind his desk and produced a small leather bound document. "The gist of what you need is in there," he said, handing it to her. "Destroy it once you have the details and let me know the results as soon as you've completed your appraisal. Use anyone you need to get this done, understood?"

Placing the document in her purse, she merely nodded once and walked slowly from the room with a seductive swagger to her hips.

*If only I were twenty or thirty years younger,* he thought.

Pulling himself together he called after her, "Oh Angelika, ask Harry to come in for a moment, would you?"

She waved in acknowledgement, and as she left, Yeung's head of security, Harry Bing, made his silent way into the office.

Harry was a powerfully built man in his late forties originating from Johannesburg, who was not only a gifted teleporter, but one of the most powerful telepaths Yeung had ever met.

In a previous life, Harry had been head of security for the "De Beers Consolidated Mine Company" at the Premier Diamond Mine, at Gauteng, South Africa.

He had attained that position because his employers were amazed by his unprecedented skill at discovering employees trying to steal company property as they left the mine. Although the company employed state of the art "Scannex" technology, Bing had an uncanny knack of spotting a thief from a hundred yards away, and over the years had personally apprehended over three-hundred thieves unfortunate enough to try and sneak past security when he was on duty.

He had been happy to pave out an illustrious career for himself with De Beers, until a chance meeting with Yeung four years previously, who happened to be visiting the mine on business.

Harry sat without invitation at the end of the conference table, waiting for his boss to amble over to him.

They shook hands and Yeung said, "Harry, I'd like you to do something for me."

\* \* \*

Fort Wainwright is home to over ten thousand soldiers and family members, comprising units of 1$^{st}$ Brigade, 6$^{th}$ Light Infantry Division, the Arctic support Brigade, the 4$^{th}$/123$^{rd}$ Aviation Regiment, along with the 23$^{rd}$ Aviation Intermediate Maintenance Unit, and the 283$^{rd}$ Medical Detachment.

The commanding officer of Fort Wainwright, Brigadier General Alan Pascoe, read the report in front of him for the third time, shaking his head. The report detailed the incredible rescue of all passengers on the Delta Airlines flight into Fairbanks just two weeks before.

To say that the powers at the Pentagon were not going to like what they read was an understatement, as they were already expressing a hostile attitude.

To know that an obviously technologically advanced, highly trained and motivated group of people existed was one thing. For them to act in the benevolent gracious way they had was commendable, and a great relief to those who had benefited from their aid.

However, their apparent gifts, or superhuman abilities were a cause of great concern to many security services around the world, and especially to those bureaucrats lurking within the Defense Intelligence Agency here in the U.S. They wailed at how these acts were highlighting the ease with which these unknown do-gooders were popping up all over the place, to circumvent whatever established protocols were in existence.

The way they had landed the jet here on the base had started alarm bells ringing. It would inevitably result in the knee-jerk reactions already seen in quite a few departments, as they panicked over imaginary threats to national security.

As if the events of that evening were not enough, he had been forced to endure an army of press from all around the world outside his base. He had also received unwanted enquiries of investigators from the NSA, Homeland Security, CIA and HUMINT, one of their specialist analytical departments.

There had been an initial enquiry from the National Threat Assessment Centre, which had been tasked to identify and research the "obvious danger" an organized group with such abilities could present in the future.

General Pascoe could only imagine what the reaction might be, as he pressed "send" on his secure terminal, to transmit the findings of the enquiry to those waiting for it deep in the bowels of the US Department of Defense at Arlington, Virginia.

As it transpired, the Guardian Angels were also the topic of conversation among a startling number of some of the world's most notorious crime bosses.

These individuals did not have the advantage or resources of entities like The Council, or the CIA, FBI, NSA, or their Australian and British counterparts, ASIS or MI5/6, but they did have their own way of getting things done.

And they wanted something done, fast!

* * *

Another development to emerge from these concerns was the sudden resurrection of obsolete paranormal research programs in one country after another.

People are not aware of how seriously some governments assess research into psychic phenomena, especially in relation to ESP, telepathy, remote viewing, and telekinesis. These abilities would be useful tools in counter espionage.

Because the scientific community of the world was now buzzing from recent events, and especially enthusiastic over the sheer range of psychic abilities the Guardian Angels obviously possessed, many old programs were brought down off the shelf. The programs were given sparkling new names, and found themselves on the receiving end of very generous budgets, including access to some of the finest military and civilian scientific staff and resources available.

In the USA, the "Angel Project" was initiated from the ashes of an old defunct World War Two program into psychic research. It was moved from Nevada to Virginia, and given the ripe pickings of a brand new underground fortified research facility, together with carte blanche authority over the acquisition of individuals with a "measurable" paranormal quotient. The Angel Project received the promise of unlimited funds if they could isolate such individuals quickly.

In Russia, The Directorate of Special Activities suddenly found itself with a lot more power and influence within bureaucratic circles, and was extended the opportunity to pick and choose whatever manpower and resources it saw fit.

Outwardly, nothing appeared to change within the People's Republic of China. Children, both pre-school, and in their first years of education were regularly tested for psi abilities anyway. The only difference was that testing was much more thorough, rigorous, and widespread.

In fact, within weeks of the startling events around the world, it became part of the curriculum for all children within China to be tested, with a new proviso stating the aim was to test twice a year from the age of four onwards. Anyone scoring above a certain percentile was whisked away to new State funded schools and all contact with their families heavily restricted.

Additionally, the selection process for employment in sensitive positions would include a "psi-test", with an even tougher process for those attempting to secure governmental positions of oversight.

It appeared a common thread was developing around the world—"I want one."

And in these early days, people were happy to see what would happen within their own borders over the coming months. After all, someone, somewhere, must have some sort of natural psi ability that they would be able to hold up and proudly display to the rest of the world and say, "Look what we've got. Have you?"

However, those aspirations hid darker motives, especially within the more clandestine departments of some governments who would not be content to merely discover individuals with psi abilities to benefit society as a whole.

This undercurrent revealed a more aggressive focus on finding individuals who would be stronger and more talented than the "other sides", and more willing to serve the goals and aspirations of their particular government's foreign and domestic policies.

Basically, they wanted "Super Spies", and they wanted better ones than anyone else.

There was a determination to achieve this goal by any means necessary to ensure they stayed ahead in the perceived race that had just begun.

Some even had aspirations of boosting their chances, by thoughts of persuading or even coercing one of the Guardian Angels to assist in their research programs.

That line of thought could only end in tears.

# 3

# Unwanted Developments

From: Guardian Lord Anil Suresh. Lord Evaluator, Guardian Operations.

To: Lord Marshall Earl Foster.

Date: November 10th, 2015

Subject:

Findings of Sector Overseers, High Grand Master Samuel Thaleton—Americas Sector & High Grand Master Park Leung—Asian Sector.

Sir,

Following my investigation into the suspicions raised by High Grand Masters Thaleton and Park, I report as follows:

At 11:00 a.m. EST USA—30th October 2015, duty Far-scanners aboard Guardian Observation Station 2, detected an emergency "May-Day" call from a Diamond DA20 trainer light aircraft experiencing difficulties above Chicago, IL, USA.

The call was allegedly made by a panicking student, stating her instructor had passed out and that she was unable to control the craft as it was only her second lesson.

Scans confirmed a light aircraft containing two individuals was indeed flying erratically over Soldier Field, Boston, apparently heading towards Merrill C Meigs Airport. As scans continued the craft went into a steep dive.

In view of the gravity of the situation, Guardian Master Lindsey Buckingham (TK) and Guardian Peter Smith (HeaL) were dispatched to assist.

Neither has natural teleport abilities and as such inserted via "T" ring.

Upon arrival they discovered two unknown occupants, one male and one female, who appeared in the best of health. (Descriptions as per appendix A)

The occupants apologized for the deception and stated they represented "interested persons" who were keen to acquire the services of exceptional and gifted individuals to undertake "employment" that would be mutually beneficial to all parties concerned.

Guardian Master Buckingham went to apprehend the individuals, and subsequently discovered they were endowed of psychic abilities, as they not only anticipated her reaction, but were able to teleport from the aircraft before being taken into custody.

Not being blessed with natural teleport ability, neither Guardian was able to follow the hyper-spatial pathway of the suspects to the point of materialization.

Once the aircraft was safely on the ground at Merrill C Meigs Airport, enquiries discovered the British registered aircraft had been stolen the previous day from Bristol Airport, UK.

Checks are still underway to discover how it arrived in the USA, but, as the distance is far beyond the natural range for the craft, it is thought teleportation is the most probable cause.

Forensic sweeps by our own Inquisitors have revealed no clues as to the identity of the two individuals suggesting a "psi-sweep" to remove DNA evidence. (Forensic analysis as per appendix B)

A psi-crystal containing the mental records of the incident by Guardians in attendance is enclosed. (AS/1)

At 03:00 a.m. local time—Hong Kong—2nd November 2015, duty Far-scanners aboard Guardian Observation Station 4 monitored a call to emergency services from the reception of the Ritz-Carlton hotel, atop the International Commerce Centre, West Kowloon, Hong Kong, stating there had been an explosion at the top of the building a few minutes previously, and that a fire was now raging.

At over 1588 feet tall, this building is the tallest building in Hong Kong, and the fourth tallest in the world. Both life and property were in immediate danger and as such this incident fitted our "Instant Response" protocols.

Scans had captured the explosion and a full Alpha Response Team was scrambled.

Insertion to target was made two floors below the incident and under the command of Guardian Master Edward Clegg. (Elm-F/E & TP)

One stick under the direction of Guardian Kerry Yip, (Tel/HeaL), was tasked to the reception/arrivals lobby of the hotel and building to assist ingress by local emergency response units, while the other stick headed by Guardian Carlos Abano, (Sh/Tel/TK) was tasked to assist Master Clegg on site.

On arrival, he found the area deserted, and a saloon bar and store heavily damaged by explosion and fire.

Within the remains of the bar were three casualties, two male, one female who, due to Master Clegg's elemental capabilities, were easily reached.

The team was surprised to find that the "casualties" were in fact free of injury, and that one of them at least was possessed of some form of elemental capacity, as they were free from the effects of blast, heat or burns.

The woman apologized to Guardian Master Clegg for the damage caused to the building, and stated sufficient funds to cover the cost of repairs would be discovered within the safe behind the hotel's main reception inside a black leather briefcase.

She went on to make a similar offer as was made at the Chicago incident, asking that all the Guardians present seriously consider the proposal, as it was unlikely such an offer would be extended again so freely.

That individual, or one of the men accompanying her, was powerfully telepathic. She was able to overhear Master Clegg's instructions to his team to arrest them. She indicated to her companions that they should leave.

At this point, they departed by way of teleportation, one of the men dropping a cylindrical device that exploded less than a second later, saturating the team and surrounding area in a corrosive, flammable jelly.

Two of our Protectors were seriously injured in that blast, as they had neither the telekinetic, shielding or elemental capability needed to protect themselves sufficiently before team members could recover from their surprise and render assistance.

By the time the safety of the team was confirmed, the teleport specialist, Guardian Master Clegg, discovered the dematerialization nexus had degraded to the point where the hyper spatial pathway was too diffuse to follow.

(Descriptions of suspects are listed at appendix C)

Forensic teams were able to analyze microscopic fragments of the explosive device, which were all but consumed, but enquiries are continuing. (Results as per appendix D) – It can be seen the substance used is an advanced compound that should be unavailable in view of current global technological capabilities.

An open briefcase was indeed discovered within the hotel's main safe, containing five million US dollars.

Analysis of the briefcase and its contents has been inconclusive so far.

A psi-crystal containing the mental records of the incident by Guardians in attendance is enclosed. (AS/2)

Conclusion:

It is evident that maturation of the human mind is in advance of what was anticipated.

Gifted individuals possessed of high ability are already present in greater numbers than previously estimated, some of whom are clearly already united in what can best be described as, an "organization" whose formation has eluded us and whose goals and aspirations are currently unknown.

Whatever this organization is, they are unclear as to our motivation and tenets, which would explain the naïve approaches and offer of "employment", however, it is clear they are well-funded and equipped, having access to superior technology than is currently available to world markets.

It is also clear that while those encountered so far do not have the strength and range of abilities of the Guardians, they are nevertheless possessed of sufficient potential to pose a threat to Protectors if caught unawares.

Recommendations:

A heightened alert status is to be initiated immediately at all stations and centers. All telepathic interchange at incidents is to be automatically encrypted from now on.

Personal shields are to be maintained at incidents as standard until the threat assessment is completed.

Re-roster duty lists to ensure a broader spectrum of abilities are available to respond to every incident, especially where Protectors are tasked to deal.

All response teams to implement forensic protocols immediately, and maintain aura scans to identify those with psi ability.

Temporary allocation of Inquisitor teams to each station to pursue and apprehend suspects when discovered.

Station sensors are to automatically employ aura micro-scan programs for the next month in response to all "remotely reported" incidents.

Lord Evaluator Anil Suresh

* * *

For anyone interested in statistics, the five weeks following the Fairbanks incident proved to be a very sobering time indeed. New directives from certain agencies within various governments had resulted in the implementation of some very public and more duplicitous forms of information trawling.

The more overt methods included "fun and personal discovery" challenges within national and local newspapers and online quizzes, tests, and games. Those interested were offered a chance to, "Find out if you are a psychic", or, "Are you the next Guardian Angel? – Find Out Now."

Countless schools had visits from various "educational agencies", (all with extremely authentic looking credentials), who ushered children through "psychic evaluation programs." Some even made family weekends of them, where the evaluators got to meet the families of all the students, and easily gained a vast amount of personal details that otherwise would have remained quite confidential.

Businesses, and especially those whose role was deemed sensitive to national and economic security, found their employees were required to undergo additional vetting procedures and team building exercises. This caused a good many people to express their concerns as to how ridiculous things seemed to be getting.

On a more worrying note, certain agencies in numerous countries had been authorized to monitor the personal e-mails and social network messages, text and telephone conversations of literally anyone they wanted.

An extremely sophisticated set of programs were initiated to monitor the unceasing chatter and clamor that filled the ether, all waiting to be activated by a very special set of key words or phrases.

Such monitoring was run in tandem with hunter/seeker programs that endlessly interrogated the computerized files and systems of multiple "secure" databases around the globe.

These programs were also spliced into the countless CCTV control centers around the world, which afforded the snoopers virtual live-time surveillance of potential persons of interest when they were using their credit cards, driving their vehicles, or simply going about their daily lives. Movements and actions were scrutinized closely for any suspicious or out of the ordinary behavior.

Personal details relating to millions of people were thoroughly researched, all for the purpose of finding those carefully selected keywords or phrases. When words or phrases were linked to an individual, that person's details were added to an ever-growing list.

Where such key words were repeated, a shorter list was compiled which found its way to analysts within a few days for comparison with any CCTV footage there might be.

If those key words or phrases wove a common thread through any particular individual's life, and especially when there was CCTV coverage to support it, they were paid a personal visit.

What happened next was usually entirely dependent upon several factors, such as, who the person was, and their standing in the community, the number of available next of kin, and their country of residence.

It is no surprise that statistics over this period showed an alarming rise in "Missing Persons" reports.

The only ray of light during this darkening period was the fact that the mysterious Guardian Angels had continued to offer their most welcome assistance at times of great need. They saved hundreds of thousands of lives around the world in situations as varied as earthquakes in China, Greece, Turkey, and the Eastern United States. Some of these quakes measured over seven on the Richter scale. The Angels were there for the flash flooding in India and New Zealand, a freeway collapse in Brazil during Rush Hour, and they rescued an injured lone climber stranded and dying from exposure in the French Alps.

Amazingly, they were also on hand to assist authorities on two separate occasions off the coast of Somalia, where pirates had forcibly taken control of several cargo vessels. They had also assisted in the mid-air release of hostages during a hijacking over the Pacific Ocean. Recently, they had even rescued a five-year old girl in Thailand, who had been abducted from outside her home by a pedophile as she played in the street.

Sadly, an outrageous incident occurred the same day the little girl was rescued in Thailand that caused quite a stir internationally.

Someone had actually tried to initiate an attack against the Guardians.

Luis Plazas, a Costa Rican crime lord from Jaco, was an unstable individual who was, for all intent and purposes, a drug abusing homicidal maniac, and not the kind of person you would like to upset.

He had literally shot, stabbed, hacked, drugged, drowned and blown his way to the top in a bloody two year take-over that had not only eliminated his rivals, but left hundreds of people, including police and magistrates, dead.

In the five years since then, the country existed in a permanent state of silent fear, especially of reprisals if any were unwise enough to cross him or disappoint him in any way.

Those years of committing atrocities without concern of prosecution, had left him with an over-inflated opinion of how untouchable he was. Like many of his cohorts, he was incensed that the Guardian Angels were now daring to interfere in the way he made his living.

Always out to make a show of himself to bolster his "Teflon" reputation, he had his men rounded up nearly a hundred people from a local village, strapped suicide vests containing five pounds of explosives to each one, and packed them into a seventy-five foot long semi-submersible drugs boat.

Once loaded, he had them sailed eight miles into the Pacific Ocean by two of his lackeys who were currently in his bad books and lucky not to have been executed already. Then he calmly calling the police headquarters at San Jose and "anonymously" tipped them off to a major cocaine haul weighing about five hundred tons that was about to go to the bottom of the ocean five miles out from Tambor, because of an explosion and fire on board.

His tip-off had the desired effect. The authorities, knowing full well who was calling and being frantic not to disappoint him, began broadcasting for the help of the Guardian Angels via radio, TV, satellite, and anything else they could get their hands on, to help them get to the boat and make the arrests Plazas obviously desired.

Sure enough, less than five minutes later, a Guardian team arrived at the boat expecting a fight with panicking drug runners, only to discover the ruse.

Notice of their arrival was immediately passed to Plazas by one of his men, who then simply threw his mobile phone into the ocean. One of the attending Guardians saw what happened, and realized what he was up to. After rendering him unconscious and skimming his mind, the Guardians looked into the hold of the boat to discover the terrified villagers, all strapped to mobile phone activated explosives.

A full scale emergency "Bio-Port" was initiated. The powerful sensors of one of the Guardian Observation stations locked on to the "life-signs" generated by the captives, and simply whisked them away, leaving behind all inorganic material such as clothes, jewelry, and the explosives.

Thankfully, this was accomplished within thirty seconds of their arrival. Plazas had since been busy ringing another number, and then entering certain validation codes to ensure the detonation of the explosive vests and an even larger bomb hidden in the hold of the boat.

The Guardian team had extracted moments before that detonation.

The two lackeys were very grateful not to have been on board when over eight-hundred pounds of explosives blew the boat and its contents to pieces.

When they realized they were as good as dead to their boss, and had been offered up as sacrifices, they were very compliant in helping identify Plazas and his location to the Guardians.

When Guardian Inquisitors materialized inside his bedroom only thirty minutes later, they found him stuffing his face with pizza, and totally absorbed in a movie on TV.

He was so shocked to discover he wasn't invincible, that he cried like a baby when arrested, and was still crying when locked in police cells under Guardian supervision.

Fortunately, this was the only openly aggressive attempt against the Guardians to make the news, and some who watched the incident and who read about it in the newspapers in the days following the attack, did so with both alarm and interest and made hasty revisions to their plans.

* * *

Several more of the resin encased messages were left at some of the more serious incidents. A startling invitation was extended following the evacuation of a chemical plant in Bamako, Mali, where a containment breach had threatened to poison the Niger River.

The invitation set the world buzzing as to its meaning and implications. It read:

*"WORLD EVENTS INDICATE IT IS APPROPRIATE FOR US TO OPEN A DIALOGUE WITH YOUR LEADERS AT THIS TIME, TO INITIATE FORMAL RELATIONS.*

*WE SEEK TO PROPOSE A FRAMEWORK IN WHICH THE SUPPORT OF YOUR LAW ENFORCEMENT AND EMERGENCY SERVICES MAY BE PERMANENTLY ESTABLISHED FOR THE CONTINUED WELFARE OF ALL THOSE IN NEED.*

*AN APPOINTED REPRESENTATIVE WILL CONTACT YOU SHORTLY."*

If this message didn't cause a sensation in itself, imagine the furor that followed every day after its release, when each and every TV and satellite station around the world had their services interrupted for a period of thirty seconds, twice a day, once at 12:00 noon GMT, the second at 9:00 p.m. GMT, with a simple worded message:

*"December 1ˢᵗ 2015 – 12:00 noon GMT – (BBC World News)"*

A date that was, at that time, just seven short days away, reducing the worlds media into an uncontrolled frenzy, especially at the BBC, whose Director and Board Members were in absolute raptures at being selected for whatever event had been planned.

Everyone was quite unaware of the covert methods currently being employed by their governments to procure an edge in the new "Psychic Race." As such, they were eagerly looking forward to whatever revelations December would bring.

Expectations of something wonderful, something amazing, were running high.

The various agencies tasked to give their respective governments that "edge", were not so enthusiastic, however. They were concerned that their plans to get a head start in the race might have been uncovered by the

Guardian Angels, and furious activity was now taking place to cover up any links to their departments, and their governments.

While several of the more amenable administrations took heed and reigned in their agents, (those being the ones who had only stretched their human rights laws minimally), many just carried on regardless, some even intensifying their efforts while preparing intricate cover stories for the inevitable press releases, "just in case", and sat back and waited for the day to arrive.

"Ostrich Syndrome" would have been an apt term to use to explain their attitudes.

# 4

# Ostrich Syndrome

*November 25<sup>th</sup>—Sicily*

Luigi Espasito, Boss of the crime family whose name he proudly bore, was relaxing on his family's small estate in Brolo, Messina, Sicily, eighty-one miles east of Palermo.

Although a resident of Paris, France, for over fifty years, he liked to return home as often as possible to the place he had been born some fifty-seven summers previously. He enjoyed spending time with his mother and father, both in their eighties as they relaxed in retirement, doing what they loved best, pottering about in their tranquil gardens with the help of a locally recommended, but elderly gardener/handyman, Gianni.

His father, Nazarino, the former Boss, was still an astute man and had recognized his advancing years had begun to take their toll about three years ago. Earlier this year, he had given up his position despite his amazing gifts, paving the way for his son to come to power. His years of planning and preparation were coming to fruition.

Leaving the American side of business to cousins in Chicago and Boston, Nazarino had ensured his gifted eldest son had attended the finest schools in Europe, and attained the highest qualifications in business law.

He then encouraged his son to concentrate most of his efforts on expanding The Council's growing influence within the legitimate side of the many businesses and corporations coming under their umbrella, as well as promoting future partnerships they may want to establish.

And his efforts had paid off handsomely.

The Council was flourishing, and their family had secured assets in over seventeen countries worth over thirteen billion Euros. They also had influence in businesses and other syndicates throughout Europe, Australia, the Middle and Far East, as well as America and Japan. They commanded the respect of the crime-world around the globe.

Nazarino had taken to the simple life with surprising ease, and had been quietly delighted with the way his son had initially been running things—until recently.

Like his father, Luigi was very sharp and had an analytical mind that could plan ahead for decades. He had the patience to set things in motion that would bear fruit many, many years later. Unlike his father, however, Luigi did not exercise the same patience if those plans did not work out as foreseen, or when it came to settling scores against real or perceived slights, preferring to make a quick example of those unwise enough to cross him.

His unique ability, involving the manifestation and manipulation of the fire element, had no doubt burgeoned from his innately fiery temperament. He had a short fuse, and it showed, as some had discovered to their cost.

He was particularly irritated by some recent happenings. The first time, a few months ago, was when two of his erstwhile employees had been apprehended by Guardians, all the way down in Australia. Those men hadn't known they were working for him, as he always ensured his connections were dealt with by proxies, which is why their sudden conversion to the straight and narrow had not brought the authorities to his door. But he still chafed at the loss of the regular supply of motor boats and launches they provided. Those items had been useful, as they were "redistributed" to their friends in the Black Sea Consortium, who looked on them as status symbols, and who would then grant all sorts of reciprocal favors in return.

He had lost face there, and although alternate arrangements procured replacement craft only four days later, he still bridled at the loss of respect it had cost him, and the taint it may have added to his dependable reputation.

If that hadn't upset him enough, the recent loss of two-hundred and fifty kilograms of heroin destined for his USA market had been an additional slap in the face.

That, and the fact that he'd then been faced down by Boss Yeung in front of the other Apostles, had led to him nearly losing control and setting fire to his damned precious table.

*Asshole!* He thought.

Still, he felt better now than he had for weeks.

Despite what that pathetic excuse for a leader had said, his preparations for revenge were coming along nicely. The humiliation he still felt over the Guardian Angels interference in his life would soon be answered, and there was nothing the old fart could do about it.

His plan for the Guardians was as simple as it was elegant. Humiliate them! Rub their stinking, interfering noses in it so the world would see them for what they were.

Yes, he'd had to call in favors from associates in China, Hong Kong, and the United States that had cost him over fifty-million dollars, but it was going to be worth every cent, and every compromise.

He'd got the idea from, of all people, his eleven year old niece, Amelia, who had been playing in the garden a week previously.

Much to his distaste, he had discovered her playing a game of "Guardian Angels."

Lost in her own little world, her heroes were rescuing her from a Nuclear plant that had suffered a containment breach that was threatening to destroy her make believe world. He wondered where on earth she had got the idea, and was reminded by his housekeeper Gianni, that there had been repeated newscasts on the TV lately about nuclear reactors and the safety of nuclear power. Japan was still trying to get its Nuclear Program up and running following the earthquake and tsunami of 2011 that devastated some of their main reactors in Fukushima.

Mulling it over in his mind led to an unexpected revelation.

He had contacts in both China and Hong Kong who would be able to procure certain guidance chips from associates in the United States. These chips were destined for their latest generation of Hard Target Penetrating, Ground Burrowing, Tactical Nuclear Missiles, the B91-11 1KT Land Buster, which was undergoing tests in the supposedly secret military research area at Oak Ridge, Tennessee.

Those same contacts had the technology to doctor the chips and replace them without discovery. This ensured that a number of those missiles would be susceptible to interference at a time and place of his choosing.

Cousins in America also had the resources to incapacitate the scientists in the test area by non-lethal means, to give his representatives a window of opportunity. They could then commandeer the missiles in flight, and reduce the chances of intervention.

Of course, a suitable distraction would have to be engineered. Only four days ago, he'd had the idea of widening the nuclear theme, by focusing his thoughts on the Waste Isolation Plant in Carlsbad, New Mexico. He knew at least two of the technicians there were in debt to the family. They would be in an ideal position to ensure a suitable distraction was initiated to draw away the attention of the authorities, and, if urgent and critical enough, those interfering busybodies, too.

Working via a chain of proxies that would ensure he was distanced from the fallout, he had given the go-ahead, and things were progressing nicely.

Yes, Luigi was in a very good mood, so good in fact that he felt untouchable!

\* \* \*

*November 28th—8:30pm—Washington DC, USA.*

Gregory Harris, Unit Director of Section 6, the CIA's Parapsychology Investigations Response & Research Unit, could not believe his continuing luck.

For the past two years, he had been marooned in the quagmire that was his department, a tiny office deep in the bowels of Langley, Virginia. It was a bottomless pit of careers going no-where, and dead end leads. His department was a token effort in the race to prove the actual existence of abilities like ESP, clairvoyance, remote viewing, and the like. In addition, they strove to locate individuals who would be able to viably demonstrate abilities in a controlled environment, which the company could then put to use in what they termed as a "productive" manner.

Events over the past few months had resulted in the expansion of his department. A team of staff had been drafted from Nevada, Harris had been promoted, and they had been given a new headquarters facility here at Langley to absorb that expansion. He was also given a remit allowing him a great deal of leeway to achieve results.

Results are exactly what had fallen into his lap.

The current Angel Project initiative had netted him six viable candidates out of a possible fifty-three in recent weeks. Three were in their mid-twenties, one in their thirties, while the most recent were an elderly couple from Nebraska.

Initial testing and reports showed the candidates to have obvious ESP abilities way beyond anything encountered before, even though he was sure that all but one of them were not even trying. They seemed more intent on passively resisting every attempt to get them to participate or co-operate.

Even the use of drugs didn't seem to speed things up. Two of the candidates appeared to be virtually resistant to all hypnotics and other drug combinations. *Interesting in itself,* he thought, *and ripe with possibilities.*

The only one keen to be there was the twenty-two year old mentally unbalanced young man from New York. He was accustomed to living on the streets and fending for himself since childhood, and he had apparently used his telepathy and TK abilities to commit petty crime for food, clothes, and comic books. He had also used it to gain entrance to buildings where he could sleep, and of course to ward off any would-be aggressors.

His complete cooperation had been guaranteed by three square meals a day, his own comfy room, a place to put his comic books, and an introduction to all the delights that "X Box" and "Play Station" had to offer.

And now tonight's gem! Not thirty minutes ago, one of his team leaders had called him at home stressing how urgently he needed to get back into work. When he had questioned the caller, the answer had prompted his panicked response, and each minute of the drive in from Washington DC seemed to take an absolute age.

His offices, now three floors underground, were isolated from the rest of the main building due to the nature of the work undertaken there.

Besides the usual security measures for entering the main building, his department could only be accessed by a swipe card and fingerprint operated standalone elevator, with standard CCTV monitoring. This gave access to a tunnel over four-hundred feet deep. From the tunnel, the complex could be entered only by passing a series of biometric and bar code scanners. This verified the ID swipe card that permanently hung from his neck, and also his handprint, iris, and voice phrase recognition, each in turn, with a different nine digit code for each security checkpoint.

All this was encased in reinforced lead-lined concrete over twenty feet thick. The construct was complete with active neural gas dispensers, and sonic dissipaters at strategic positions, to drop any unwanted visitors in their tracks.

Quite excessive really, if you considered the new guest they now had staying with them in the interview cell behind the two-way mirror.

"What have we got?" asked Harris excitedly.

Ryan Lee, the duty team leader that evening, handed a report to his boss. "Turns out the little girl was in class yesterday at Holly Meadows Elementary School, Alexandria, when she suddenly starts freaking out in the middle of class for no apparent reason, bawling her eyes out evidently, and crying 'No mommy no,' over and over again, poor little thing. The teachers were so concerned they tried to contact her mother, Karen, when she suddenly goes all quiet, looks at the teacher, and quietly whispers to her, 'Mommy won't be coming, she's gone.'"

"And?" asked Harris, still confused.

Excitedly, Lee replied, "The thing is, when she was freaking out, they say her hair was almost standing on end, like she was electrified, and the furniture in the classroom was shaking all over the place as if there was an earthquake.

"Her mother was the victim of a hit-and-run auto accident at Landmark Mall. Witnesses say she appeared to be suffering from a real heavy head cold or something like that, and she had just finished loading shopping into the back of her car, and had some sort of sneezing fit. She stepped back from the car as she was sneezing and into the path of some old guy in an antique Buick whose registered blind but who, apparently, keeps driving. He didn't see her. She didn't see him, and it was over before she knew anything. Those old cars are built like tanks, and he took her down and went right over her without realizing it, or so he says. Witnesses say the woman was alive for about a minute before she died and the old guy's still in custody over at Alexandria Police Department while they work out exactly what to do to him that won't bring on a heart attack."

"Does the girl have family?" queried Harris.

"None we know of, it was just her and the mother. Preliminary checks reveal that the mother, Karen Selleck, was orphaned when she was nine, coincidentally when her parents died in a car crash. We're trying to look into a possible chance she had an aunt who was adopted, but at the moment that comes up blank as there are no records to support it.

"The parents were Canadians living and working in the US, but Karen was born here. Birth name Karen Renoeuff, she survived the crash, and because no other living relatives could be found, she was brought up by the state. She kept very much to herself, and didn't have a lot of friends. She was married briefly to an Edward Sellick, an only child and ex-Army Ranger who died on active service a year after his daughter's birth."

"What about his parents?" Harris asked.

"They both died last year, boss, father from colon cancer, and mother just pined away. Looks like Karen lived off part-time work, to make time for looking after little Becky, and that supplemented the Army pension of her late husband. This fits the profile perfectly."

"So, what's with the daughter?"

"Aaah, this is where it gets even more interesting," Lee replied. "The CCTV footage and witnesses put the time of the accident at 2:28 p.m. or thereabouts. Guess what time little Becky started freaking out at school?"

"2:28, by any chance?" asked Harris with mounting excitement.

"On the nose. We can be sure of the time as it was just before recess by a few minutes. That little girl knew something had happened to her mother and that she wouldn't be coming home. This fits the profile we've been tasked to look out for, which is why when this report was initially filed by Alexandria Police, we were on it in minutes."

Harris was jubilant. "Good work, Ryan. We need to act on this quickly to see what we've got. Do you know if the school or police also contacted the Department of Human Services and Child Protection Services?"

Lee didn't have to look at the report. "That's a definite yes. There's already an application in with the Family Fostering Services department because of her circumstances. All the schools here are very strict in their child welfare protocols, so we've got a very narrow window."

"We'll see about that," Harris muttered. "We've waited all this time for an opening like this, someone young we can mold, and we're not going to waste it now. Who knows she's here?"

Lee thought for a moment. "No one, boss. Maggie Creegan was on call at the time, and was there in sixteen minutes, posing as Veronica McMahon, one of the Child Welfare Department councilors to gain access to her. She got them to call into the office on the chameleon line to check her credentials, and after checking with us, they were quite happy they were speaking to the real deal. She was in and out in eight minutes.

"After all, it was close to bed time, and we've got to get her settled," he added, smirking.

Harris slapped his colleague on the back. "Good job all round, Ryan. Where do we stand with her now?"

"Well, to keep her comfy and calm her down, Maggie's stayed with her to reassure her everything's going to be alright, that we're her friends and she can trust us. We were going to let her try and relax for the rest of the weekend, and then we can start testing on Tuesday morning when the rest of the team gets back. They've already been notified and will be in bright and early December first to set up."

Nodding, Harris said, "Excellent. Ensure we have the DNA profilers in, too. I want to check for any commonalities between our subjects here. Oh, and make sure we check out any resistance she has to drugs. We need to see if that's a problem were going to run into in future."

"Okay, sure. How far do you want us to go with her?" asked Lee.

"To the max, Ryan. Even in a child, we need to know what we're dealing with. If we can't control them passively, we'll have to resort to more aggressive methods. Talking of which, how are those new AC stun guns working out?"

Lee shrugged his shoulders. "We're getting there. Several of our guests seem to be able to withstand the usual incapacitating charge, so we're playing with the voltage to see what's effective to drop them first time."

Harris was thoughtful for a moment. He turned back to the little girl inside the reinforced cell. "Make sure we find out what our newest addition can handle, too. Do it early on so we can get any unpleasantness out the way. After all, we can't have our new girl thinking she can keep us waiting for results, eh?"

Lee nodded. "Are you going home once you've signed the permission forms?"

Harris looked back at the little one last time. "You know, Ryan, I think I will. Things are going to get busy from Tuesday with this BBC News thing, so

I want to make sure I'm fresh on the day when all the fun starts. I can't wait to see what new stuff they'll come up with."

And with that, he ambled off to his office suite feeling invincible, with his jacket slung over his shoulder and whistling a little tune.

* * *

Five-year old Becky Selleck, a slightly built mousey-haired girl with large blue eyes, whose whole world had changed so drastically the day before, stared vacantly at the dolls and selection of books and comics in front of her. The tuna pizza and half-drunk soda lay discarded on the table along with the toys and various other items that had been provided to keep her entertained. Staring off into space, Becky replayed over and over again in her mind the moment her life had changed.

She had been coloring the beach scene they had been asked to draw by her teacher, Mrs. Cooper, when suddenly her mother's mind shout flooded her senses, blotting everything out.

*Becky? PAIN! Becky, darling, is that you? Aaaaaagh! PAIN! Becky?*

Frozen in fright at the shared pain she felt, Becky saw an overcast sky, strangely red, and then her perspective seemed to change. She found herself looking across the ground as if she were lying down, before looking back up at the red sky.

"Mommy?" she replied, then mentally. *Mommy, what's happening?* Her alarm began to mount.

More quietly now, her mother's mind spoke. *Oh, my darling. I'm so sorry, I don't think I'll be able to come and get you.*

With rising panic, Becky's mind responded. *What do you mean, Mommy? Why can't I see you? Why are you hurting?*

Her mother suddenly gained strength for a moment. *Becky. Listen. Please, I don't have much time. I've been hurt. PAIN! Remember what I said you must do if I ever had to go away? Do you remember? TELL ME!*

*I remember, Mommy, but why are you going? Don't leave me!* Becky replied mentally and then out loud for the class to hear, "No mommy! What's happening?"

Her mother began fading rapidly, but her urgency was tangible. *I love you so much, my darling. My big strong girl . . . I've been hurt really bad.*

"NO, MOMMY!" Becky screamed.

*Becky, I love you, but you must do what I said . . . .*

"NO, NO!" Becky screamed in sheer terror as she felt her mother's mind begin to slip from her grasp, "NO. MOMMY, DON'T, MOMMY, NOOOOO!"

She reached out with all her strength, refusing to sever the bond between them, feeling power surge through her mind and body. The world began to darken and her mother's personality turned translucent and seemed to slip away from her perception.

Becky heard one last faint whisper. *Don't forget, my darling. I love you. Do what I said to stay safe and you'll know who you can trust when you . . . .*

And she was gone.

A huge black void filled Becky's mind as she suddenly realized she would never feel and hear her mother's mind again, never hear her voice, and never feel the warmth of her mother's arms around her.

The world shifted again, and Becky became aware of her classroom once more. She could hear the murmurs of her classmates and she saw the shock on their faces. Mrs. Cooper walked slowly toward her, arms held out in invitation. "Don't worry, Becky, we're calling your mommy to come and get you."

Looking slowly around the classroom, Becky saw all the tables and chairs had been turned over, as if someone had been throwing them around. All the shelves were tipped over, too, and Mrs. Cooper was still edging forward. "Don't worry, darling, your mommy will be here soon."

Looking solemnly at her, tears filling her eyes, Becky replied, "Mommy won't be coming, she's gone."

And with that, the floodgates opened, and the devastated child collapsed to the floor in floods of inconsolable tears.

* * *

*November 28th –11:45 p.m.—Langley, Virginia.*

Maggie had been very nice to her, Becky recalled as she finally drifted off to sleep, although the woman told many lies.

Becky could see that she was tired, but even so, Maggie had stayed with her, read her stories, given her cuddles, and tried to make her as happy as she could be.

Mommy had always told her how important it was to be polite, and so Becky had done her best to listen, and smile when she could, to show she was grateful.

But Maggie kept telling her that everyone there was her friend, and that they were all going to look after her, because she was special. And that was what frightened her the most, because they were trying to get her to break her promise to mommy.

Becky knew she was special. She was like her mommy in that way. They could speak to each other's minds when they were in different rooms, or when Becky was sleeping over at her friend Megan's house, or even at school. They used to play games when they were with other people, to see how much they could still speak to each other and not get distracted. It was hard at first, because people didn't realize they were thinking out loud sometimes with their minds, and they would think about the weirdest things. Becky soon learned to cut out the distractions, and think and talk to two people at once, and mommy was very pleased how grown up she was at doing that without anyone knowing.

Mommy had told her it was something only the very best, only the most special people could do. Something only a real friend could do, and, because they were "different", she had to be careful because people would be frightened of them, even her best friend, Megan.

Mommy had always been right when it came to their secret. When the "special people" had started to save others, many of her friends at school said lots of nice things about them. They were good, they were kind, and they used their special powers to help people.

All her classmates had begun playing Angel games at recess, rescuing each other from monsters and fires and things. It was good fun.

But Becky soon learned that what people said, and what some of them thought, were very different, especially the grownups.

Some grownups had come to the school pretending to be nice, to play special games and quizzes. But they were really there to find people like her, and take them away and make them do things she didn't understand. Some were even secretly scared of who they might find, and had nasty thoughts about what they would like to do to "special people." And there were a lot who thought like that.

Mommy had told her to be very careful while they were there, and had helped her get lots of wrong answers to their quizzes like everyone else, even though they were easy.

The grownups were watching them very closely, staring at them like cats waiting for a bird in the tree. If it wasn't for mommy, Becky might have made a mistake and she was sure they would have pounced on her. It had been very scary.

She had to be extra careful that week, because she had recently discovered she could move things without touching them. It was a delightful discovery, although it didn't always work when she wanted, and mommy said it was because it was new, like riding a bike. Mommy said that once she had practiced, she would be able to do it all the time whenever she wanted. But until then, she had to be careful, because when she got upset, things kept moving without her wanting them to, like yesterday at school.

That thought brought it all back to her again, and the tears returned, as she cried herself gently to an exhausted sleep.

But Becky was a strong little girl.

She had promised her mommy she would stay safe, and she would do just that. All she had to do now was keep waiting for someone to come and find her, to tell her everything would be alright, someone who would take her away from those who wanted to hurt her and use her because she was different. Someone she could trust.

When the right person came, she would know who they were.

# 5

# Retrospect

*November 28th – 09:00 a.m. – (local time) – Old District, Tokyo*

Lei Yeung read through the report again that Angelika Papadakos had submitted for his attention the previous week, and couldn't help but express his disappointment by mulling things over and over in his mind.

*It's to be expected,* he thought, *but we had to try.*

*There's no conceivable way they would reach that level of professionalism and sophistication without some kind of indoctrinated conditioning included within their training regime to ensure they all behave like good little robots.*

*But they can't all be that committed, that angelic, it's not natural!*

*I mean, look at my beloved Council. While most of them are dark through and through, many could be said to be quite straight-laced in comparison to the stone cold killers like Angelika, and Sebastian, or Alexander come to that. We're not automatons incapable of expressing individual thoughts and actions, far from it.*

Member Luigi Espasito's face loomed large in his mind.

*No, the fault is mine. I should have anticipated this obstacle and formulated a better strategy for our initial approach. They won't be caught off guard like that again. Still, at least we know where they stand.*

Pausing for a few moments, he savored his favorite Daiginjo-shu sake. The elegantly light and complex blend of herbs and spices were quite aromatic and always managed to soothe him when he needed to think things over.

Sipping his drink, Yeung's attention was caught by the headlines of several of the newspapers on his desk, some of which were covering the dismal failure of the Costa Rican crime boss Luis Plazas, and his ill-conceived attack on the Guardian Angels.

Plazas was appearing in court next week for an initial listing of a trial date, and his attendance was guaranteed by Guardian escorts, who would ensure proceedings were conducted with a minimum of fuss.

Yeung couldn't help but stifle a morbid laugh as he read through the article.

*What have you done, you naïve fool? How short sighted, to imagine they would be that easily killed. All you've done is speed the day our world is brought crashing down on us.*

That when he had an epiphany. Smiling to himself, he thought, *why are the most obvious, simple things hidden under our noses? That's the path we need to take. It will mean change, but we'll maintain our power base, our influence, and we'll be in the perfect position to take advantage of the changes that are bound to come.*

Feeling pleased with himself, he turned his attention back to Angelika's report.

Flicking through it again, he had to admit, there were positives in there if you looked.

For example, he now knew these Guardian Angels were not invulnerable. While it would be very, very difficult to catch them with their guard down, time might make them complacent.

Additionally, it was clear that the easier targets were those less experienced who were still under some degree of training.

Cogs began turning again within his mind.

*So, if we can't entice them, we can at least look for opportunities to ensnare those who aspire to be angelic little Guardians.*

The cogs kept turning.

*That's a point! How do they select those they recruit? How are they discovered? They clearly don't live in some commune, so where do they live?*

He realized something else was right under his nose.

*Where are they? They obviously don't pop into the office on a nine-to-five basis, so just where do they go? It must be something huge to be able to handle their resources.*

*Is it something orbital? Underground, hidden in plain sight?*

Then, something in the back of his mind made him pause.

*What was that I read the other day in one of the British papers? Something about the first public contact being made in that small English town where a child's life was saved?*

*Why was that the first time they acted?*

Tossing down the rest of his sake, Yeung put in a call to another of his people in London without giving a thought to the time difference.

Retrospect could bring a refreshingly new way of approaching obstacles that you couldn't fully appreciate until you'd tasted defeat.

A voice answered the phone.

"Aah, David, I do hope I'm not disturbing you? There's a little task I'd like you to perform for me. This one's easy. Think of it as information trawling, if you will . . . ."

\* \* \*

*November 29th–2:00 p.m., (GMT + 12 hours)—Pacific Ocean*

Pacing up and down the conference room of the heavily cloaked and shielded Training Academy, in front of the floor to ceiling panoramic window overlooking the Pacific Ocean, the athletic blonde woman could not hide her agitation.

Her long hair was tied in a ponytail, static discharges snapping and crackling through it as she paced. She held several copies of various newspapers from around the world, still in the "Nike" sweat suit she liked to wear during heavy workouts. She had been enjoying a particularly rigorous aerobic session only five minutes previously, before receiving the mental summons to attend this meeting of divisional heads, or "Lords" as they were commonly known within Guardian circles.

Those same circles referred to her, Corrine Jackson, with deep affection as the Lord Healer, head and chief instructor of perhaps the most respected department they had.

Fiercely loyal and devoted to both her calling and its ideals, she had the strongest healing abilities ever seen in one person. Those abilities together with her driving passion for excellence made her the ideal motivating force behind one of their busiest wings.

All of them appeared youthful, but looks can be deceiving. In the case of these exceptional beings, no one would have been able to guess their real ages.

Turning to her superior, she nodded at the papers and fixed him with her electric blue eyes. She spoke in an accusatory tone. "So, are you still confident we've done the right thing, Earl? I said this would happen, didn't I? People will start to rely on us every time there's even a minor accident, every time there's problem, they'll turn to us, and they'll keep turning to us without waiting for a genuine crisis or disaster."

She gestured to the many newspapers, and a bank of flat screen televisions covering the inner wall of the conference room, each showing the news highlights from over a dozen countries around the world.

"Isn't that the objective we set out to achieve, Corrine?" Earl Foster replied. Otherwise known as the Lord Marshall, he was second in command of the Guardians, and chairman of this hastily convened meeting. At well over six feet tall, this muscular powerhouse of a man, with his dark skin and close-cropped black hair, was one of the most imposing persons you could ever wish to meet.

"They needed to know we exist and what we can do. Of course they're going to react this way initially," he reminded her.

Gazing steadily at the Lord Healer, he waited patiently for her to fight down her agitation, and motioned for her to take a seat with the others.

She countered by slapping some of the articles down onto the table in front of him and, standing over him, she snapped, "That's all well and good, but are we really ready to do this?"

Throwing her arms in the air, she continued. "We're talking about global cover, for goodness sake, and my healers will bear the brunt in any disaster where lives are lost or people are hurt because we weren't quite quick enough to respond. This is already happening because we're playing nanny all the time. Ask Anil—we've only just got enough manpower to cope with the real disasters as it is, let alone all this other stuff."

Mentally, she displayed some of the more "mundane" incidents they had assisted in over the past several months as part of their effort to introduce themselves to the world. She highlighted the attempt to kill one of their Alpha Response Teams off the Costa Rican coast earlier that month. She also brought up the strange attempts by unknown gifted individuals to recruit some of their number.

Turning to the man on her left, Corrine mentally invited the Lord Evaluator, head of Guardian Active Operations to back her up and offer his opinion. She emphasized her growing frustration by throwing herself down on the couch next to him.

Anil Suresh could best described as a coiled spring of a man, always serene, but like a cobra ready to strike at a moment's notice. He was continuously drinking in the details of everything taking place around him.

Lean almost to the point of being anorexic, he had lightning fast reflexes and a mind to match. He had been listening to the exchange and sipping tea from a bone china cup, the saucer balanced on his crossed legs, until his fellow Lord had flung herself down next to him. Anil exploded into a frenzied burst of movement to recover the saucer and spoon from mid air. He returned to his former posture within the blink of an eye, without having spilt one drop of tea.

Pausing to place both his cup and saucer onto the table out of harm's way, he glanced at his fellow Lord as she mouthed the word "sorry" at him. He smiled briefly, his white teeth lighting up his Indian features, before fixing his eyes on the Lord Marshall.

"Corrine is right about one thing," he said flatly.

"And that is?" asked the Lord Marshall.

"Earl, launching ahead of schedule as we did, and with the way things are at the moment, we're going to have to emphasize to some of the larger world news agencies exactly what we do, what we're here for. While we have managed so far, it's been a stretch, especially with the law enforcement issues we've already become embroiled in. We knew there was going to be a period of adjustment by going public, even partially as we have, but we have cut things too close on several occasions now, and I am concerned we may have jumped the gun a little."

The Lord Marshall spoke quickly. "We will be addressing one of those concerns later today, Anil, but why do you think we've jumped the gun?"

"One, we need more Guardians to provide the right kind of cover, and two, we have to ensure we make the most of the teams we already have, by making better use of the full spectrum of their abilities. I touched on this aspect in my recent report. Just because we have an exceptional healer, for example, doesn't mean we need ignore their slightly less impressive telekinetic or teleportation skills. No matter how tasking it is, we need to extend each phase of training to ensure the teams have the broadest range of skills available once they graduate."

"I thought that prolonged overall training by about a year, though?"

A striking woman cut in. "Not necessarily, if the latest data is correct, but even if it does extend training, it's worth it in the long run." The Lord Procurator, Jade Heung, was the youngest of them, but she had been responsible for the training, discipline, and nurture of her students for over eighty-five years.

She knew her division intimately, and when it came to expressing opinions on training methods and the results they produced, everyone listened.

Looking at her now, the Lord Marshall urged, "What's on your mind Jade?"

Jade paused for only a moment. "Until recently, I would have agreed with you. We just don't have the resources. But over the past year I've compiled the results of a remarkable program demonstrated to me by the Overlord, oh, several years ago now. It's a program that accelerates both the learning and training curve, and the psycho-energetic potential of the candidate by compartmentalizing different areas of the psyche, and allowing them to be utilized twenty-four hours a day, actively complimenting mental synergy, even when the subject is sleeping."

"You didn't mention this before Jade, why?"

"I didn't think to mention it, Earl, sorry. It's my area of responsibility, and as you know, I like to see the results before making any announcements, no matter how long it takes. I've been waiting to see how this year has panned out, especially with the implementation of the preceptor training for expectant mothers. I was going to include the findings in the New Year's board meeting. It's proved quite revealing."

Displaying the results mentally in the air before them, she unveiled the startling results of the new training techniques in comparison to the old.

She began with the previous year's statistics. "As you know, our latest version of the psychic assay device—the Compilator—provides us with a very accurate measurement of a candidate's actual abilities and future potential. Those achieving a rating of C4, Protector Class, or C5, Guardian Class, qualify to undergo the five year training program." She paused to highlight specific points. "You can see that in former years those aspirants didn't really gain that much strength or potential during basic training. It wasn't until they underwent the enhancement phase that their powers bloomed to perhaps, C6 Master Class or C8 Grand Master Class level. Obviously, there have always been those specially gifted few like us who managed to rate much higher on the C scale. Some even reached C10 High Grand Master, but that was extremely rare. Now look at this."

She paused to bring up the new results, causing all of them to gasp out loud.

Corrine, who knew the brain and its limitations better than anyone else in the room said, "Am I seeing that right, Jade? Our candidates are completing the basic training phase at Master or Grand Master strength, sometimes stronger? Before they've even undergone the enhancement programs?"

Jade was delighted at her friend's response. "Oh yes, something about the accelerated techniques amplifies the nexus of each individuals Psi Well causing it to bloom exponentially. The earlier we introduce it, the better the results, but even a year on this program would prove invaluable. Imagine what we'll get with full term graduates in the future."

"So that's why we included the expectant mothers!" stated Corrine intuitively.

"Exactly, the earlier we catch the fetus, the greater the potential and the wider the range of abilities. How the boss knew this would work is beyond me. Do you know we've even had two of the latest Protectors re-assayed at Ultra level at their Guardianship Inaugurations? True, they only achieved that level in their prime abilities at the moment, but goodness knows what we'll see as they mature and reach their full potentials."

"What are they Ultras in?" Corrine couldn't help asking.

"The young man is an Ultra Healer, which will please you no end I'm sure, and the young woman appears to have Ultra level teleport capabilities."

Anil's face suddenly became serious. "Are they future transcension candidates, Jade?"

"We don't know yet, Anil, but if they continue maturing, they may reach the minimum nexus threshold to undergo and survive the change. So who knows, inside a few years we may witness the first new candidates to survive transcension from High Grand Master to Ultra in nearly a hundred years."

The feeling of euphoria was palpable among the group. They couldn't resist grinning at each other like children in a secret sweet shop.

It remained that way for a good few minutes before the Lord Marshall spoke. "So basically, we thought we'd jumped the gun a little and it transpires we've gone public just as our potential has coincidentally jumped along with it, eh?"

Anil smirked. "I suppose you could say it was perfect timing, my friends. Or the astounding out-workings of our omnipotent Overlord again!"

The mere mention of the capabilities of the founding leader of the Guardians sobered everyone instantly.

The Lord Marshall said, "That reminds me. There's another reason I called you all here today. I do apologize. Jade's surprise made me completely forget. Adam has completed his final assessment of the candidates for the new post of Lord Concilliator and has asked me to convey the results to you."

"So who got it?" Jade asked. "Vladimir, Victoria, or Andrew?" These were the only Guardians beside themselves with psychic abilities rated above the nexus threshold who had survived the transcension process.

"Vladimir," Earl announced. "He feels he'll be perfect for dealing with all the PR hurdles we're bound to run into as we go public from Tuesday, and his particular history and character will assist in our integration into their everyday lives."

Vladimir Arihkin was an old Muscovite, who looked like a cross between Albert Einstein and Colonel Saunders. He was an unusual case in Guardian circles, having fully matured, and completed twenty-two years in the Imperial Russian Army the previous century before his vast latent abilities broke through into awareness following his treatment for a head wound.

He was a strong telekinetic and self-healer, which is why so many were surprised when he insisted on retaining the look of a bespectacled graying grandfather when he could have easily appeared younger, as his colleagues did. His fatherly image was sure to trusted by the public.

"I hope Victoria and Andrew aren't too disappointed." Corrine sighed.

"I shouldn't think so," Earl said. "They both seem to be waiting for the positions still vacant in Shadow Operations and the Inquisitors. In fact, I'm sure they've been holding out for them for a long time now, which is why they've turned down promotion so often before."

"When do you think he'll fill the Deputy Marshall post, Earl? You could do with a hand as things get busy," Jade asked.

Shrugging his shoulders he replied, "Beats me, I've given up trying to work out how his mind works."

Anil suddenly made a connection. "Funny that, isn't it?"

"What's funny, Anil?" Earl asked.

"In retrospect, it seems we always seem to be in the right place, at the right time in history, with just enough resources to successfully ensure our safe transition to the next phase of Adam's grand plan. And here we are, after all these years, going public at long last, just at the time our recruits are experiencing an expansion of strength and ability that virtually guarantees the success of our global targets. I mean, anyone looking in from the outside could say there was more than a bit of manipulation going on here, eh?"

They all paused, staring at their colleague as the weight of what he said sunk in. Each of them reflected for a moment on the awesome precognitive ability of their founder and leader, the Guardian Overlord, Adam.

None of them knew his last name, how old he was, or anything about his family heritage. No one knew where he had come from, only that he had been among the very first of them centuries and centuries ago. He had been guiding them, leading them, protecting them, and he always seemed to know where to be and when, what to do and how. He ensured those initial gifted individuals were safeguarded, and allowed to thrive, away from the fear and prejudice of those who didn't understand.

No one knew how strong Adam was. Even his so-called weaker abilities were off the charts, rating far stronger than the machine could calibrate at that time.

All they knew for certain was that he requested the Guardians concentrate their efforts in certain areas. Eventually, an incredible harvest would occur, completely at random. Adam was humbling them with the sheer vastness of his plans.

Snapping out of their collective daydream, Corrine suddenly asked, "Hey, has anyone been tasked to do anything about the reports we've been getting regarding the abduction of people suspected of having psychic abilities?"

Everyone looked toward the Lord Marshall, who nodded his head slowly. "That's a definite yes. The sad fact of the matter is, no matter how much we show we're here to help everyone, there will be a twisted minority of those in power who fear what we represent. They want what we've got. And if they can't get it fast enough, it would appear they are ready and willing to go to any lengths to procure it before someone else does."

"Makes you wonder how Adam will choose to solve the problem before it gets out of hand, eh?" Jade asked.

"Oh, I'm sure our illustrious leader has an excellent solution in mind," replied the Lord Marshall. "Just wait and see."

"Makes me wonder what he's already got in place. Knowing him, I bet you it involves something very public, and very spectacular," Anil chipped in, a huge grin on his face.

The Lord Marshall smiled at his friend. Standing to dismiss them all from the meeting, he added, "I've learnt never to bet against you, old friend. But don't be shocked if this time his solution takes even you by surprise. Tuesday should be an interesting day, and I think our new Lord Conciliator is going to find his job getting busier a lot faster than he anticipated."

And with that, they filed out of the conference room waiting to see what would be revealed in the days ahead.

# 6

# Good Cop

David Collins, an I.T. technician employed by the Ministry of Defense at Whitehall, London, couldn't believe the way things had gone recently.

This past weekend, he was supposed to have met the parents of his new girlfriend, Lindsey, for the first time at their home in Kent.

He'd been forced to work late again on Friday at the office. Luckily, he had the following Monday off. He had been on his way to pick Lindsey up from her flat in South Kensington when his mobile phone diverted a call to him from his home number.

The caller had been none other than Lei Yeung, The Council's founder and leader. Soon enough, David had been forced into cancelling the weekend entirely, much to the disgust of Lindsey, who was refusing to answer his calls. That same night, David traveled to Exeter in the West Country.

For some reason, he had been tasked to find a little boy, one Joshua Drake, who by all accounts was the very first person to receive the "open" attention of the Guardian Angels.

Yeung wanted to know why, and that was where David's particular skills came in.

David had a psychic shielding capability that allowed him approach people totally undetected. His ability didn't render him invisible to CCTV, but it could effectively cancel out his existence in the minds of those he met.

This was very useful to him when paired with his other amazing gift. He was also a "reader": he could touch someone and read the history of their lives, a very useful skill when it came to gaining information, which is why The Council had ensured he found employment within the Ministry of Defense.

His gift also revealed the psychic capabilities of the target, whether that person was aware of those gifts or not.

Instead of enjoying a comfortable weekend in the sumptuous home of Lindsey's parents, who were reportedly very affluent, he'd had to endure the quaint charms of one of Exeter's finer hotels. Instead of relaxing, he'd worried about how much damage had been caused to his relationship, as well as following up on newspaper reports about the boy.

Also, he'd been forced to wait outside the police station in the cold for hours, trying to catch readings taken from police officers as they entered and exited, so he could discover the address of the little boy and his parents.

Yesterday, he had struck gold. Armed with the stun gun he liked to carry in case things went wrong, he had gone to their home in the Beacon Heath area in a hired vehicle.

Parking nearby with his iPod and portable DVD player to while away the time in some degree of comfort, he had extended his shield to encompass the vehicle, and sat back to wait unobserved by neighbors or passers-by.

As bad luck would have it, the family had been away all day visiting the boy's grandparents, and when they returned at 11:00 p.m. later that evening, they got indoors before David could reach them.

Deciding that direct action was needed, he had returned this morning and intended to ring the doorbell.

When they answered, he planned to use one of the fake IDs he carried for Council business. He would use the one stating he was from the local Child Welfare Services, and simply ask to see Joshua to check that he wasn't suffering from any delayed trauma from what must have been a very frightening experience for him.

If they got funny, he'd just tase them.

The first thing he had noticed on approach was the "Hide-a-way" infrared surveillance camera positioned to capture all visitors, cunningly positioned by some guttering.

So much for getting in and out undetected.

Returning to the car, he had placed a band aid over his nose to distract attention from his face, selected a suitable hat, some thick-rimmed glasses, and an extra padded coat to make it appear he had a heavier build. Thus attired he returned to try again.

Joshua's mother and father had become incensed at the army of press who had camped outside the door for weeks after the boy's salvation. They had taken out a court order to prevent further intrusions, added security, and would not answer their door to any strangers, not even "official" ones, without a confirmed appointment and prior telephone call.

Peeping at him through the crack in the door over the top of the security chain, Joshua's mother demanded, "What do you want?"

Showing the ID, he smiled as he went into his routine, remembering to turn his back to the camera as much as possible. "Oh, hi, Ms. Drake, I'm here to see Joshua. Just a brief visit, to see how he is and make sure he's settled down after all the drama."

"Who are you again?"

"I'm Danny Hollings with Social Services, Child Welfare. Please don't be worried, it's just a quick visit. We're filing the report on the incident and I've been asked to drop by and just see that he's totally back to normal."

Narrowing her eyes, the suspicion obvious on her face she had replied, "They told me it was already closed, so why are you here?"

"Like I said, it's so we can finalize the report. You won't see me again after this, I promise."

"Where's Sandra and why didn't you call before you came?"

"Sorry, that's my fault. I just transferred here from Plymouth and forgot to bring your number with me. Sandra got tied up with another case. Look,

I'm really sorry, I can see this is obviously annoying you. I tell you what, I'll wait here, just bring Josh to the door, and I'll take one look then be out of your way, okay?"

She still wasn't convinced. "Wait there, I've got Sandra's number so I'm just going to check with her before I let you in."

"Okay, but don't be long, it's freezing out here," he added, stamping his feet to add to the effect.

As soon as the door closed, he was gone, walking briskly from the house and into the street where he employed his shield to ensure no one witnessed his departure.

*Shit, so much for trying to play the nice guy! I guess I'm going to have to play it harder. I'll come back later when they're not expecting it and just take what I need.*

\* \* \*

*December 1ˢᵗ – 11:55 a.m. London–England*

Expectations mounted at the BBC News Centre in London as 12:00 noon approached. Preparations over the past week meant that every BBC news correspondent all over the globe was on standby, just in case. Favors had been called in, and every sort of transport was available, should news teams have to go mobile at a moment's notice, ranging from private jet or helicopter, down to bobcats and motorbikes.

The newsroom itself had also been rearranged. The main news desk dominated the center as usual, but now positioned toward the rear of the room, with formal and informal interview areas left and right. They were ready for unannounced visitors, with space left vacant should there be a need for it.

Since 9:00 a.m. that morning, a special report had been aired in tandem with other major news broadcasters in different countries around the world, highlighting the exploits of the mysterious Guardian Angels over the past several months. Various experts were providing their advice and opinions on a range of related topics, such as the possible agenda and motives of the worlds' new benefactors. They also discussed the Guardian Angels' range of psychic powers, and what impact their actions and technology may have on a global scale.

The various messages left by them at the locations of a number of rescues and interventions were also the topic of hot debate. The most recent one appeared to hint on matters of law enforcement. A lively discussion had just ended via satellite link, with one of Australia's top policemen, Commissioner Gordon McMenamin of the Queensland Police Service. The Commissioner had been citing the rescue at Coolangatta, on the Gold coast, Australia, several months previously. A family had not only been rescued by the Guardian Angels, but the perpetrators of a related crime had been apprehended and left for local Queensland Police Officers to deal with.

The various police services in Australia were trying to decipher Guardian Angels' message pertaining to law enforcement. It was especially important because the two criminals responsible for the theft of a motor boat which caused the accident, Tom McAllister and Michael Thompson, had been the bane of both the Queensland Police and New South Wales Police for some years. They had made their unwelcome presence felt in Victoria from time to time, specializing in the theft of boats and marine equipment.

They were compulsive thieves, already on the road to a lifetime spent committing crime and serving successive prison sentences. Commissioner McMenamin had gone to great lengths describing the overwhelming compulsion both men felt to tell the truth and confess to previously unreported crime. It was totally out of character for the two men. The Commissioner stated that if this was a taste of what was to come, he would be giving his wholehearted support to their newfound friends.

Now, with just over two minutes left, the floor manager drew everyone's attention to the clock and directed everyone to stand by. News crews around the world were asked to finish last minute preparations, and complete final signal tests and equipment checks.

Screens went to the digital countdown, while the two presenters chosen for the occasion, Robert King and Sophia Davies, had the finishing touches added to their make-up.

As the clock hit the one minute mark, the intro music was queued, and the "Special BBC World News Broadcast" along with its presenters, was announced to the millions of people tuning in.

Robert King watched the floor manager's fingers count down from five to one, and began his introduction.

"Good day, you're joining us live here at the BBC, where we await the final few seconds to the deadline the entire world has been waiting for."

Sophia Davies chimed in. "Yes, the waiting is almost over, and we're about to discover if we're going to receive another broadcast from the Guardian Angels, or perhaps something even more astounding."

As she finished speaking, the wall screen behind them flicked to the red and white BBC Logo with the timer still counting down, now showing just twenty seconds.

"We're not sure what to expect, but our teams around the world are on standby, to provide as full as coverage as possible," Sophia added.

Robert then looked slightly off screen and said, "We now have just ten seconds to go, and an expectant world may begin to get some answers as to . . . . ?"

His voice faded as the studio lights suddenly dimmed dramatically. Power wasn't lost, but something was obviously affecting electrical circuits.

"One moment please, we appear to be having some difficulties here in the studio," he murmured.

As he spoke, the floor manager, Katy Greene, was frantically shouting into her microphone to her assistant, Amy Smith, up in the director's booth. "What's the problem, why aren't the backups kicking in, are we still broadcasting?"

Amy's voice sounded over the earpiece. "That's a yes. It only seems to be affecting the studio lights."

"Well, get it sorted, we've got the world watching here." Greene was suddenly shaken roughly on her shoulder by one of the floor cameramen standing next to her. "What?" she demanded.

He was pointing over to the informal interview area, where three large couches were arranged in a box shape with a large coffee table in the middle. "Look at that!" he gasped.

Sophia pointed. "Something appears to be happening right here in the studio, ladies and gentlemen. Can we get the cameras on it, please, so everyone can see?"

Greene shouted into her mouthpiece. "Don't worry about capturing any floor crew; I want those cameras on it."

In the dim lighting of the studio, what looked like a ball of plasma, the size of a small plate had appeared hovering over the coffee table. It was glowing and sizzling like a multicolored electrum, and casting eerie shadows over the rest of the set.

Ribbons of light seemed to wash and condense into it in concentric waves. The ball glowed more brilliantly, and grew in size. It changed color to blue white, creating an even starker contrast within the confines of the studio.

Both the presenters were struck dumb. They, along with the rest of the millions of viewers, watched the eerie display unfurling in front of them in silent awe.

The ball kept growing, and after a few seconds, it floated down in front of the coffee table, continuing to grow, until it was big enough to encompass a person, whereupon a black dot appeared in the middle of the cascading ribbons of power.

The dot grew bigger, until all that could be seen was a halo of cascading energy like a corona, encompassing a void of utter blackness.

Suddenly, a person stepped down out of the void, causing it to collapse in on itself into nothingness. As it did so, the lights returned to normal.

The abrupt return of glaring studio lights only added to the shocked silence that greeted the arrival of the visitor. Everyone, both in the studio and around the world, knew instantly what stood before them.

The stranger was dressed head to toe in black, and wore a cloak with the hood drawn so far forward so that a face was undistinguishable. His hands were cross-linked in the posture of a monk. He was a Guardian Angel in the flesh.

Robert was the first one to regain his composure, and managed to break the silence with a timely jibe to the camera, aimed at his co-presenter. "Well, everyone, it looks like Sophia got her wish and something much more astounding *did* happen. It's taken us a little by surprise, but hopefully we can make our guest feel much more welcome now."

He turned to the representative of the Guardian Angels. "Hello, and welcome to the BBC, and of course to the rest of the world."

The figure slowly lifted its arms, and pulled back the hood to reveal the smiling face of a quite unremarkable man who appeared to be middle-aged.

He was powerfully built. Despite this, he looked more like a university professor than a legendary "Guardian Angel." The gentleman standing before them had neatly trimmed grey hair, a moustache and beard, with silver glasses perched on the end of a generous nose.

Shrugging, and raising his arms in an almost apologetic way, the man chuckled. "I'm not what you expected, am I?"

His rich, deep, accented voice contained a hint of self-mockery and easily filled the air without the need of a microphone. He gestured to one of the couches. "May I sit down? Perhaps we'd all feel more comfortable if we relaxed and chatted over here."

Both Robert and Sophia almost fell over themselves in their haste to cross the floor to the informal interview area. As they did so, Katy Greene was hesitantly stepping forward toward the Guardian Angel, holding out a button microphone.

Tentatively, she asked, "Do you even need one of these?"

The Guardian Angel smiled amiably. "If it makes you more comfortable, my dear, I shall gladly wear it, although you will have to help me put it on. I've never had to use one before, and it looks a bit fiddly."

She leaned over him nervously. Her fingers trembled as she attached the microphone to his robe on the third attempt.

"Fiddly for you, too, eh?" His humor seemed to put her at ease. As she began to step back, he asked, "May I be so bold as to ask for a cup of tea? I feel I may be doing a lot of talking in a minute, and need something to help."

"Of-of course, do you like biscuits?" Katy stammered.

The Guardian's face lit up. "Why, thank you very much, I must confess I'm more than fond of custard creams." He patted his stomach. "Perhaps *too* fond—I have to be careful now. I can't burn off the calories like I could in my younger days."

Katy couldn't help but smile as she returned to the floor area. Before she had even turned around, she heard good old reliable Amy yelling, "I'm on it."

Both Robert and Sophia had now taken their seats. They had originally opted for the couch opposite the Guardian Angel, but moved closer to him at his insistence. He repeated reassurance that he wouldn't bite.

Despite the uniqueness of the occasion, everyone present couldn't help but relax in the presence of this "ordinary", extremely chatty, approachable man. Everyone quickly settled down, ready for the interview to start.

Sophia began. "First of all, can we say, on behalf of the BBC and indeed the rest of the world, thank you so much for coming. We weren't sure what was going to happen today, but it's lovely to get to meet one of you at last outside of a disaster or emergency. Do excuse me, but we've been calling you Guardian Angels—what do *you* prefer?"

The Guardian Angel removed his spectacles. He looked at them warmly before raising his arm so they could see the wide scarlet band with a thin inner gold stripe near to the end of his sleeve.

"Officially, I'm the Lord Concilliator, spokesman for the Guardians, but that's quite a mouthful to get your head around, isn't it? I prefer Vladimir. It's my name, and sounds much less formal, eh?"

Robert couldn't help but laugh out loud. "Vladimir it is, then!" He introduced himself, and then indicated his co-presenter. "Robert, Sophia. If you don't mind my saying, your name and accent sound Russian?"

"You're quite correct," Vladimir replied. "I was born and raised in Moscow, ooh, some years ago now. I've not been there for a while, and don't miss the cold at all."

"Do you still have family there?" Sophia asked.

"Yes, certainly. But I haven't been home in a long time."

"So, the world has dubbed you Guardian Angels, but what do you call yourselves?"

"We just prefer to use the term Guardians, to be honest, because we're fully aware of our limitations and are under no illusions about being angels. We just thought it time to properly introduce ourselves and hopefully open some doors for a closer relationship in the future."

"So that's why you're here today?" Sophia stressed.

"Yes, to say 'hello' to you all, and to reassure people that we're here to help. We also ask for your patience and understanding as we plan our initial approach to your leaders to prepare a framework for future co-operation. I suppose you could say we're eager to lay out some ground rules that will allow us to do our job properly as we try to implement the changes this will bring."

"Changes?" interjected Robert.

"Yes, of course. How else will society adapt to the introduction of, in the words of some in your media, 'Super beings who defy the laws of time, physics and nature'? One minute, you're going about your business, dealing with the stresses and challenges of everyday life on your own, and then, all of a sudden, 'tah-dah', we turn up doing all sorts of things that seem extraordinary."

"And you think this will mean changes?" Robert persisted.

"Yes of course, Robert. The world is, like it or not, a very different place now we're actively involved with it. That's why we deliberated so long before making ourselves known to you."

"So you've planned this for some time, then?" Sophia asked.

"It has been our aim to introduce ourselves for quite a while now, Sophia. But as I hope you can appreciate, with something that will have such a huge impact on all of humankind, planning the timing of it took a lot of forethought and, quite frankly, involved a high degree of risk."

"What do you mean by risk?" she asked.

The Guardian thought for a moment. "Let me put it this way. It's like trying to decide when to rescue people from a sinking ship. If you go in too quickly, unprepared, you end up managing to rescue some of the passengers, only to find out that you don't have enough lifeboats available for everyone. So many people die, because you jumped in too soon. But, if you wait a while, and make sure you have enough lifeboats, and enough properly trained crew to operate them, then, although you may lose a few passengers initially, you end up saving virtually everyone once you do start to help."

Robert added, "So you're saying that although you wanted to help sooner, you were forced to wait until your resources matched your desire?"

"Exactly. There have always been tragedies and natural disasters. History is full of incidents where good people have lost their lives. We have to watch the terrible loss of life, knowing that if only we had been ready, we could have done so much to help. But we couldn't. If we'd started trying to help sooner, we wouldn't have had the infrastructure in place, or indeed the range of abilities we now have, to be of a genuine help to anyone long-term."

"That must have been difficult," Robert commented.

The Guardian nodded in reply, a sad look on his face. "You'll never know, my friend, you'll never know. In his wisdom, the one who leads and directs us ensured everything was in place before we introduced ourselves to a world in desperate need. He ensured that all of us are fully trained, properly equipped, and correctly motivated. He ensured a proper infrastructure was in place to enable us to respond, very quickly, at any time to any place in the world, because to him, every soul is precious and deserving of the best quality care we can give."

"And you can guarantee that?" Sophia gasped.

The Guardian twitched his eyebrows. "Well, we promise to do our best. It is a stretch, I admit, especially in these early days, but part of the reason I am here today is to assure the world that we offer you all a full global response to emergencies and the occurrence of natural disasters should you wish us to continue to do so. Now, I must stress, we can't be everywhere at once, but we'll do our best to be there if you need us. And soon, we hope to offer much more."

The Guardian was interrupted briefly by Amy bringing tea and biscuits for everyone. After placing the tray in the middle of the table and pointing at the custard creams, she raced off to the safety of the control booth.

The Guardians face lit up with delight at the prospect of refreshment. He indicated to his hosts that they should follow suit, he took a handful of biscuits and began dunking them unceremoniously into his tea.

Quite a few people couldn't help but be surprised at how ordinary this man was.

Robert lifted his cup, obviously running something over in his mind.

Around a mouthful of biscuit, the Guardian asked, "You wanted to say something, Robert?"

"Vladimir, are you hinting there's more to come?" Robert asked. "It's just that before Amy brought the tea, you mentioned the Guardians were hoping to offer much more than you're doing at the moment."

"You are quite correct. As I mentioned, we had to wait before revealing ourselves to the world to ensure that our resources were sufficient to meet the demands that would be required of them. Now we've done that, we look forward to improving our services by asking for your help, because that help is something that will assist us to integrate into your society."

"How so?" Sophia asked.

"Well, as you know, we are now in a position to provide emergency cover, but I must stress, it is *only* emergency cover. Although we have the technical and strategic resources in place, we now have to wait for our human resources to catch up."

"So you're saying you need more people?" Robert inquired.

"Precisely, and that's where you all come in. There seems to be a huge increase of people being born in recent years with the genetic potential for higher psychic mental function, or 'Psi-function'. That's our term for those who have the capability of utilizing genuine, measurable psychic powers. Thankfully we have the means to distinguish the potential for such abilities, and can accurately measure the strength and range of those abilities in each individual. We don't catch everyone, but we do our best to locate as many as possible so their gifts can be fully enhanced by our specialized training."

"So how do we actually help?" Sophia asked.

"The more people let us know of gifted ones in their families, the more opportunities we will have to train up future Protectors and Guardians at our training academy."

Sophia's face couldn't hide her surprise. "Sorry to interrupt you, but you have an academy? And what are Protectors?"

"Yes, we have a very special academy, Sophia, and 'Protector' is the title bestowed upon our candidates when they graduate after five long years of training. Think of it as an active, but probationary rank, where the newly trained Guardian is given further on-the-job training and experience. After a few years, if they continue to mature, they are entitled to wear the black uniforms that have become quite infamous recently and subject of all the 'Jedi' nicknames that seem to have stuck like glue."

"So where is your academy, how many students do you have? Just how many of you are there out there?"

Raising his hands in a placating gesture, the Guardian shook his head. "I'm very sorry, Sophia, but that information is quite sensitive at the moment. One day we will reveal more about ourselves, but for the moment we have to remain a bit of a mystery to everyone, as we have done now for many years."

Robert looked thoughtfully at his guest. "It must have been very difficult to keep it secret all this time."

"It has been, Robert. It has put our candidates and their families under a great deal of pressure. Put a good few off too, I can tell you. But hopefully that will become a thing of the past as we move more freely among you and more of you join us in the future. It will be nice to widen the services we can offer."

"Widen the services?"

Vladimir nodded. "For one thing, our technology is far in advance of what is currently available around the world. We are looking forward to the time we can begin pointing your scientists in the right direction, regarding such things as clean energy solutions, and transportation and construction methods that harmonize with the environment instead of harming it. Health care is another area we can assist with, improving your screening techniques and treatment of certain diseases, your handling of trauma victims, and those born with genetic abnormalities."

"So you're going to solve or eradicate many of the problems we now face?" Sophia asked.

"No, I didn't say that, but we will point you in the right direction to help your scientists discover things for themselves. There's that old saying about the starving man: 'Give a man a fish, and he will feed himself for a day, teach a man how to fish, and he will feed both his family and himself indefinitely!' We intend to ensure you are pointed in the right direction to fully understand the things you will develop, and use those developments as a springboard for greater things."

"So what you're saying is, the help you provide will speed up the means by which we learn to reduce or eradicate our own problems. You won't actually do it for us, but you'll help us learn to do it for ourselves?" Sophia clarified.

The Guardian nodded vigorously and leaned back in his chair. "That's right. And by working along with us, you'll make our job easier too. For example, think of aircraft that rarely develop faults, mining processes that avoid the need for people being underground in the first place, and buildings that can withstand earthquakes or tornados, eh?"

"Prevention being better than cure," agreed Sophia.

"Exactly right, which will leave us free to assist in other ways, so long as we get the blessing and co-operation of your governments. Hopefully they will come on board without too many problems."

Robert couldn't help but interject. "This all sounds very nice, Vladimir, but we're talking about dealing with politicians. There are bound to be problems, yes?"

"Let's be realistic about this, Robert. You know as well as I do the world is full of all sorts of different people, from all sorts of different backgrounds, yes? By and large, most people can be described as "good", while a minority is labeled "bad." However, whether good or bad, what unites most people is their tendency to be fiercely protective of their own individual little bits of the planet. You look at this world from above, and you see an absolute jewel in space. Despite what mankind has done to it, the earth is still beautiful, and has the potential to be even more beautiful in the future. It's not until you start looking in books that you see all those dotted lines appearing everywhere. Man has been intent on carving out chunks of it for himself for thousands of years now, and then jealously guarding it against all sorts of threats and dangers, some real, and most imaginary."

"So you think some will dig their heels in at the offer of change because they'll view you as a threat?" offered Robert intuitively.

"Precisely—despite our best assertions and actions to the contrary, there will always be those who question what we do. That's why we chose to introduce ourselves at all those accidents and disasters in so many places around the world. Hopefully it's emphasizing we're here to help everybody, no matter where you're from. If you need our help in an emergency, then dotted lines on a map aren't important. Lives are!"

"That's very reassuring to know, but sadly suspicions are bound to exist, aren't they?" Sophia added.

"Yes, they are, Sophia, which is why I've been assigned to you to act as a mediator, to help ease any transition.

"Over the coming months, I will introduce you to my team. We are the ones people will be able to bring their questions to, and hopefully, have any fears and concerns allayed. Of course, a proper means of putting those questions forward will have to be formulated once we've liaised with your world leaders, but we look forward to helping even the most obstinate ones see the obvious. We're here, and we're here to stay, and all we want to do is help. We dearly want emerging ones around the world to join us, and extend an open invitation to them. If certain individuals or groups of society get so petty that they refuse our offer, or deny our full integration into society in their particular country while others forge ahead of them, well, that's up to them, eh?"

"So you're here for the long haul, then?" Robert asked.

The Guardian leaned forward. "Of course we are. We're not about to offer our help, save a few lives, and then disappear and leave you alone, are we? Of course, neither will we force ourselves on you. Our help is freely given to all. Everyone deserves the same standard and quality of help. Our people are all volunteers, from all the countries of the world you can think of, and so we offer our help to everyone. But if your leaders refuse our help, then we won't force the issue."

"And are you categorically stating, here and now, that you have no hidden agenda, or hidden master plan to get one over on us?" stressed Sophia.

Looking over the top of his glasses, the Guardian smiled. "A very good question, Sophia, and a very legitimate one. We thought such a question may arise, and as such I have been authorized to answer it in a very direct way."

"How so?" queried Robert.

"Let me put it to you as succinctly as possible.

"We are a very special, very powerful group of people. Helping others is what drives us, and motivates us to improve ourselves. We want to help, and we want to share that with you, so the world as a whole can grow and achieve its full potential. It could be a wonderful future, but to achieve it, you have to make a choice."

"What choice?" Sophia asked.

"To step into the future with us Remember, more people are breaking through into psychic awareness these days. Your future is our future. We need to unite to achieve it. Future Guardians are being born all around the world at this very moment. Think about it—who do you think has been saving you lately, Martians?"

Both presenters were too stunned to say anything for the moment, so the Guardian continued.

"That's why we need no hidden agenda. Your future will determine our future. We don't need your technology, your weapons, or your earthly resources. We are so far ahead of you that, not to be rude, it would be like asking a caveman to assist in building new warp engines on the Starship Enterprise. Not just ridiculous, it would never ever happen. You have no secrets that we can't find out if we want to. When we make contact with your leaders, we will demonstrate our integrity by presenting documentation to them regarding the military and industrial strengths of all countries. Obviously, we don't wish to cause unnecessary alarm, but hopefully it will prove, 'look, if we were after your secrets, there's nothing you could do because we've got them!'

"We can find out anything we want about you, and if you were thinking of planning a nasty surprise on another country, well, it's not going to work, because not only will we warn them about it, but we can easily remove your potential to cause harm to others. We're not going to steal any of your secrets and sell them to fictitious highest bidders, or use them to further any hidden agenda. We just want to help you adjust to our presence, so that as your society gets used to the concept of people helping each other, you'll be better placed to help yourselves.

"Psychic abilities do not discriminate between skin color, language, or race. They are neutral to a person's standing in society. They are here, now, and you are not prepared or equipped to deal with those people or help them reach their true potential. We are."

Both Robert and Sophia were still too stunned to answer or formulate a question, so the Guardian continued more gently.

"Imagine a future society where no-one ever need fear disasters or major accidents again, where the world was an absolute paradise, free from pollution or industrial scarring. Imagine a world free from sickness. Free from the dangers of organized crime."

"Crime too?" asked Robert in disbelief.

"Yes, Robert, but as I've mentioned, that's something for the future, as everyone would need to be on board before we could implement changes."

"What do you mean?"

"Think of all the countries in the world today and the differences there are in their judicial systems. Some seem barbaric, while others appear too lenient. Some are influenced too much by crime lords or by corruption.

"Some countries have problems that create all sorts of hurdles. All those conflicting laws and standards would need to be unified into one pure codex, one balanced standard for all. Yes, it would take a lot of work to unify the process, but it would be well worth it."

"That sounds …incredible," Sophia murmured. "To think that type of unity would even be possible."

"Well, it's a long way off yet, as I say, it's something for the future, and only when we get world leaders to unite. Remember, manpower will be an issue, as we would have to introduce any agreed changes gradually over a period of time, for example, by incorporating our Inquisitors into investigation teams like the FBI, National Crime Squads, and so on, so the world can see the impact the inclusion of our skills would have in such investigations."

"Inquisitors? What are inquisitors, Vladimir?"

"They are our version of policemen, Sophia, although we prefer the term 'investigators'. They are highly trained operatives who can use their specialized psychic powers to investigate a wide variety of incidents to establish the factual truth of what actually happened.

"Not only can they gain that information from people's minds, but they can support it with evidence from the environment, and also with the enhanced technology we have."

Robert nodded emphatically. "That sounds marvelous, Vladimir. People wouldn't be able to lie. It's like that example earlier today from Commissioner McMenamin in Australia, where those criminals were what, compelled to tell the truth?"

"That's right, Robert, although that incident does highlight the ways in which laws would need to change if we assist in law enforcement issues."

"What do you mean?" Robert asked.

"Well, the statute books would need to include clauses, or specific Acts covering the 'legality' of psychic questioning and examination."

"Oh, I see—it would be easy to allege someone is guilty 'because their mind said so,' but we need an acceptable framework in place to fairly and legally establish the truth."

"You see the dilemma, Robert? That's why we're developing a mechanical form of verification, so it can confirm the validity of any psychic findings."

"Sounds like a mind-field to me," Robert quipped.

"An apt expression though." The Guardian chuckled. "It's going to be a long haul, I think, but one that will be worth it in the end, especially when you consider the other side of the coin."

"What other side?" Sophia asked.

"Not everyone who develops psychic abilities wants to join us. We think that number is very small, but there are those out there who are not part of our organization, and of course like every other member of society, what type of person they are is largely down to them."

"So you're saying there are other strong psychics out there who are not Guardian Angels?"

"Are they a threat?" Robert asked fervently.

"Sophia, Robert, please remember we're talking about normal people here—people with an ability that sets them apart. Yes, they are out there, and whether or not they use their abilities for the good of all is up to them.

"The big difference is that they live a very difficult life at the moment, in fear of discovery by others, even by someone within their own families sometimes. There are those who would exploit them should they be discovered."

"Exploit them?" Sophia repeated.

"Of course. I imagine you're both aware of current initiatives in schools, in the workplace, and in the media to discover if anyone out there is a potential Guardian Angel, yes?"

"Yes, they're quite widespread," Robert affirmed.

"You're both reporters. What do you honestly think would happen to anyone out there who was discovered by some of these governments, or other interested parties, to possess psi abilities? Because I have to admit, we Guardians are quite concerned at what we're seeing."

Robert's intuition suddenly kicked in. "Do you have something to tell us, Vladimir?"

The world held its breath, as a totally different atmosphere descended on the studio, and they waited for the Lord Concilliator of the Guardian's to reply.

# 7

# Bad Cop

Making his way across the muddy fields behind the house of the Drake residence, David Collins had to smile to himself in satisfaction.

Sure enough, while the family had beefed up security at the front of their home, he had been correct in his assumption that they wouldn't bother much with the back.

The low wire mesh fencing separated the home from miles of open farmland bordered by statutory brambles, thorns, and thistles.

They obviously didn't think anyone would try to get through. And they were right—who in their right mind would traipse through this muck?

David amused himself with the fact that he probably wasn't in his right mind. The people he represented were not just *anyone*.

That's why he couldn't afford to mess about any longer. They would want results, and he was here to get them. Heavily shielded, a taser tucked snugly in one pocket and a dart gun in the other, he was determined to come away with answers.

*No more Mr. Nice Guy,* he thought.

Coming at last to the back fence, he looked around to ensure no one was in a position to see it bend under his weight.

He climbed over. A dirty plastic swing and a deflated plastic paddling pool in the back yard confirmed he was in the right place.

Other toys were littered around the poorly kept garden—a bike, a ball, some cars along with a few "Action Man" figures, all scattered and abandoned along the concrete path. The back door was conveniently ajar.

Perfect!

Removing both the dart gun and the taser from his pockets, he started along the path, quickening his pace as he drew nearer.

*Burst in, stun them, read them and then out through the front door with my face covered until I'm out of camera shot, then I'm away,* he thought.

A rear window was also open, and he could hear the mother shouting to the boy inside to shut up, as she was trying to listen to the BBC Broadcast. He thought he heard something about her wanting to hear what the Guardian was saying.

He was surprised. *Oh, they turned up then?*

However, that wasn't as surprising as what happened next.

He was about three yards from the door when he suddenly heard a thrumming sound and found a glowing, golden blade of light held about two inches from his throat.

He froze, looking along and over the long blade at the startling woman who held it there, her magnetic grey eyes boring into his soul, a look of warning flashing in their depths.

At six feet tall, and with a physique that looked as if a goddess had somehow been poured into her black uniform and molded into liquid marble, David knew instantly who had figured him out. *Shit!*

He felt an invisible pressure hold him still.

A voice in his mind spoke. *Hello, David, my name is Victoria. Do I have your attention?*

His eyes darted about, flicking from the blade to her, then to the house before returning to the blade again.

The same voice spoke again. *Don't worry about the people in the house. They're blissfully unaware of our presence and we're nice and safe within your chameleon shield. I asked you a question, David. Do I have your attention?*

"Err, yes!" he replied, too shocked to utter a full sentence.

He looked more closely into the face of his adversary. Her dark flowing hair was tied back, cascading over one of her shoulders. Strong features highlighted just how beautiful she was. But those intensely grey eyes terrified him; they burned with a barely restrained power that caused his teeth to ache.

Taking a deep breath, David repeated more fully, "You have my full and undivided attention, yes."

He relaxed as the Guardian sheathed her plasma baton, and David found he could move again.

*We believe you may represent a group of people who have made several uninvited approaches to our members recently in the vain attempt to offer positions of employment to them.*

*While every member of the Guardians is free to do as they wish, you should be aware that we are very loyal to the cause we serve, and none of us appreciate your attempts. While we don't know your reasons, we feel they must be of a somewhat darker disposition than we would prefer. Otherwise, you would have openly made contact with us.*

*Make sure you tell those you serve that they would be foolish to confuse our restraint with weakness. Just because we choose to act with patience does not mean our patience is limitless, understood?*

"Yes, I understand."

*I hope you do, because we do not expect to have to bump into you, or your people again under these circumstances. Understood?*

"Yes."

*Oh, David, not to labor the point, but that includes circumstances like this one, yes?*

"Yes, I understand clearly. I'll make sure that's passed along."

*Tell those you serve that this boy is protected. He is not only important to us, but to the whole world. If your people make another ill-advised attempt to gain access to him, not only will they regret it, but those making the attempt will never be in a position to harm anyone ever again. Am I making myself crystal clear?*

"Yes, Ma'am"

*Also, while I am fully capable of mind-reaming you where you stand and leaving your skull empty of information or coherence, I won't. Instead I will extend to you and your people something you have failed to extend to us, simple courtesy.*

*It is clear you are all gifted in some way. The world needs people like you, now more than ever. Seriously think about the path you are on, because if you don't, you will all face the consequences. Is that clear?*

"Yes, very clear."

And with that, David experienced a moment's disorientation and found himself standing on the sidewalk next to his hired car more than a mile away.

Needless to say, he was on his phone and updating his superior within seconds, very glad to be away from that compelling woman who was so terrifyingly beautiful.

\* \* \*

*BBC World News Headquarters—London—England*

The Guardian's eyes had a faraway cast to them as he deliberated over his reply. They waited for what seemed like an age before he at last nodded fractionally, and returned his attention to the studio.

"Sorry about that," he conceded. "I was just checking to make sure it's okay for me to explain a few things."

"So do you have something to tell us?" repeated Robert.

A wan smile crossed his thin lips. "Let's be honest for a moment. We've asked you to take quite a lot on faith, haven't we?"

"What do you mean?" Sophia asked.

"Well, we turn up out of the blue, start saving people all over the place, leave mysterious messages, and when we say our first very public 'hello,' we make all sorts of predictions that the worlds going to be a better place 'IF' you do what we say, yes?"

"Yes, but what are you getting at?" stressed Sophia.

The Guardian cocked his head and thought for a moment. "Let me put it this way. What do you imagine would happen if we were actually able to demonstrate the truth of our concerns?"

"That would go a long way in boosting public confidence, of course." Sophia was intrigued, wondering where the conversation was heading.

Robert agreed. "In fact, it would do a whole lot more than just increasing your popularity or public confidence. It would show we could trust you, and your claims of uniting people toward a better future. That's something the world's leaders have tried to do for years and failed quite miserably at."

"If you can claim to do better and actually prove it, well, bring it on, please!"

The Guardian nodded. "Very well. As a matter of fact I do have something to say, and without being rude to you both, I need to address the people of the world to do this properly. Am I right in saying your mobile teams are already in place, and ready to respond to anything that might develop in a number of countries?"

"Yes—why?"

"That will help facilitate what's going to happen in the next few minutes." The Guardian turned to face the cameras and the waiting world.

At that precise moment, at a number of covert facilities in various countries around the world, an irrepressible cold shiver was working its way down the collective spines of security agents.

It was a similar feeling being shared by another group of talented people, although for very different reasons. This broadcast was being used by them to gather valuable intelligence on those they thought of as their opposition.

In fact, so high were those concerns, that the energy generated by the sudden burst of e-mails, phone calls, and video links between them would have been sufficient to run a small city.

Back at the studio, most of the lights suddenly dimmed again as the cameras zoomed in on the representative of the Guardians. One bright light isolated him from everyone else, and added an ominous undercurrent to the increasingly tense atmosphere.

His initially open and friendly face now showed the steely resolve of someone clearly in control. His eyes began smoldering like burning coals to emphasize that fact as they bored into the cameras.

"People of the world, we came to you today as friends, ready to open a dialogue, and work with you toward a future that will have far reaching implications for the good of this planet, and for future generations to come. We can only achieve that future if we work together, and if you trust us. You will have listened closely to the discussion so far tonight, and will no doubt dissect it in minute detail once it has ended. However, we feel that you should all be given an opportunity to see the truth of our worries, because it is a truth that concerns us all.

"As you will be aware, since we revealed ourselves to you, along with a hint of our potential, certain initiatives have been implemented by various governments to uncover people who might possess abilities like ours. Some of those initiatives have been conducted in plain sight as referred to earlier, in your schools, in your places of work, and in the privacy of your own homes when you took part in those tests in the newspapers or on the computer, just for the fun of it.

"However, what the majority of you will not be aware of is the fact that along with those tests, an incredible amount of covert and quite frankly illegal snooping was taking place. Literally millions of you have had your movements, conversations, texts, and e-mails monitored in a focused attempt to identify people who have measurable psi abilities.

"To show the accuracy of this statement, and prove our integrity in this matter, certain classified documents will shortly be delivered to the heads of state of the respective countries concerned. Quite a number of your leaders were totally unaware of the procedures those security services were employing under their noses. In addition to this, sanitized copies will be delivered to all major news companies globally. We ask you to scrutinize those copies closely. Obviously, you will find certain details have been omitted from those files to protect the privacy of those subjected to illegal activity, and of course, to extend a degree of respect for the security of those countries concerned.

"A majority of countries involved had the foresight to take note of the last message delivered by us, reading between the lines of what it implicated, and have discreetly extended a number of invitations to us to visit their facilities to advise, and to ensure the best care is given to those individuals possessing true psi abilities. Such people exist. After all, I was one of you before my abilities were discovered.

"However, it is both disturbing and disheartening to realize that a number of facilities, particularly in Russia, China, Japan, Switzerland, Israel, and the United States are continuing to function, with little or no regard being given to simple decency or human rights. Some of you may wonder what right we have to interfere in the matters pertaining to citizens within specific borders, so, I would ask you all to consider this.

"At some of the disasters we have prevented, you have witnessed a mere glimpse of our potential. You have only seen a fraction of what we can do—a shadow of the power we possess.

"I referred to a simple fact earlier this evening, that we appear to have reached a pivotal time in human history, where a startling amount of people are being born with the capacity for higher mind function. Potential Guardian Angels are living among you.

"Indeed, we as Guardians are among you today, in a position to help only because we were discovered by those with abilities like ours and invited into a wonderful family of men and women who, instead of living a life of self-centered luxury by abusing their powers, were motivated by a superior vision to put their abilities to use, by serving others.

"Who would you prefer to guide those among you who are discovered to have the potential to cultivate such awesome power? People like us, who have demonstrated our integrity, or those who would ignore your rights? Who would you rather be in a position to influence such fledgling super minds, those who have many years of experience in helping, and nurturing, or those who have no experience whatsoever and are puppets to be used for the dictates of the state?

"Would you feel comfy knowing that people with psi abilities were being manipulated, intimidated, and forced by threat of violence to be a good little soldier?

"How secure would you feel knowing there were individuals out there who were capable of taking advantage of you in all sorts of ways that you were powerless to prevent or resist?

"Gifted people can be a great blessing to society, or a deadly cancer. How they turn out can be largely influenced by us all. To help you see exactly what we mean, we are going to be taking direct action very shortly against those who do not have your best interests at heart."

He sat back slightly, and the full lights of the studio returned, drawing the collective gasps of Sophia, Robert, all the staff, and many millions of viewers. Standing behind the couches in the interview area were six figures, dressed head to toe in black, heads bowed, hoods forward. At some unheard command, they suddenly removed silvery grey tube shaped devices from under their cloaks. Sweeping them in a circular motion seemed to activate them, and beams of green light instantly sprang from both ends of the tubes.

Simultaneously, the six figures slammed the ends of their respective plasma staffs into the floor, causing the whole studio to shake, and a deep "boom" to reverberate throughout the building. They stood there motionless, waiting.

Without blinking, Vladimir Arihkin gestured to his colleagues. "Ladies and gentlemen, may I introduce you to some Grand Master Guardians, the team leaders of today's operation. You will have noticed they were able to teleport into the studio without making it obvious, as I did with my entrance.

Hopefully this should indicate that no one who breaks the law, or who commits crimes against humanity is beyond our almost instantaneous reach. When I arrived here today, I did so slowly, and in a manner that created a theatrical entrance. My colleagues have just demonstrated one of the ways we can execute an instantaneous tactical insertion into any location without drawing any attention whatsoever."

He turned to the floor manager. "Katy, isn't it?"

"Err, yes." She stammered in reply.

"Don't be nervous, my dear, I was wondering if you would be so kind to ensure your mobile teams in the following countries I'm about to list are watching. If you don't have a team for any specific country, let me know, and we can improvise with a team that is available, okay?"

"Yes, certainly."

Standing, and walking to where his colleagues waited in silence, the Guardian paused for a moment. He spoke slowly. "Russia; China; Japan; Switzerland; Israel, and the United States of America."

As he said the name of each country, one of the Grand Masters stepped forward in turn and swept back their hoods, revealing their individual faces. It seemed as if the team leaders, two men and four women, were in their late twenties or early thirties and every one of them was in excellent physical shape. They gave the impression of concealed competence, confidence, strength, and ability.

Turning to Katy again, the Guardian Lord asked, "Are your news teams ready?"

"Yes, they're all on stand-by to go. But we couldn't get permission for an independent team in China. We have to have a representative of the People's Party with them at all times, and we weren't allowed any freedom of movement in Russia, either."

"That's no problem, the People's Party representative will be most welcome to go along, and . . . ." He paused for a moment as his eyes lost focus.

Suddenly, he asked, "Do you have any of your representatives on standby in Norway or Sweden, or somewhere like that who are watching and who are prepared to assist us at short notice?"

"Yes, we do, in Norway I think," she replied.

"Excellent. Please advise them to expect this Grand Master and her team in a few minutes." He indicated an exceptional looking pale woman with beautiful electric blue eyes, and a blonde bobbed haircut. She made a point of stepping forward and looking directly into the camera. She waved slightly and nodded once to ensure she could be identified. As she raised her arm, the two silver bands on her sleeve became clearly visible.

"Will do," Katy replied, as if she were carrying out an ordinary everyday task.

Stepping back, she began speaking rapidly into her microphone, and disappeared off toward the back of the studio.

The Guardian Lord turned back to the camera, and in a slow deliberate voice, made an announcement.

"People of the world, I am speaking slowly now, to ensure that my words are fully understood. As I speak, Guardian technicians are implementing a voice over sub routine into the signal. This will ensure that my exact words are accurately translated into the tongues and dialects of the people manning the target facilities.

"In a few moments, these Guardians will join their respective teams, whereupon they will teleport to the various cities where the BBC News Teams are located. Once they have introduced themselves, and provided essential instructions, the combined Guardian/BBC groups will then teleport to the facilities in the aforementioned countries where people are being held against their will. Once there, they will facilitate the release of all those who wish to leave. Should any express a desire to remain at any of the facilities we visit, their wishes will be respected. Be under no illusions; we will know with one hundred percent accuracy if any individual wishes to leave, or if they or their families are being coerced."

Suddenly, his eyes shone brighter, the light almost dazzling for a moment before he made an effort to reduce their luminosity to a gentle glow.

"To the people currently manning those facilities we will shortly visit: we will extend to you the courtesy of arriving outside of your main facilities. Once there, we will approach any representative you may have on hand, and request your co-operation to enter. If you exercise good judgment, matters will progress very smoothly, and your governments will no doubt be viewed more favorably by the world.

"If you seek to deny us entrance, be advised we will gain entrance without your support. Please do not view our restraint as a sign of weakness. Additionally, do not try to use force to prevent our access. If you attempt to use force, we will incapacitate you in the gentlest way possible."

The camera zoomed out again to show the Guardian Lord standing next to his colleagues behind the settees. He nodded briefly to them, whereupon they sheathed their staffs, and, at some unseen signal, simply vanished.

Smiling to his hosts, he walked back round to his seat and sat down. "More tea, anyone? It should still be quite hot."

"Err, no thank you," Robert mumbled.

Sophia just shook her head. "What happens now?"

"Well, now we wait a few minutes and then we see what happens. Where would you like to watch live?"

"Live?" Sophia asked.

"Yes, of course, that's why we joined up with your news teams. We want a third party to capture what takes place live on air at each respective site, so the simple truth is revealed. We can follow along with what takes place here in the studio."

"May I make a suggestion?" Robert asked.

"Please do," the Guardian replied.

"A lot is bound to happen if we try to go live to six different venues from here. If it's all being recorded anyway, why not stick to just one location now, so it doesn't overwhelm the viewers. Then we can show either the highlights after, or show each location in turn, if not today, on special programs over the week."

"That's an excellent idea, Robert. So where would you like see?"

Robert turned to his co-host. "Lady's choice, Sophia?"

Sophia thought for a moment. "Well, it would be a safe bet to go to an English speaking location, so America it is."

The Guardian Lord cocked his head slightly to one side for a moment and was obviously communicating with someone mentally, before nodding and looking back to his hosts. "Ready when you are. Would you like to announce it or shall I?"

Both presenters shook their heads and held their hands up in unison, causing the Guardian Lord to laugh out loud and mutter, "Chickens!"

He turned to the cameras once again. "Ladies and gentlemen, we are about to go live to the joint Guardian/BBC team visiting the USA, as they begin their operation to free a number of people held against their will. Please, try not to be upset at what you may see. These events are happening live, and persons at these establishments will be under a great deal of stress due to our arrival, and may act out of character."

He nodded, sat back, and helped himself to more tea and biscuits while the cameras of the world captured events that would go down in history forever.

# 8

# What a Difference a Day Makes

*BBC Studio—Washington DC*

In the few minutes it had taken for the Guardians to collect their respective squads and then join the various mobile BBC news teams on stand-by, last minute instructions had been given, and everyone was ready to go.

Cathy West, a twenty-six year old Languages graduate from Birmingham, England, still couldn't believe her luck.

She had only been with the BBC for four years, before landing what she thought was a plum assignment in the USA just a year previously. She was fluent in French, Italian, Spanish, and a number of South American sub dialects. This earmarked her as a prime future candidate for "The America's" correspondent's position, when it became vacant.

Up until yesterday, she assumed she would have nothing whatsoever to do with such an important occasion, even though her immediate supervisor, Henry Gould, a thirty year veteran of the BBC, had been taken ill with pneumonia only two weeks previously and still lay bedridden at his home.

She thought that if anything important did happen, they would naturally turn to a more senior correspondent.

That morning, she was awoken by a call from the Overseas Director himself, stating that she was not going to be replaced by a seasoned correspondent from New York as initially planned. They wanted to see if she was up to the challenge if it came her way. Evidently, Henry Gould had been loudly declaring she was just the person for the job, and that she should be given a chance.

And they had listened!

Initially, she didn't know whether to be elated or terrified.

Fortunately, Cathy's assigned camera man, Mike Turner, had experienced reporting from South Africa, Palestine, Beirut, Baghdad, and more recently Columbia, and had been able to help keep her exuberance in check. He reminded her that the odds of them actually being chosen for anything meaningful today were next to nothing.

She had managed to fight down her excitement until about ten minutes ago, when they realized that odds didn't come into it anymore.

The USA was on a short list mentioned by the Guardian representative, which meant they had spent the scant minutes since then in frenzied preparations.

The Guardian had gone on to clarify that a whole group of them, actual Guardians, were going to be stopping off at their studio, before taking them on to some unknown location in the United States.

*What a difference a day makes,* she thought, as four Guardians materialized out of thin air in front of her.

\* \* \*

*Old District – Tokyo*

Lei Yeung sat in his office, transfixed by the bank of TV screens before him, each tuned to a different channel from various countries around the world.

*My God!* He thought, thunderstruck at the direct action the Guardians were proposing. He would definitely have to revise his initial plans regarding how the Council would meet the danger they obviously presented, and especially after the call he had just received from David in the UK.

Trying to sort the implications out in his head, he was disturbed by a light rapping on his door. A familiar telepathic hail caught his attention.

*It's me, Sir, may I come in?*

Yeung extended a verbal and mental invitation to his trusted aide and head of security. "Come in, Harry. What have you got?"

Harry entered. Yeung could see his aura was tinged with a neon red—a sure sign he was highly emotional, angry, or excited.

"I followed Espasito to his hotel, and then the airport the next day as you requested, and managed to stay in close proximity without being seen. Over that time I was able to observe his thoughts clearly up until the time he was called through to the executive lounge," Harry said.

"And?" Yeung inquired.

"It's as you suspected, Boss. He thinks you weak, and a fool for not taking a more aggressive line. He's planning to do something about it himself to raise his status in the eyes of the other Apostles."

"Oh, really? What is he planning, do you know?"

"No, Sir, he went beyond my range before I could ascertain those details. The only thing that's certain is his desire to act. But, I did find something else you might be interested in. That's why I've been so long getting back."

"Go on."

"When I was scanning him, I saw definite signs of a compulsive matrix within the sub layers of his psyche. It was faint, as it's designed to fade as time passes, but someone has been fucking with his mind and ensuring his naturally bluff and aggressive tendencies are hard for him to resist at the moment. I spotted it because he's been under that compulsion for a few months now and it's left a mental scar that's slow to heal."

Intrigued, Yeung asked, "And do you know who it is that's been tampering with our brash newest addition?"

"I'm sad to say that I do. Although she tried to hide the evidence of her tampering, the mental signature belonged to Member Connor. That's where I've been, checking out things on her end."

Geraldine Connor was your typical blonde bombshell.

She was thirty-two years old, and highly empathic and compulsive. Hailing from Los Angles, in the United States, she had been a gifted member of The Council for two years now following the death of her father, and had ensured their coffers were well funded by the considerable revenue her porn agencies generated.

Yeung was nevertheless genuinely surprised by this revelation. Only yesterday, she had calmly been attempting to get him to visit her in America and sample the delights of her home town.

"Are you sure about this, Harry?"

Harry opened his mind to his boss, displaying the indisputable evidence of betrayal he had painstakingly uncovered over the past few weeks.

After double checking the information before him, Yeung said, "Thank you, Harry. That will be all."

Once his security manager had left, he spent some time using his considerable intellect to run through a number of scenarios in his head, before arriving at an acceptable solution for each of his problems.

*My suspicions are confirmed. They are choosing candidates from among the populace, and have been for some time. I've just got to determine how.*

*This training academy of theirs may present us with possibilities we haven't considered yet, especially if we can discover where it is.*

*And, if we can't follow that line, at least we know there are those out there who have been approached, and declined their offer for whatever reasons. Perhaps they might prefer our proposals?*

Making a few notes to himself to follow up on later, Yeung then turned his attention to the problem of Member Espasito.

*He lacks stability and good judgment, and she is obviously counting on that to divert our attention.*

*However, he does have considerable resources at his disposal. If I wait to see how this foolish attempt at revenge turns out, I'll be in a better position to determine our official response, because after all, his attempt could work!*

*Still, if he's discovered, we can simply deny any involvement.*

Yeung reached for the telephone to place a vital call to Member Papadakos, who he was sure wouldn't mind delaying the start of her current assignment.

He knew she loved the sunshine and warmer weather, so would no doubt enjoy a little side trip to Los Angeles in the States, even if it was on Council business.

*What a difference a day can make to your plans*, he thought, as the phone began to ring and he turned his attention to a more immediate solution to his other problem.

* * *

*Langley, Virginia.*

*Section 6, Parapsychology Investigations Response and Research Unit—Angel Project*

Gregory Harris could not believe how quickly the world could turn upside down when it hated you. Just yesterday, life had been good, great in fact, and it had ended on a very high note with approval being granted for the initial tests on their prize catch.

Those tests were scheduled for later today, and he had gone to sleep on the fold-out bed in his office. He was looking forward to what this new day would bring, only to be rudely awoken by yesterday's shift leader, Ryan Lee, just after seven a.m. Ryan was asking him to come and see what was happening in London.

It was just under an hour before shift change, and the others would usually come in from seven-thirty a.m. onwards, but they had obviously decided to come in early to see what the fuss was about across the water.

The atmosphere was quietly tense and everyone was on edge. The Guardians obviously had an awareness of exactly what was going on in the world, which would put most intelligence agencies to shame.

Liz Watkins, the team leader for the day, was glued to the TV, as were most of her team, Ian Cooke, Brian Hooker, and Colum O'Hagan. Sarah Smith, the only one missing, was already in the interview room with Maggie

Creegan being briefed on the preceding day's events, and the planned activities for the child that day.

Even then, the small portable TV was on, and the two women were obviously paying attention to the broadcast.

Initially, they had been quite relaxed when the Guardian appeared in the BBC studio, because the quaint, middle-aged looking man appeared completely harmless.

However, it quickly dawned on them just how powerful and how technologically advanced they must be, and Harris felt the blood draining from his face as he began working out the implications of what was surely going to happen.

As the phones in the office, and his own mobile phone began ringing almost in unison, his team was not surprised to see him turning purple in rage. He rushed into his own private office, slamming the door behind him to field the flack that was no doubt flying their way.

Looking through the glass window at Harris as he argued with whoever was on the other end of the phone, Liz Watkins called over to her fellow supervisor.

"Hey, Ryan, what do you think they'll tell him to do?"

"Hell, Liz, I don't have a clue, although I think it's obvious they'll come for us. We were on the list."

"We don't stand a chance. Did you see those light sabers they had?"

Brian interrupted. "Plasma Staffs, they call them plasma staffs, and they look a nasty bit of kit."

"Whatever," Liz replied. "I bet those things would slice through the titanium doors of this place like a hot knife through butter."

"Or us," Ryan mumbled with a worried look on his face.

"What?"

"Think about it Liz, if we're told to resist, do you seriously think anyone will come and help us, or give us Guardian killing ray guns or anything like that?"

"Shit! I didn't think of that."

Colum, who was still glued to the TV, called out, "Looks like they're on the way, they just disappeared from the studio."

Everyone jumped as Harris slammed his way out of his office. "Listen in, everyone, you're not going to believe what we have to do."

As he began filling them in on the delights about to come their way, they could all see the stress etched upon his blanched, sweating face.

Lee thought to himself, *He's ready to pop. And to think only yesterday he was the happiest I've seen him in a long time. What a difference a day can make!*

\* \* \*

*Langley Virginia*

*Outside "New Building"—CIA Headquarters.*

The New Headquarters Building at Langley was built to blend into the Old Headquarters with seamless grace. The new frontage had flowerbeds, landscaped gardens, and walkways separating the headquarters from the huge parking areas.

The entrance area itself, all glass, with aesthetic waterfalls on either side of the sliding doors, made it look more like the entrance to a university. If you took the time to look up, over the skylight walkway, the two towers of the old building were a reminder of what went on there.

At this time of the morning, the staff was arriving for work, travelling in from the suburbs or from Washington DC, which was only nine miles away. The walkways were beginning to get busy. Extra staff had been drafted in because of the BBC broadcast. Only a few minutes before, the place had become a hive of frenzied activity, especially for the security department.

Red lights had begun flashing throughout the building, warning everyone that a possible lockdown may occur and that security protocols were to be initiated.

Fortunately, it wasn't too busy outside, as the sudden arrival of six additional guests on the main concourse caused the few employees entering the building to jump in surprise.

One was a middle-aged man with a calm face. He was carrying a camera with the BBC logo on it. Beside him was a younger woman with the statutory microphone in hand, who looked like she may explode with excitement.

It was their companions that caused the most reaction; the earlier broadcast had made it clear who they were and what they represented.

Four black clad Guardians stood with the reporters, two men and two women. One of the female Guardians stood very close to the reporters initially, with her hands on their shoulders as she moved with them, obviously their assigned protector.

The leader, recognizable to some from the earlier broadcast, motioned with his hand and they began walking slowly as a group towards the main doors. The small crowd parted like the red sea.

The leader smiled warmly to passersby. "Good morning. Please don't be too alarmed, we're only here to pick up a few people, and then we'll be out of your way."

As they walked, Cathy kept going through the leader's instructions in her head, given to her just before their arrival. "Just relax as much as you can, and simply report what you see and hear as it happens around us."

He had indicated a dusky Mediterranean woman, identifying her as their protector. "Helene will be looking after you, so the rest of the team and I can get in and out with the minimum of fuss, and not have to worry about you, okay?"

"Okay." She still wasn't sure that she was really there, or that any of this was real.

Mike, the cameraman, had just nodded for a moment before continuing to check his equipment, clearly unfazed, a fact not unnoticed by the Guardians.

The leader had then identified their call signs for the operation.

"So you don't have to remember names, just refer to me as Alpha. Helene is Bravo. Remember, she will shield you from anything unpleasant. Nothing will touch you, okay?"

Cathy had nodded mutely at the reminder of what might happen. "That man there is Charlie," the Guardian continued. "He's our specialist healer, and the other lady is, believe it or not, Delta. We will be communicating mentally, as it's a lot faster, but will speak out loud if we need you to do anything specific. Do you both understand?'

Both Cathy and Mike had nodded their confirmation. Just like that, the world changed. One moment, they were in the studio, then there was a moment of disorientation along with a pins-and-needles feeling along the nerves, and what seemed like blindness. Suddenly, they were standing in the cold morning's sunshine, outside a glass fronted building in the middle of a group of shocked people. Bravo's steadying hand was on her shoulders, whispering that they were outside the "New Building Entrance" to the CIA Headquarters in Langley.

Alpha motioned for them to move forward together towards the sensor operated doors, all the time reassuring bystanders who were doing their best to get out of the way. The power had been cut.

Inside, armed people in and out of uniform were fanning out into a defensive cordon.

Alpha turned to Mike. "Are you getting the aggressive reaction to our presence, Mike? Please note in particular, they are not only armed with handguns, but there appear to be people joining them with both low and high caliber assault rifles. If I'm not mistaken, are those stun grenades?"

Zooming in and panning across the growing number of people inside the reception area, Mike remained calm. "Getting it all, just do your stuff."

Nodding, Alpha returned his attention to the doors, paused for a moment, waved, and called out to those inside. "Hi. Look, you know who we are and why we're here."

In response, several of the more determined security staff lowered their centre of gravity and trained their weapons directly at him.

The Guardian pointed to the door. "And I'm sure you're equally aware that cutting power to the door isn't going to stop us. I'd prefer to open it without damaging the motor mechanism, so if one of you would be so kind as to *think* where the power control is for a moment, I'd be very grateful."

Sure enough, the reception staff couldn't help but think about the controls to the door and how they could be isolated or operated.

"Thank you very much." With a gesture of his finger, Alpha restored power to the doors.

They opened, and the group began to walk in only to be met by four stun grenades, and half a dozen taser darts.

None of the percussions or blinding flashes caused any disorientation to Cathy or Mike whatsoever. Cathy was calmly narrating everything she saw and heard, concentrating on the aggressiveness of the response in particular. Mike, the ultimate professional, calmly captured everything in digital Technicolor for a stunned and disbelieving audience to see.

All of the tasers darts fired at the news team halted in mid-air, about five feet ahead. Those aimed at Alpha, Charlie, and Delta struck home and delivered their one hundred and sixty-thousand volts of electro-muscular disruptive power.

Although the taser operators kept their triggers depressed, they had no discernible affects whatsoever upon any of the Guardians.

Repeated dart strikes from other taser operators also met with similar failure.

Throughout the attack, the Guardians stared calmly back at their aggressors.

Noting their mounting shock and disbelief, Alpha spoke. "There is no need for this, you know. You're just tickling us and we're only here to retrieve some people who shouldn't be here. Now are we going to start communicating?"

His statement was met with a full on fuselage from the security staff, who let rip with everything they had. The deafening assault continued for nearly a full thirty seconds, in which time, some of them fanned out further to each side for a better angle, doing everything they could to take down the Guardians.

During the deafening assault, Alpha calmly turned to his companions, briefly looking to each of them in turn.

Cathy thought, *issuing instructions.*

Alpha's mental voice answered in her head. *That's right. In a moment Charlie will disappear for a few minutes to retrieve the documentation we require that shows exactly what's been going on here and by whose authority. Don't worry when he suddenly leaves us. For now, though, I'm going to end this silliness. It's gone on long enough!*

Looking first to Delta, who grinned and nodded, and then to Bravo, Alpha returned his attention to the security staff and raised his hand.

Everything suddenly went silent as the shooting instantly stopped. The camera clearly captured thousands of bullets hanging in mid-air in front of them like a swarm of angry wasps, before they dropped to the floor in a cascade of tinkling metal.

In the silence that followed, Alpha's whisper could clearly be heard, each word like a hammer falling on an anvil. "Are you really that stupid? Do you realize what would have happened to you if we'd erected a hard shield instead of a density barrier, how many of you would have been cut down by ricochets and your own lack of self-control?'

Comprehension dawned on quite a few of the faces looking at them.

A few even had the decency to appear ashamed.

"Enough!" He shouted loudly, at the same time mentally signaling to Delta.

She stepped forward two paces, and raised her right hand, clenching her fist. This caused a number of the security staff to resume their firing postures.

By the time they brought their hands up, their weapons had been sucked out of their grasps, slings, and holsters, into what looked like mini spinning vortexes or black holes floating in the air before them.

Shocked again, they stepped back, staring at the vortexes before them. Quite a few wondered if they were powerful enough to suck a person into them.

Alpha's voice cut through the silence. "Don't worry. Despite your totally unjustified aggression, we value human life, which is why we're going to make sure you don't do anything to hurt either yourselves or anyone else."

Both he and Delta suddenly brandished their plasma staffs, the beams bursting to life as they appeared. Slamming them in unison into the ground, they unleashed a rippling green wave of energy that rolled outwards from them in an ever expanding circle. Everyone the ripple encountered fell to the ground unconscious.

The building shook from the concussion, and continued to vibrate for nearly ten seconds before the rumbling faded away.

It was only then that Cathy realized that Charlie had vanished, off doing whatever his part of this mission was.

After the Guardians had removed the taser darts from their uniforms with telekinesis, they moved forward again at Alpha's direction, past the now unconscious security teams, and down the corridor toward the older part of the building. As they moved, Bravo began to draw back a few paces. "Don't worry, I'm just giving myself room to move should I need to," he explained. "You'd have to be over fifty yards away to start leaving my protective shield."

"Okay," Cathy replied gratefully.

Mike nodded, busy concentrating on capturing everything he could.

This drew a smirk from the other Guardians; they were enjoying the total calm he seemed to radiate in the middle of such a tense situation.

They reached the end of the corridor, turned left and continued on past startled workers toward the old building. A few minutes later, at a point close to where the old and new buildings merged, they found Charlie waiting for the rest of them by an armored door. He was being carefully watched by several members of the security team and a number of suits who were busily talking on mobile phones. They were in no hurry to offer resistance.

Cathy saw Alpha raise his eyebrows at Charlie, obviously asking a question telepathically, only to receive an almost instantaneous nod in reply.

Turning toward the camera and indicating his colleague, Alpha spoke. "For those of you watching, and wondering where my colleague has been, he has just secured all documentation held at this facility relating to something called the Angel Project. Those documents will be delivered to this country's leader in full later today. Heavily sanitized copies will be delivered to your major Broadcasting Companies.

"That project is the reason we are here today, because through the door where my colleague is standing we will eventually find a number of American citizens, ranging from just five years of age to eighty-four. They appear to be here against their will, most by illegal means. These people have varying degrees of psychic ability. It is our understanding that they have been subjected to invasive scientific procedures that amount to torture. This has ensured their cooperation regarding their continued grooming for deployment against the enemies of the United States.

"It may also amuse you to know that one of the gentlemen in front of us just offered my colleague a job, and asked that he pass that invitation on to the rest of us."

Smiling, and shrugging his shoulders, he added, "Fortunately, our diaries are full!"

With that, he turned to Cathy and Mike. "My scans of the area show it gets confined as we go in and down, so stay close. We will give you as much room as possible to capture what's going on down there, okay?"

Both of them nodded, and unconsciously moved closer to Bravo as they all followed him toward the door.

Charlie turned to the armored titanium doors, looked at the keypad control for a moment and concentrated. A faint thrumming was heard for a few seconds before the door opened, sliding into a recess, and drawing shouts of alarm from the watching suits. The security detail looked to them for guidance, but a warning gesture from Delta caused them to withhold their permission to engage.

Evidently, the spitting, coruscating ball of plasma, the size of a watermelon that she generated about two feet in front of them, was enough of a reminder for them.

As the Guardian team entered the hallway behind the door, Delta moved the plasma ball into the doorway, and expanded it until it blocked either entry or exit.

"Should hold for at least fifteen minutes," she said, grinning. They turned to the simple elevator doors at the end of the short corridor.

"Power's been cut," Charlie pointed out.

"I'm on it," Bravo spoke suddenly from behind Cathy, causing her to startle.

She closed her eyes, and concentrated for a few seconds before power was restored. Bravo then moved her attention to the handprint scanner and swipe card security ports. After concentrating again, they too came to life, displaying two green lights.

The doors to a very spacious lift opened, playing background music. A soft jazz version of "Fly Me to The Moon" made them pause and look at each other in disbelief.

Shaking her head, Bravo turned to Alpha. "I've looped the power supply so it can't be disturbed for about ten minutes. I've also neutralized the charges on the cables and breaks, just in case they get silly."

Delta addressed Cathy and Mike. "It wouldn't pose a problem to us, anyway."

"Telekinesis?" Mike queried.

"He speaks," Delta replied, punching him on the arm in a playful manner.

"Right the first time; all of us have it in varying degrees," Bravo explained.

Delta hadn't finished teasing him. "Yeah, so keep the noise down, Michael. God, some people just don't know when to shut up!"

Despite the gravity of the situation, everyone burst out laughing.

The sound of their receding laughter caused the suits and security detail to wonder what on earth was going on.

\* \* \*

The unfortunates trapped within the secure rooms of the Angel Project over four hundred feet down could only wait and listen with mounting trepidation as the Guardians made their inextricable way toward them.

Each successive reverberating boom signaled the destruction of one of the security check points. As each one was obliterated, the groaning and shrieking complaint wrung from the structures weakening integrity grew louder and louder.

The vibrations following the demolition of each post became more and more pronounced, until eventually, amid the flickering lights and falling dust, the assault seemed to reach its crescendo, and everyone held their breath. They waited for the final nail to be driven into their coffins and the inner doors to be blasted open in triumph.

In the deafening silence that followed, the simple knocking sound, along with the grinding protest of the armored door was a complete anti-climax.

# 9

# Someone You Can Trust

The team opened the door and filed into the office, while Alpha calmly walked over to the people kneeling in submission on the floor.

"Please get up," he said calmly. "It must be uncomfortable enough for you as it is without having to do that. If someone would be so kind as to get some refreshments, I think we can resolve the situation over coffee or tea, if you have any."

Several faces turned toward one of the men, who was still kneeling on the floor and staring at the ground. His face was ashen, and his pupils were dilated. His head was wagging vacantly from side to side.

Alpha scanned the outer layers of his mind and saw the conflicting emotions there, surging anger and fright, overwhelming fury and helplessness, suppressed authority and embarrassment, along with a huge weight that seemed to be sinking like a hot spike into his head. This confused his thoughts, and was concentrated on one side of his brain.

Alpha instantly recognized the onset of a stroke and quickly sent a mental summons to their specialist healer, Charlie. Alpha knelt beside the stricken man, closed his eyes, and sent his ultra-senses into him, searching out the weaknesses and the choke points within his brain.

He quickly catalogued years of bad diet, appalling sleeping habits, hypertension, and a tendency to push himself too hard.

The rupture about to take place within the major blood vessel of his brain would certainly damage all twelve of his cranial nerves. Alpha, a qualified healer himself, simply froze his entire system within a hyper spatial teleport matrix, suspending him within a micro-second of time. He conferred with his more qualified colleague who was already at his side and assisting in the unfortunate man's treatment.

To everyone looking on, Harris had appeared to turn to stone while the two Guardians hunched over him with their eyes closed. Their hands supported his skull and back.

Bravo was explaining to the members of the office what was taking place. One of the people who had just got up off the floor hurriedly explained. "He's been under a lot of pressure with this damned initiative we've been working on, and with the way he is anyway, it was only a matter of time before he had a stroke or a heart attack."

"Ryan, isn't it?" Bravo asked.

When he nodded, she continued. "They may be busy for a few minutes, so why don't you all relax a bit while we ensure the place doesn't come down around us. A coffee would be nice."

Bravo concentrated for a while, obviously speaking mentally to someone. A few moments later, a dozen silver tube-like devices with fold out tri-pod legs appeared on the floor in front of them.

Bravo and Delta began placing these around the facility at strategic points, and once finished, activated them simultaneously, causing a deep thrum to be heard. They could also feel a tingling sensation over their skin.

"Don't worry, that's just the force field keeping us safe," Bravo explained.

Everyone seemed to relax. "Well, tea and coffee all round then," Brian said cheerfully. "Is it okay for me to use the kitchen?"

Both Bravo and Delta quickly scanned the area. "No problem," Delta affirmed. "In fact, I'll help, and you can give me the chocolate biscuits to take care of."

Brian looked at her quizzically. She tapped the side of her head, grinning. "You can't lie to me; I know you've got some. And you keep them in the fridge, too, just the way I like them."

Shrugging his shoulders in resignation, Brian led her toward the kitchen area as she began to regale him on the benefits of chilled chocolate biscuits.

When they were gone, everyone was surprised to find Alpha was already standing up, nodding his head in satisfaction.

Harris was lying on the floor with his head in Charlie's lap, and people began to crowd round, getting in the way of the camera.

"Will he be all right?" Ryan wondered.

"Yes Ryan, he will be," Alpha assured him. "I'm a Master Class healer, amongst other things, but my colleague Charlie is a specialist healer, borderline Grand Master Class, so he's in very good hands. We've just initiated a cathartic nexus to siphon off the pressure, and as it reduces over the next few minutes, Charlie will repair the weakened veins and capillaries. He'll need to sleep for a day or two once he's home, but there will be no lasting side effects. Just give them some space, and we'll move him into his office. I believe there's a bed in there?"

"Yes, there is," Ryan said. "Is it okay if I sit with him? We've been friends for over twelve years now."

"No problem, I can ask your colleague, Liz, to help. I understand she's your counterpart."

"Yes, although she hasn't been briefed on our latest arrival yet, the little girl who came in over the weekend."

"We already have some copies of your documents available, and we can use those to go over your guest's history and check them out before we leave."

"That's good," Ryan replied vaguely, his concern for his friend clearly distracting him.

Tapping him on the shoulder, Alpha pointed to Harris, who was sound asleep and floating in mid-air toward his private office.

"We'll get him comfy and leave you two in peace," Charlie told him.

Alpha paused, and looked Ryan in the eye. "I would be grateful if you would do something for me."

"What's that?" Ryan asked.

"Just tell him how lucky he was that we were actually here today. It might not seem like it, but even had we not paid you a visit, that stroke would have happened. Maybe not for six months, maybe not for a year, but it would have happened. His lifestyle is killing him. Get him to think about a career change or he won't live to see his retirement. Trust me!"

Ryan glanced at his friend as he floated past and onto the bed in his office. "Oh, believe me, I trust you. Thank you for saving my friend. Many people wouldn't have done it given the circumstances."

And with that, Ryan went into the office, closed the blinds, turned off the main lights, and sat next to his friend in the darkness until the Guardians left.

Back in the main office, Bravo had been arranging the organized release of the people held in secure rooms a floor below.

Copies of their files lay on the desk in front of Bravo. She was discussing the first subject, Robin Johns, with Liz Watkins as Alpha rejoined them.

"So he's been on the streets for what, seven or eight years now?" Bravo asked.

"So far as we know," Watkins affirmed. "Records confirm him at Trinity Island School back in 2008, but after that, he simply dropped out."

"Any family?" Bravo inquired.

"None to speak of. His mother, Ellen, was a single mother and an alcoholic. There were a string of abusive boyfriends, many of whom were also abusive to Rob, so he was left to himself most days. He had to cook for himself, get himself to and from school. It's a common neglect pattern, sadly. When he dropped out and disappeared, she didn't even know he'd gone."

"And you picked him up how?" Alpha asked.

"Part of the initiative was to correlate out of the ordinary behavior, patterns, and reports. We found a very well fed, very well dressed street bum who had all sorts of stuff in an Aladdin's Cave of a den, who simply didn't get hassled by any of the other homeless strays in the area. It stood out a mile. Looks like a combination of neglect, having to fend for himself on the streets and the emergence of his abilities tipped him over the edge."

"So how did you get him in?" Bravo wondered.

"Big Macs mostly," Watkins replied.

"Sorry?" Bravo was trying not to smile.

"Big Macs. He has quite a telekinetic ability, and he would use his abilities to fend off anyone bothering him, or to get food, clothes, and toys. So when we brought gifts and food, and offered him a place to stay, he just got up, walked past the Snoop Team and straight up to the unmarked, supposedly covert wagon out in the street, and got in. He was our first find, been with us over a month now."

Bravo looked at Alpha and mentally asked, *How did we miss him?*

*We'll find out when Charlie does an initial assay of his abilities,* Alpha replied. *But don't be surprised if we find he has strong shielding capabilities. If he got into the habit of hiding himself from others over the years, it stands to reason he would do the same unconsciously as his abilities emerged.*

Alpha spoke out loud. "Let's get the ball rolling, shall we? Quicker we get this done, the quicker we can get out of here."

Bravo nodded and turned to Watkins. "We can do our own full assessment of your guests once they are at one of our facilities. I'll come with you to fetch Robin, to make sure he stays in a good mood."

As both women got up and began walking to another security door at the back of the office, Watkins said, "Pity you don't have a Big Mac with you, he loves them."

"Oh, I've got something much more fun for him," Bravo replied, patting her side.

Turning to Cathy and Mike, Alpha said, "Could you two please wait here? He's been held here for a while and might feel pressured to see a camera straight away. You can record them as they come into the office, and see what Bravo's surprise present is."

Several minutes later, an extremely happy young man was escorted into the office waving his very own, very lifelike Jedi sword around, heavily engaged in fighting off imaginary foes that were attacking him from every side.

Cathy and several of the CIA agents appeared quite shocked, until Alpha pointed out the plasma staff could be locked onto different settings. It was quite safe to play with at the moment, even with one of the beams deployed.

This statement was met with concerned disbelief by all the women present. All the men stared at the baton with envy in their eyes.

The main office area was rearranged so that the guests could await their release in comfort, drinking tea, coffee, or juice, while watching TV. Some of them ignored the television, finding plenty of entertainment in Robin protecting them from invisible Imperial Storm Troopers.

Bravo would escort one of the staff down to the rooms, ask them to get ready, and once they were dressed, would bring them up to the office to quickly verify their story and have Charlie check out their health.

One thing the civilians didn't know was that Charlie was not only a very strong healer, but also had an aspect to his healing ability that related directly to a person's "psi-well." He could sense the range and strength of the abilities they possessed.

Every human being generates an electromagnetic field. It surrounds their body, and many refer to this field as an aura. Although invisible to most, a person with psi ability can see this field by shifting their mental perspective. Depending on a person's state of mind and physical well-being, that aura can vary between a gentle nimbus surrounding the body, with brighter concentrations around certain meridians that some refer to as chakra points, or, if that person is unwell, it can be murky and flecked with muddy darker colors.

In those with psychic abilities, the nimbus is much more pronounced. It becomes a glowing halo of radiance, with bright concentrations at the chakra points.

If a person is endowed with powerful abilities, that nimbus blooms outward in petal shaped arcs, and can be mentally blinding. Where the individual is very strong, their energies can shine like miniature suns.

The color of the aura will reflect both the person's predominant psychic qualities, as well as their energy level.

Charlie's ability was even more refined. He was able to read individual auras with a clarity and precision that enabled him to evaluate a person's psychic strength, range, and achievable growth, or "ramping" as it was referred to, with a high degree of accuracy.

As Charlie checked each person, he was also able to assess and deliver a psychic profile for Alpha to present to the Lord Procurator on their return. His report detailed the range and current strength of abilities each individual had, and their ramping potential.

As he chatted to Robin, with the frequent interruptions that were necessary because of his fight against the Imperial forces that were threatening to overwhelm the group, he could clearly see the mental imbalance that crippled the young man.

His natural pink and vermillion aura, the sign of a telekinetic, intertwined with the blue of the intuitive ability of an empathic telepath, was marred by cloudy tendrils that seemed to leech the strength out of his natural radiance and mental balance.

It was something that could be overcome with care, allowing Robin to reach out for his potential. The bright yellow flashes edged with black was a sign of blocked energy that bloomed repeatedly from him, especially when he got excited.

Those flashes almost masked a very special ability that Alpha had asked Charlie to look out for, the velvet blue/black color of a natural mental and physical shielder, which explained why the scanners had missed his distinctive aura.

Very carefully, Charlie mapped his psi-well and complexus, highlighting where the Lord Healer and her staff would need to concentrate their effort to free him from his illness.

Yes, this young man had the potential to join the academy in future years. Charlie couldn't help but smile at the thought of Robin's reaction on earning his very own plasma staff, and one that could do some real damage to Darth Vader himself, let alone his puny Storm Troopers.

The next people brought up were the elderly couple from Nebraska, Earnest and Margaret Hemmingway, who had been married now for almost sixty years.

They had been discovered because, of all things, the garden surrounding their home was an absolute paradise. To say they had green thumbs was an understatement; all manner of flora and fauna thrived under their protective care. People gossiped at how they were always winning prizes for their flowers, fruits, and vegetables, and how they had an uncanny way with animals, even wild ones.

They might have gone completely unnoticed were it not for the current initiative. Their yellow and orange auras confirmed their elemental abilities. Earnest showed the strongest capacity for manipulating the earth and water, while Margaret's stronger orange and green tinged aura revealed an aptitude for influencing the health of living things.

They had been totally unaware that they had any special abilities. Their joy of gardening had channeled their energies in a mutually productive way that effectively hid their gifts from everyone, including themselves. Charlie could also see they were weak telepaths, but again, his scan of their minds proved they had no idea. They believed their years together had made them naturally intuitive to each other's thoughts and needs.

Thankfully, this couple had only been here about a week. They would be able to return to their home later that day and enjoy a peaceful life, free from further intrusion. The Guardians would see to that, and ensure an appropriate cover story was provided. With the CIA's willing assistance, they would announce the "mistake." After all, they just happened to be very experienced, gifted gardeners.

Jose Antonio Calderon, a thirty-four year old ex-con from Huston, Texas, was an entirely different sort. His distinct red aura, tinged with green, revealed him to be a highly compulsive individual, able to influence others by force of will. That, together with his self-healing ability and lack of early direction in life had made him a natural criminal. He was a thug who extorted others to further his own interests.

He had come to notice his talents when several hits on him had been unsuccessful, despite claims to the contrary, each asserting that he had been successfully gunned down. The news of his self-healing ability had pre-warned the Snoop Team, who used multiple weapons to bring him in. Even then he had presented quite a problem. Drugs had little effect on him. The teams on the Angel Project always tested him with two fully armed response teams on standby.

Fortunately, both Bravo and Delta were deliberately letting their own vastly superior compulsive capabilities deliberately leak out in his direction, and it was keeping him as quiet and compliant as a lamb.

Next to emerge from below were twenty-six year old Paul Cole, and twenty-four year old Sandi Windsor, a young couple from Alaska.

Sheer bad luck had led to their being discovered a few weeks prior.

Alaskan weather can be cruel, especially in the Northwest, and they had crashed their pickup truck on the way home from the small settlement of Wiseman during a snow storm. They preferred the seclusion of the "Great White", their cabin, a mile off the Dalton Highway and close to the Arctic National Park and Preserve, as it allowed them to live in utter tranquility.

Isolated, they had huddled within a protective shield against the side of the truck, generated and heated by Sandi, who kept her strength up by absorbing healing energies transferred to her by her boyfriend.

Once Paul had realized the storm was passing, Sandi had blasted away the snow covering them, and they had set out using his remote viewing ability to guide them. They had calmly strolled into the Rangers office at the reserve requesting help.

The recovery vehicle was dispatched to recover their truck. The driver noted the human shaped blistered paintwork where they had huddled against the side of the van, and drew it to the attention of the Rangers. Although they were able to explain the damage quite easily, the details in the report were pounced on by the Angel Project.

The next day, a fully armed tactical team was sent to retrieve them.

Fortunately for that team, both Sandi and Paul were quiet and gentle people who were not in the least bit aggressive. Paul saw them coming in three helicopters from over two miles away, and Sandi could have easily blown them from the sky when they hovered overhead, despite the fact that she was untrained.

Charlie could see Paul's green and violet radiance, the sign of a strong healer, intermingling with the ochre and blue/black blooms of his girlfriend. Her strong elemental abilities were quiet for now. They relaxed side by side, basking in their regained freedom.

*Yes,* Charlie thought, *today had been a very good day.*

And the best was yet to come.

* * *

*Holding Room 2 – Angel Project*

Little Becky Selleck had eventually fallen into an exhausted sleep in the early hours of the morning, dreaming of home and her mommy.

In her dreams, she was in the safety of her warm and cozy room, buried under the quilt, half asleep. She was waiting for her mother to wake her as she did every day, coming up the stairs projecting thoughts of love and security, humming the tune from the radio in her head.

Telepathically and out loud, she would come into the room and say, "Now where's my Becky today?" She always made a point of standing in the doorway as if she was searching every corner of the room with her eyes.

Looking at the moving mound on the bed, with the quietly giggling child inside, who was trying to shuffle into an even smaller ball, she would say, "Oh, she's not in bed, it's just the quilt."

Becky's mommy would walk over to the bed, get on her knees, and look under the bed. "She's not hiding under here, either. I know, she'll be in the closet and will try and jump out and scare me. Well, it won't work today because I know where you are, and I'm going to . . . ."

Throwing open the closet door, she would feign further surprise. "My, my, she's not here. Oh dear, I suppose I will have to eat her favorite breakfast for her. What a shame—she sooo loves Wheatyflakes as well. Never mind, if I can't eat them, I can always give them to Barney next door."

At the mention of Barney, the neighbor's very fat and affectionate dog, who loved having Becky give him tummy tickles that lasted forever, Becky would usually leap out from under the quilt. "Here I am! You never find me!"

Lately, she had taken to using her new gift by moving something small on the other side of the room with her mind, making it go "bump."

Mommy would play along and say, "I heard you, now I've found you." She would look and exclaim, "Oh, she's not here. I know—it must have been a mouse wearing Becky's shoes. I do hope the mouse asked Becky first?"

One time, Becky even made the quilt jump into the air as she revealed herself, much to their delight.

She would miss mommy, she would miss being woken by her thoughts, and she would miss her cuddles . . . .

*Becky?* A voice said.

Still half asleep, buried as usual under the quilt, Becky tried to hang onto the dream of mommy and home.

*Becky, where are you, little one?* The same voice spoke again; it was a man's voice.

*Go away, you're making mommy disappear.*

*I'm sorry, but I can't go away, your mommy wanted me to come and find you.*

Becky suddenly became wide awake and went very still, realizing she hadn't actually been speaking, just thinking, and that the man's voice was not a voice at all, but only inside her head.

*Hello?* She whispered with her mind, not daring to move.

The same warm mind replied. *Hello little one. Who's been a very good girl, then? Who did exactly what mommy said and kept herself safe until someone came to take her to her new home, a special home?'*

Not daring to reply, Becky suddenly remembered what her mommy used to say to her over and over again when they were together.

"Darling, if ever there's a time when I can't be with you, remember never to trust anyone who can't speak to you in the special way I do."

At first, the little girl had been confused by her mother's caution. "But why won't you be there? Why would you leave me alone?"

Mommy would always reassure her. "I wouldn't want to leave you, my darling, of course not, but this is important."

Gradually, over time, Becky had come to realize that mommy was just being very careful. Mommy was special like she was, and she wanted to make sure that Becky would always be safe if there ever came a time when she couldn't be there. Safe from others who couldn't do the things that they could.

"Where are the other special people?" she would ask.

"They are everywhere living in houses like you and me. Some very special ones live all together in a big home."

"Well, why can't we live there?" she would ask, employing a child's logic.

"Well, mommy nearly did when she was younger, but she was just going to get married to daddy, and so we ended up living in our own house. And now, I like living here, and I like it you have all sorts of friends at school, and mommy has her friends at work."

"Aaah, but the people here are not special like us, so we have to keep it secret from them. So couldn't we live there now?"

"That would be lovely, but it would mean leaving behind the friends we have here, so I thought we would wait until you're a bit older."

"Then we're going to go and live with other special people?"

"Hopefully, yes. But until then, we have to stay secret. And if I ever do have to go away, do you remember what I told you?"

"Yes." Becky would reply in a serious tone. "Be careful who I make friends with. Be careful who I talk to. If they can't speak to me with their mind, I must not tell them I can do it."

"And what else?" Mommy would emphasize, tuning in her aura so Becky could see it.

"Look at them carefully to see if they can shine." Becky would reply proudly, making her own aura shine brightly in return.

Mommy would then scoop her up in her arms. "Well done, my good little girl! They are the only ones you can really trust Becky, never forget that."

Special home! The words struck a powerful cord in young Becky's little heart. Still hardly daring to move, still trying so hard to do exactly what her mommy had told her, she carefully thought. *Why can you hear what I'm thinking?*

Feelings of warmth and a broad smile registered strongly in her mind as the voice replied. *Aaah, that's because I'm special like you. Like your mommy.*

*You're special?* Becky thought, still being careful.

A powerful feeling of approval radiated toward her from the unknown mind.

*Good girl. Your mommy would be very proud that you listened to her. If I could just find you, I would give you a big hug to say well done. But the people upstairs must have tricked me, because they said you were still in bed. You're not there, all I can see is the quilt. I know, perhaps you're hiding in the closet over there.*

The sound of his footsteps walking past the bottom of the bed toward the single closet in the room caused Becky's spine to tingle as she recognized the game she would play with her mother.

She exerted her farseeing faculty very gently and saw a man dressed in black, with pretty stripy things on his sleeves. He was opening the closet door. He was shining like the sun, surrounded by gold and dark blue bands of light, with greens and oranges and reds and purples of different shades, all swirling around and around.

*A SHINING MAN! A BRIGHT SHINING MAN!*

He was peering into the almost empty closet now and shaking his head sadly.

He turned to a woman still standing by the door, one of the ladies who worked there. He winked at her and said, "No, she's not in here, either. Oh well, I shall have to go without her then, what a shame."

The quilt exploded upward from the bed as little Becky launched herself toward his arms, shouting loudly with mind and voice. "No! Don't leave me, here I am."

Laughing loudly, the man caught her, held her up and looked into her hopeful face, his eyes shining like two warm suns. "Don't you ever worry about that, Becky. You'll never be alone again. Trust me, you're safe now."

Becky looked him straight in the eye and simply said, "I know." She snuggled into his chest and held on tight. She felt truly safe for the first time since her mommy had had to go away.

\* \* \*

Charlie was absolutely stunned when they walked back into the main office.

He expanded his own assessment faculty, so the others could see Becky through his mental eyes. Everyone was astounded.

Although she was only five, and totally untrained and unschooled by the Guardian preceptors, her mother's obvious input had a dramatic effect on her natural strength and range of abilities.

When Alpha put her down on the chair, explaining that Charlie was a special doctor who wanted to make sure she was okay before going to her new home, her unique distinctive aura became clear for all to see.

A huge golden nimbus surrounded her, interlaced with violets, indigos, blues, greens, and a strong pink, even flashes of vermillion, showing her huge reservoir of ultra-senses, empathic, telekinetic, and healing abilities. Some were haloed in white exploding mini stars, showing the abilities that had not yet manifested, especially the healing and teleport capabilities.

It wasn't the fact that her complex aura radiated with the brilliance of an individual whose abilities would easily mature beyond High Grand Master level, unprecedented in one so young and untrained. On the contrary, it was the ribbons of brilliant silver shimmering throughout all the colors of her aura that shocked them all. That color was a clear and rare indicator of someone with a vast psychic talent awakening and coming to fruition, someone capable of the ultimate transformation on maturing, someone capable of transcension!

To see those indicators in one so young and unaware was like being granted a glimpse into heaven itself. It was wonderful beyond description, and something they might never witness again.

The Guardians all exchanged surprised glances, a fact not missed by Cathy and Mike, still busily recording.

"Is everything all right, Alpha?" Cathy asked.

Alpha cleared his mind of the wondrous vision of Becky's aura. "More than all right, Cathy. This little girl is very, very special, and I've got a feeling that one day she may help to change the world."

Becky beamed at the compliment. "When are we going home, and why are they calling you Alpha when your name is Alexander?" she asked.

Everyone who heard her comment burst out laughing, while Alpha/Alexander had the decency to look embarrassed. He stooped down by her and spent the next few minutes trying to explain why the others were calling him by a different name.

Thankfully, she tired of making him suffer, and gradually became absorbed by what Robin was doing with his light saber over in the corner of the room.

She giggled and whispered, "He's funny." Suddenly her eyes popped as she shifted her telepathic perception and gasped. "Ohhh, he's special, too!"

Looking around the room, she instantly recognized the other people in the room who were special like her, and added, "Are they all coming home with us?"

Nodding, "Uncle Alexander" replied, "Some are, Becky, but some like Grandpa Ernie and Grandma Margaret over there say they're too old to move, and just want to go to their own home. They especially like their garden there."

She nodded. "But they can come and visit us when they want to, can't they? Or we can visit them?" She sent them a telepathic query.

Margaret got up from her chair, tottered over, and patted Becky on the head. "You can visit us any time you want, sweetie, and when you do, you can help me feed all the birds we get in our garden. They're always friendly, and always hungry and they love to sing for us when we feed them."

The elderly lady and small child then walked back to the other side of the room where they proceeded to chat away as if they had been friends for years.

Bravo quietly stepped over to Alpha, and spoke out loud for the benefit of the camera next to her. "They're getting inquisitive upstairs. We've been down here for a while and they want to know what's going on. It looks like they're about to send a team down the shaft to check things out."

"Let them come," Alpha replied. "We won't be here when they arrive anyway, and it will be good for them to get one of their own doctors in for Mr. Harris." He turned to everyone else. "If everyone would please gather round me, we're about to leave and I want to make sure everyone has everything they need."

Looking around, he surveyed his eager audience.

"From here, we will teleport to one of our Operations Centers. From there, you will be taken to where you need to go. Mr. and Mrs. Hemmingway, before we take you home, we'll be having a chat with you and introducing you to a liaison officer from the Lord Concilliator's office who will make sure you don't get hassled once you're home, okay?"

They all nodded once to indicate that they understood. "Thank you, son, that will be fine," Ernie added. "But would it be too much trouble to ask you take us to our local store as well? We've not been gone long, but need some milk and bread."

Alpha couldn't help but smile; it was one of the hazards of the job to be called son or other such terms by people who were far, far younger than himself.

"That will be no problem at all, Sir. Consider it done."

Turning to the Angel Project team, he said, "Don't worry, the place won't collapse for at least an hour, so it will give you all plenty of time to get what you need before you leave."

Before another word could be spoken, they were gone, winking out of existence in less time than it takes to blink an eye.

The bemused CIA agents were still sitting there, some ten minutes later, staring at each other in bewilderment and wondering what would happen. Their equally stunned colleagues eventually entered the offices via the wrecked approach tunnel.

"I thought this place was supposed to be impregnable?" said one of the recovery team members as they entered.

Liz shook her head as she beckoned them in. "You have no idea. Can you imagine what would have happened if they had been pissed at us?"

# 10

# Myth and Legend

Most people do not realize that many of the beliefs and rites found in a number of religions nowadays were formed from the myths and legends of ancient times. This isn't surprising when you remember what people in the ancient world had to contend with.

For sure, life was simpler then, but it was also a lot harder.

If you were hungry, you had to hunt for hours, maybe days on foot to snare, trap, or bring down your prey. You would have to understand the nature of your quarry, know its habits and its characteristics to ensure your chances for success were good.

If you couldn't hunt, you might have to bend your back from dawn to dusk scratching a living from the land, or through the animals you tended. You might toil to bring in the yield of the sea.

You would have to use those resources to make clothes, homes, tools, and weapons to protect your home and loved ones from those who would try to take what you had worked hard to produce.

Nature brought hardships, such as droughts, storms, eruption, earthquake, and so on. It's no wonder that in many cultures the gods evolved from the daily toils and struggles faced by people as they fought to exist.

The Pantheon of the ancient Assyrian and Babylonian nations prescribed the belief in superhuman beings in human form, all immortal, and each charged with oversight of an aspect of heaven or earth.

Some of the first to be worshipped among mankind were Tammuz, Ea, Asshur, and Enlil, who were said to control the harvest, the yield of the waters, supernatural powers, fertility, war, and the weather.

Marduk, chief among those gods, was said to exercise control over all the other gods below him, and was said to have the capacity to fulfill the role of all of them combined.

It is perhaps not surprising that those same qualities were also reflected in the Pantheon of another ancient civilization, Egypt.

The earth and its yield, fertility, storms, chaos, war, protection, even the personification of supernatural powers within humans, were embodied in such gods as Geb, Isis, Set, Horus, and Werethekau.

Again, this culture had a chief god, one who was above and who directed all those below him, Ra, God of the blinding sun, giver of life to those on earth.

As humankind spread across the earth and became more cultured, the gods they worshipped also took on a more philosophical and romantic aspect.

According to Plato, the earliest of the heroic Greek kings who rose to godhood and saved his people was Atlas, whose name was recorded in their earliest writings as king of fabled Atlantis. Others believe Atlas was a Greek name prescribed to an ancient fabled Egyptian pharaoh, Wa-n'ka-reh, or Achtoes III, or, in some more ancient references, Adem'uhn.

He was attributed with leading a society, blessed with highly evolved arts, literature and way of life, far in advance of those to follow, even thousands of years later.

According to Greek mythology, his characteristics as life giver and protector were reflected by Zeus, a being of such position and authority that he was more powerful than all the other gods combined.

His was said to control the storm, wind and life-giving rain, and of course the thunderbolt, which he wielded in his hands. He also encapsulated the finest of godly qualities, those of irresistible power, majesty, soaring vision and life and wore the fabled Aegis, the breastplate of protection and authority, so awful and awesome to behold that no-one could look upon its magnificence.

He was ruler of Olympus, home of the gods. He was lord of the sky, thunder and rain, and was also known as the cloud gatherer.

Zeus had many children, some from among humans, and those children were mighty in their own right.

The twins Apollo and Artemis are two such offspring of note who endured through the ages.

Apollo's qualities are encompassed within the radiant sun and light, in imitation of his father, along with the bow and arrow, and the dolphin.

He stood for truth and prophecy, medicine and justice.

His twin sister Artemis was thought by some sources to pre-date even the time of Greek legend. She was the chaste goddess of the hunt and wild animals, and of the athlete, whose qualities were represented by the bow and arrow, the torch and wings denoting her speed, and dolphins, which she loved dearly.

In some of the more obscure sources, it was thought that Artemis also served as an attendant to her father as standard-bearer and recorder, a task attributed to the Nike, the goddess of swift victory and military prowess.

Some sources claim them to be different aspects of the same goddess, able to overcome all obstacles to achieve victory.

The Romans saw Zeus's attributes reflected in Jupiter, their sky god, and god of thunder who was represented by the immense power of the bull.

The attributes of the pine tree are also linked to him for its ability to endure where other trees cannot.

Apollo remained "Apollo" to the Romans with much the same virtues, other than some interesting references to his warrior-like attributes, or brave and manly qualities.

Indeed, the Greek word Andros/Andres is reflected in a very common name, Andrew, and is still linked to those reflecting manliness in its most masculine form.

The Greek huntress Artemis, (or Nike) who wielded the bow and arrow with unceasing accuracy, and yet who loved animals, was named Diana/Victoria by the Romans.

As a quiet contrast to her father and brother, her qualities were represented by the moon, the mighty oak, and in some accounts she had wings on her feet, such was her speed and uncanny ability to achieve victory over death.

Myth and legend can provide a wealth of common denominators that help explain why certain beliefs or practices are so prevalent today.

Interestingly, they also reflect another common denominator.

A group of exceedingly powerful and very gifted individuals were believed to have existed throughout history, all of whom appeared to be united or otherwise under the leadership an even more powerful guardian.

Whatever the origins of these legendary individuals, be it human or divine, they were known to predominate for a period of time, guarding and shepherding mankind, before waning from public popularity. They were replaced by similar gods in other cultures, who coincidentally held the same or very similar attributes.

Some say such myths and legends may have a basis, jazzed up to make them more romantic or acceptable.

What do you think?

# 11

# Perspective

As the offices of the Angel Project disappeared, the feed was cut and the screens went blank for a moment. The broadcast switched back to the studio.

Robert appeared to be in conversation with the Guardian Lord. Sophia looked to Katy for direction.

"Welcome back to the studio," Sophia began, "After what can only be described as unprecedented events in America. We need time to absorb exactly what's happened, so we will be going to your local news stations, and we will return to you live at three o'clock. Join us then for a brief round-up of these incredible events, when we will discuss the impact of the direct action taken today by the Guardians, and what its implications are. See you then."

As the camera zoomed out and away, the BBC News theme was played before switching to the multitude of local channels that serve communities in most countries.

Millions of viewers had to endure over thirty minutes of torturous everyday drivel, weather and travel news, before returning at last to the reason they were on the edge of their seats.

During that time, telephone companies made huge profits as lines were jammed by just about everyone wanting to discuss what they had witnessed.

\* \* \*

Upon returning to the BBC studio, viewers were surprised to see the third couch was now occupied by two guests, the presenters having been joined by the young woman reporter from the American incident, Cathy, who was still obviously hyped up from the events surrounding the rescue. Alpha, or "Uncle Alexander" as he would later be called, the leader of the Guardian team who had so dramatically freed the people held in the fortified CIA facility, sat beside Cathy.

Robert opened the questioning. "Alexander, how do you feel the operation went today?"

"I feel today's venture was a success for several reasons," the Guardian replied. "Firstly, we set out to free individuals who had been held against their will, in clear violation of the actual laws of most countries. Now, I know some may argue that State or National Interests were involved that justifies in some way the measures they took, but, if I may be direct, the law is the law, people are people. Everyone deserves to be treated by the same standards and with the same level of respect. When ordinary folk are going about their daily business, they deserve to be protected, whether or not they are gifted. So, in that respect, we achieved the goal we set out to accomplish. The freeing of those held illegally.

"Please don't take us the wrong way. We really do respect and uphold the law. When laws are just and reasonable, they are a healthy guide for society to live by. We need set standards to guide us, but the law should also protect us. If you wanted to bend the rules to support or justify a certain line of action just because it suits a particular agenda, well, just imagine the nonsense that could be explained away with pathetic excuses. The law would become a millstone around the necks of those it was designed to protect, and a convenient tool for those who are prone to misusing power.

"That's another reason why I feel that today was such a success. It demonstrated that the same standard of law and protection applies to you regardless of what color your skin is, what tongue you speak, weather you're rich or poor. You deserve the best, and we want to set the world on the path to achieving that ideal."

"I can relate to what you're saying," Sophia agreed. "But do you think the world will perceive what you did as justified, seeing the violent reaction and opposition your presence caused?"

"Good point. I don't presume to speak on behalf of the world, so we'll see their reaction on the news in the following days. Personally speaking, I feel good about what I did today. None of the people we rescued wanted to be there. The mere fact they reacted violently has nothing to do with the rightness or wrongness of what we did."

Cathy looked a little embarrassed as she interjected. "I hope you don't mind, but I was there today with the Guardian Team, and although my footage will no doubt be the subject of a televised report later, I just wanted you to know how I felt."

"And?" Robert asked.

"Well, I'm just a reporter, and a relatively new one at that, and although we obviously surprised everyone at Langley, I was absolutely horrified when they started shooting at us. I mean, really, why they did that is beyond me." Indicating the team leader, she continued, "Alexander was openly communicating with them, asking for their assistance, trying not to damage things. And then they just started shooting and shooting. It was obvious they had something to hide and this is supposed to be one of the most civilized countries in the world. I'm sorry, but that was disgusting, especially when it was revealed they had children and old people in special cells deep underground. Talk about over the top."

"So how do you think the people will respond?" Robert inquired.

"I think they'll support what happened because people aren't stupid. They saw how violently the Guardians were resisted, and how gentle their response was. Just imagine what would have happened if they had responded in kind. And we all saw the people that had been imprisoned—I mean, please, a little girl? If this is the way America reacted, what happens if terrorists or even criminals get their own psychics, or are psychic themselves?" Suddenly a thought came to her. "Can I ask if any of the other teams got the response we did?"

Robert looked toward the control booth for direction while the Lord Concilliator replied. "We already know the answer to that question. Although we went to great lengths to emphasize our non-aggressive intentions, we were met with resistance amounting to deadly force at the Russian facilities as well and . . . ."

Robert cut in. "Actually, we have just received copies of that incursion by the Guardians. Would you like to see it?"

A few seconds later, the clip was loaded and ready to go, and a frozen picture appeared showing the blonde Grand Master Guardian. Everyone recognized her from the studio earlier that day.

The caption beneath the picture described the location as an FSB facility on a small island at a point where the Neva, Mal, and Reka-Bol Neva Rivers converge, just south of Leningrad Zoo Park, in St. Petersburg, Russia.

The picture was taken about ten yards behind her and to her right. Her plasma staff was in her hand, the blades were glowing bright emerald green, and two of her colleagues stood slightly behind her. They were facing outward on either side, with their staffs held in similar positions.

Their postures made it clear they were in the middle of a battle.

Everyone jumped as the picture came to life and the sound of heavy and sustained gunfire filled the studio. A man's voice was heard. "Remember, stay close to me to ensure you remain within my protective shielding and let Alpha do her job."

The camera panned left and right as they moved slowly forward, revealing they were crossing a bridge spanning a frigid looking river.

On the far side, about one hundred yards away, a plume of smoke suddenly appeared from the nozzle of a T-90F tank, as it recoiled from firing.

The camera paused on the most modern tank the Russian Army had, and then a split second later, there was a deafening explosion. The Dual Headed, Kinetic Energy, Armor Penetrating High Explosive Round struck home, causing an orange/yellow and black ball of flame to bloom over an invisible shield erected three yards in front of Alpha. The circular dome of her shield appeared, outlined in boiling flame.

The blast caused her to take a step back, then with a grimace her left hand shot forward and the barrel of the tank suddenly began to bend upwards. It stopped when it had reached a ninety degree angle. The tank tipped quickly onto its side, then onto its roof, keeping pace with the speed and motion of Alpha's hand, clearly visible, a pale contrast against the dark sleeve of her uniform with its silver bands near the cuff.

It came to rest, stuck solid on its roof, bent barrel driven deeply into the ground by its weight, where it stayed like a stunned beetle—minus the wriggling legs.

Alpha nodded to her two companions who began gesturing, and suddenly a huge amount of guns, rifles, and hand held anti-tank weapons appeared on the floor in front of the team, accompanied by sudden silence.

Walking up to the weapons, Alpha looked toward the people on the other side of the bridge, and then made a point of wagging her finger slowly at them.

She then raised her hand, and coruscating bluish white beams sprang from her fingers, melting the weapons so quickly that the rounds inside them never had a chance to explode.

She then motioned to everyone, and the team began walking forward again. They had only covered five or six yards before a huge portion of the bridge thirty yards in front of them exploded, showering debris over everyone, and out into the river.

The faint pattering of debris striking the shield could be heard, along with the occasional thump of a bigger chunk of masonry.

Suddenly, they all heard a very distinct and loud *"whump"*!

One of the Guardians pointed upward, and the camera caught a particularly nasty looking chunk of metal and stonework that had been serenely sailing through the air out toward the Neva River. It had suddenly changed course and, with increasing velocity, came crashing down on the camera crew.

This was followed a few second later by other chunks of debris, all being flung at the crew with uncanny precision.

Bravo could be heard reassuring them. "Don't worry, relax, it's nothing I can't handle. Alpha's just spotted the source of our mysterious rock throwers and sadly it appears to be a couple of people we were here to help." He paused, obviously receiving information mentally before continuing. "Yes, two young men, strongly gifted in telekinesis are diverting those larger pieces down on us."

There was another pause as a particularly large chunk of stonework and masonry bounced off the shield, before Bravo continued again. "Alpha is communicating with them now."

There was another pause as a tongue of flame curved out from the doorway of a building on the opposite shore, to spatter harmlessly off Alpha's shield.

"Aah, looks like one of them has some degree of elemental ability as well. It was a big mistake to direct it at Alpha, though. Keep going, you'll like this."

The reporter with that Guardian team, Warren Shaw, called out to Bravo. "We'll like what?" Suddenly, two very startled young men appeared just in front of Alpha, obviously teleported by surprise away from their secret vantage points.

Both of them sported crew cuts and were wearing military uniforms. They immediately dropped into fighting crouches and began gesturing with their hands. They were met with an equally instantaneous response from Alpha, who slammed her staff into the floor, sending out a familiar boom, and an expanding, rippling wave of green energy.

The energy wave lifted the young men off their feet and caused the whole bridge to lurch. They came crashing to the ground, clearly unconscious, and as the boom died away. Silence descended once more.

As Alpha walked forward and passed them, one of the Guardians with her, another young woman stooped to check on the two men. After a moment, she smiled and patted them both on the cheek, before encasing them in a glowing red cocoon of light. She looked across to Bravo, who gave a quiet laugh.

"What's funny?" Warren asked.

Bravo gestured to his colleague. "Charlie was thinking, 'Boys! When will they *ever* learn?' They're both out cold. No harm done, just a bad headache when they wake up and realize that they aren't the biggest fish in the pond."

"What's the red thing?" Warren asked, referring to the cocoon.

"We call them Dream Webs. It keeps a person unconscious and prevents them from hurting themselves or anyone else."

And with that, they continued on toward the gap where the bridge had been blown apart. A few seconds later the gunfire started again.

Bravo sighed. "Aah well, it looks like someone's brought some more guns to play with."

The footage stopped, and they returned to the studio.

"I must confess, the level of violence I've just witnessed is not like anything I've seen before, and it made me feel quite uncomfortable," Sophia admitted.

The Lord Concilliator nodded. "I don't blame you, Sophia.

Today we visited a total of six locations and only five people of the forty we offered to rescue expressed a wish to stay with their captors. Two of those wishing to stay and work with their governments were actually being held at the Russian facility, and they are the ones we've just witnessed using their abilities in an attempt to thwart the rescue of others held with them. Some are already being turned into super soldiers who are clearly ready to use violence to serve the purposes of their masters."

"It's lucky no one was hurt today!" Robert exclaimed.

"Thankfully, despite the use of deadly force against us, no one was hurt at either venue, the only casualty being a person suffering the onset of a stroke in the CIA facility. He was successfully treated on site by Guardian healers, and will make a full recovery.

"Once all the footage is in and you have had an opportunity to analyze our actions, I am hoping you will recognize the fact that you can indeed trust us. We will not neglect that trust in the way your governments do."

"If I may interject?" Alexander asked.

Both the Guardian Lord and Sophia nodded, so he continued. "This touches on my earlier answer as to why I felt today was such a success. I think the fact that we now have thirty-five additional gifted individuals who can contribute to making the world a safer place is one of the greatest victories we've had. Now, it remains to be seen whether all of them are suitable candidates, but all of them have volunteered for training.

"Just think of the impact that will have on the quality of protection we can give in the future. In future years, when some of these new ones are present at the scene of a disaster, people will be sooo relieved that they were given their liberty today and given the opportunity to join us."

Both Robert and Sophia were nodding. "So, do you feel today's actions have already produced results?"

"Certainly. Two of those who could have been future Guardians were actually persuaded to fight. It confirms what the Lord Concilliator said earlier today regarding the potential for danger."

"That's a very good point," Sophia agreed. "People like that would be very difficult to control or subdue by normal methods should they go on a rampage."

"Not that we're saying that just because they don't join the Guardians they will automatically become a menace—far from it. But we have seen how some are being induced to serve the political aims of the country where they live. This is something we are determined to counter in the future, to ensure we don't have psychic spies or soldiers on the loose conducting all sorts of clandestine activities to the detriment of those we would protect."

Alexander added, "And of course don't forget, if some of those other countries they oppose just happen to have their own psychic soldiers, well, imagine the potential for disaster. Just look at how powerful those lads were who opposed the team. Imagine what they could do to a normal police or army squad. It's frightening, because it shows just how far along the Russians have progressed their own psychic warrior research, and how they're prepared to use it."

The Guardian Lord joined in. "That's why documentation regarding each nation's agenda regarding this Psi Race will be collected by us and then delivered to each and every other country in the world. People need to appreciate this is not a race between individual countries."

"So each and every country with such an initiative will be visited?" Robert asked.

"Certainly, how else can we reveal the extent of the problem and make our recommendations," the Guardian Lord stated.

"Which are?" Robert pressed.

"Today's events confirmed that super soldiers are being molded. We need to ensure the law is changed to set guidelines that acknowledgement that psychic gifts are real, and that those people need to be properly trained so that they know how to use their gifts in a safe way, and in a manner that does not breach psi-etiquette."

"Psi-etiquette, what's that?" Robert asked.

"It's the term we use among those who are gifted, and refers to a proper and accepted standard of behavior.

"This is why we're so keen to help. We are the ones in the best position to ensure all those with gifts are discovered and recognized as early as possible, and then to train them to act properly and develop themselves their fullest potential. No one else has the expertise, experience, or resources to do this successfully. You stand at a crossroads in human history and need help. And we are here to give it."

"Well, you've certainly given us a lot to think about, Vladimir," Sophia said. "Is there anything else you feel should be highlighted?"

"No, not at this time, Sophia. People will need to see just how widespread the cause for concern is to provide some perspective to those world leaders who might be reluctant to work together. We look forward to seeing if society would like us to expand our input into everyday affairs."

"You mean the expansion into law and order?" Robert queried.

"Eventually, yes. Before that, we can broaden the fields of education, science, medicine, and so on. Of course, this will help us lay solid foundations before that huge expansion into your legal systems. The Overlord likes to remind us to take it one step at a time."

"When will we get to meet the Overlord?" Sophia asked.

The two Guardians exchanged the merest fraction of a glance. The Lord Concilliator replied, "We honestly can't answer that. Not to be difficult, Sophia, but he's quite a mysterious and solitary figure, even among Guardian circles. He's been working so hard that he tends to think and act at on an entirely different level. That's why he's ensured there are high ranking Guardians like myself who can speak on his behalf. Perhaps you'll see what I mean one day, perhaps not."

Robert had just received instructions via his ear piece. "I'm so sorry, but we have to round things off due to scheduling and time constrains.

"On behalf of all of us here at the BBC, and the viewers who joined us from around the world, can I say 'Thank you very much' for revealing a little about yourselves and your intentions, and for inviting the world to join you in taking the direct action we've seen. It's certainly given us much to think about. I'm sure it will continue to do so as further details come to light from the documents seized at the various locations you've mentioned. I'm sad to say our time is almost up, but hopefully we will have an opportunity to meet again as things develop and further details come to light?"

Both Guardians climbed to their feet. "I'm sure we'll all speak again soon, Robert, Sophia," Vladimir said. "And may I return that 'Thank you', as it's been very pleasant to be here and help you see a little of what we're about. Good afternoon."

He nodded to his colleague, and they both vanished from sight, thankfully remembering to take Cathy with them.

Robert looked briefly to his co-presenter, and then to the camera. "I think it's going to be a time of adjustment for us all in the weeks and months ahead, especially with people who can just appear and vanish like that. It takes some getting used to, I can tell you.

"So, join us again at six o'clock tonight where we will review the action taken today around the globe by the Guardian Angels, and bring you edited highlights of the events at each facility. For now, from us here at the studio, have a very good afternoon."

The picture faded to the BBC logo, the music queued, and that was the end of that day's entertainment for the world's public at large.

* * *

During the next few days, quite a few of the world's leaders personally experienced how unnerving it was to have people suddenly appear out of thin air in front of them. True to their word, the Guardians ensured each Head of State was paid a personal visit, briefed on that day's events, and provided with their own copies of some very sensitive documentation.

It didn't appear to make a difference where they were, or what they were doing, or who with.

Neither did it appear to matter what security measures were in place around them.

The day after the last of the world's leaders had been visited, all major news agencies around the globe received their promised copies of those documents. Even as sanitized as they were, they made eye popping reading.

December fourth dawned to the glaring revelations of secrets being laid bare, and the world couldn't get enough of it. The term "Read all about it" was true for once, as just about everyone could do just that!

# 12

# The Way People Think

*December 4th*

The day started much like every other day, with embarrassing headlines that dish the dirt on those in power, revealing a little of what they truly are.

People appeared to have an endlessly voracious appetite for what the newspapers had to say, and newsstands were soon emptied of virtually every publication on sale.

TV schedules were also adjusted to accommodate the many additional special reports, which were willingly devoured by a hungry public.

Such was the intensity of people's attention upon the events of December first that other daily staples were almost unanimously ignored.

For example, a number of newspapers and magazines around the world had been running articles on the unusually strange weather experienced that year.

Everyone seemed to accept that things had been getting warmer, wetter, and much more unsettled for a long time, and weather extremes were becoming part of everyday life.

Flooding, storms, high winds, even earthquakes, were more commonplace in lands where they had never been encountered before. Areas prone to seasonal wintery conditions were being crushed by extremely heavy snowfalls and deep penetrating freezes that were bringing Canada, Northern United states, and Northern Europe to a standstill. People were beginning to realize that when it came to the weather, forecasters couldn't really accurately predict ahead as they used to.

Australia was experiencing their sixth year of devastating flooding on a scale previously unheard of, along with Bangladesh, Spain, France, and many of the Greek islands. Huge thunder and electrical storms and high winds were striking throughout Southern Europe, and even into parts of Northern Africa, where they were just not ready to deal with it.

Even in the United States, where a well-equipped infrastructure was in place along Tornado Alley, the unseasonal storms there were causing havoc.

And for those living in Texas and Oklahoma who had been distracted by the events of December first, the weather was about to remind them of how fickle it could be, and how quickly headlines could change.

The day began with strong, warm winds from the southwest, which encountered unsettled colder winds from just about every other direction. Massive clouds caused heavy downpours followed by periods of bright sunshine, with temperatures several degrees above average, and heavy traffic warming up the desert roads. There were thunderstorms followed by sunshine and rainbows, with the oppressively sweaty, cloying air that makes it difficult to breathe at times.

The warning signs were there if people had been looking.

The oppressive weight of the clouds didn't seem likely to clear. The winds, gusting at over sixty miles an hour, seemed unable to freshen the air; they were more determined to test the fortitude of fences and sheds and the more fragile of structures belonging to the residents of Oklahoma and Texas in particular.

By mid-day, when the fifth increasingly violent thunderstorm had passed in the area bordering the two states and people were surveying the damage caused by the winds and marble sized hail stones, they were beginning to get worried. The horizon between Fort Worth and Abilene to the south, and as far as Wichita Falls to the north, was getting progressively darker and darker, and the thick churning, billowing clouds were piling higher and higher and fanning out into the anvil shape that heralds a really big storm. The interior of the clouds glared brightly, with increasing frequency, as bolt after bolt of lightning was unleashed with merciless abandon.

So concerned were the local authorities in northern Texas, New Mexico, and Oklahoma that they began initiating an evacuation plan.

Amazingly, they found that many people didn't want to leave their homes or businesses.

Winds suddenly leapt to over seventy miles an hour and those who had remained with their properties rushed to prepare for the inevitable.

\* \* \*

Four hundred miles above the earth, Guardian Observation Station Two was parked in geostationary orbit over Brazil. The cloud mass and building winds had attracted the attention of duty far-scanner, Guardian Naomi Cruiz, a former resident of Sao Joaquim, Brazil, and a graduate of the academy only three years previously. Fortunately, Naomi had the ability to compartmentalize different aspects of her consciousness and complete multiple exercises simultaneously. It was a skill that had not only earned her the respect of both her peers and tutors alike, but one that would prove to be a godsend as the day progressed.

Already, the unusual conditions were generating lightning strikes of over three hundred kilovolts. Naomi's ultra-senses, and her equipment—far superior to anything in the possession of NASA, or the military—were accurately recording core temperatures of each strike at over thirty-two thousand degrees Celsius, with energy in excess of five-thousand mega joules. They were occurring with alarming and increasing rapidity.

She had been watching the strikes go in with her far-sight for over three hours, and had just finished sending a Standby Alert Warning to the American Sector under High Grand Master Samuel Thaleton, as well as to Headquarters. Suddenly, her ultra-senses noticed that three areas towards the west side of the super cell thunderstorm were condensing rather alarmingly. The winds were increasing again to over one-hundred miles an hour. Because of the temperature differences of the colliding winds, they were beginning to rotate into three distinct vortexes.

If these increasingly unstable winds continued to accelerate, they would each spawn an EF5 strength Tornado.

She exerted her psi-faculties and mentally focused on the western edge of the storm, at the same time adjusting several of the monitoring sensors to ensure she could check her findings against them.

The periphery stretched from the edge of Fort Worth west toward Abilene, nearly a hundred and fifty miles distant, and a similar distance northeastward past Wichita Falls.

While it was not the custom for the Guardians to provide weather warnings, she felt it prudent to do so on this occasion, especially because of that area west of Wichita Falls where the pressure was dropping dramatically. The winds were beginning to converge into the three distinct vortexes she had previously noticed.

Homes and property were being battered relentlessly, not just by the winds, but by hailstones now measuring just less than two inches in size. Windows, vehicles, and other frailer structures were being badly damaged.

People were also being hurt, either directly by the winds and hail, or by vehicles, as drivers were beginning to lose control when their windshields were shattered by the freak hailstones.

Activating the Alert Alarms, she sent a condensed mental burp of information to the Standby Teams in the USA and Headquarters, as well as to the Alpha Response Teams on the station. She focused even more closely on the area of concern, as the vortexes had now touched down and were building in strength and energy.

At the sounding of the alarm, a mental query arrowed into her mind from the Station Commander, Grand Master Anatt Yasin.

*Why weren't we notified earlier, Naomi?*

*Up until two minutes ago, nothing to tell, yet another day, yet another set of storms with tornado potential, nothing their resources can't handle. Then within a minute, the winds jumped to over a hundred miles an hour and now we have three Class Five tornados formed and getting stronger!* Naomi explained.

*Three Class Five tornados, so quickly?*

Naomi was using her boosted far-sight in tandem with station sensors to zoom in even closer to the storm. She watched in amazement as the tornados appeared to rotate around each other, growing even stronger, before beginning to fuse into one vast vortex of incredible power. Ground zero was a two mile swathe of fury midway between Burkburnett and Frederick, to the northwest of Wichita Falls.

She scanned the monster tornado, simultaneously broadcasting her findings to the commander. The winds were now howling at over two hundred miles an hour and increasing. Intermittent purple flashes were visible along with the lightning strikes, indicating the storm was strong enough to create bursts of gamma radiation.

*Things are going to get busy—starting now!* Naomi replied, as she activated the Immediate Response Alarms.

Grand Master Yasin severed the link. She began issuing multiple commands to lead the teams that would be first on scene at the emergency, leaving Naomi to notify the civilian emergency service centers at Wichita Falls, Lawton, and Oklahoma City.

At the same time, she updated the Guardian Command Centre at Headquarters who confirmed they would now take charge of the incident from the station itself, and co-ordinate all available Guardian resources to optimize their response.

Free to make her final assessment before returning to Observatory Scan Mode, Naomi was greeted to the sight of a giant vortex, with winds now in excess of three-hundred miles an hour. The vortex seemed to gouge a groove out of the earth as it passed; it leveled everything it could touch as it headed for the next major city at its mercy, Lawton, containing over one-hundred thousand souls.

\* \* \*

High Grand Master Samuel Thaleton stood as motionless as a statue before the bank of monitors at the darkened American Sector Control Centre.

He was drinking in the constant stream of information from both the instruments before him, as well as information provided telepathically by his Silver Commander on scene in Texas and Oklahoma, Grand Master Yasin.

Although his hands rested on the console, he didn't move a muscle, operating the many instruments with telekinesis. The gold rings on his sleeves were swathed in an eerie blue/green light from the panels and computers as they went about their multiple calculations, making it look as if they were infected by some insidious disease.

The tornado had grown in size to over three miles across at its base, with winds in excess of three-hundred and fifty miles an hour. It had generated its very own unique storm front, and was preceded by a lethal Super Cell, where the hailstones were measuring in excess of three inches in diameter. The lightning bursts of over seven-hundred mega joules and over four times hotter than the surface of the sun, were striking every few seconds, causing actual bursts of gamma radiation. Such was the speed of the lightning strikes that the supersonic shockwaves they produced were multiplying together, resulting in an ear splitting acoustic roar of deafening proportions.

Samuel didn't like what he saw, and requested further help from polar Observation Stations One and Three to assist ground teams with evacuations. The storm seemed to be travelling at ninety miles an hour, veering away from Frederick and heading toward the main interstate highway, Route 44, somewhere between Geronimo and the next main city in its path, Lawton.

They could not afford to let it reach that city, and so the Guardians made ready to hold the tornado at bay in an area between Geronimo and Lawton itself if their attempts to neutralize it failed.

The Guardians had begun handling the disaster in stages. They organized smaller rescue teams comprising of Protectors and Guardians along the way at Burkburnett, Grandfield, Loveland, and other smaller towns, to assist those injured or trapped by the approaching maelstrom.

They had been fortunate. There had only been a handful of ruptured eardrums, a dozen casualties with broken bones, four with concussion from hailstones, and amazingly, only two victims of lightning strikes.

Many homes and other properties had been ripped to pieces and thrown almost a mile from their original locations.

The Guardians had to remove some people against their will, especially one group who had been determined to stay with, of all things, a barn full of clothing and sports equipment that they were trying to load into five huge trucks before the tornado arrived. Several were even on their mobile phones to lawyers in an effort to make the Guardians wait.

Assessing the situation as too dangerous, the Guardians had to forcibly transport them away en masse. Had they not responded when they did, all of those people would have died, either directly from their injuries as the building collapsed, or from the ferocious Tornado that arrived only minutes later.

As the Guardians stood ready to face the most devastating storm ever witnessed, there was no doubt they would be further hampered in their efforts by the small number of news crews who had sped to the scene, wrongly assuming that the mere presence of the Guardians would automatically guarantee their safety.

How strange the way some people think!

\* \* \*

*Paris – France*

Luigi Espasito couldn't believe his luck.

He'd done well patiently waiting for all the pieces of his plan to fall into place. At last, the day of the intercontinental missile tests had arrived, where he would stamp his mark on the world, proving to The Council that actions spoke louder than words.

Those missiles would provide the catalyst to expose the interfering Guardian Angels as the frauds he was sure they were. The guidance chips for five of the B91-11 Land Busters, doctored and replaced only four days ago, were ready to be activated and sent on their merry way to the new co-ordinates he'd chosen—co-ordinates that he was sure would never be forgotten.

A pre-arranged and timed diversion had also been prepared and initiated just several hours ago at the U.S Military Waste Isolation Plant in New Mexico. Two employees, eager to pay off a longstanding debt to the family, had created a diversion to keep the Guardian Angels occupied when they arrived.

A simple power outage had been activated, and at the same time, a short-term computer virus had been introduced. This ensured a catastrophic systems failure took place within the main plant. As this occurred, an additional Trojan Horse was added that had knocked out all the security sub routines.

During the panic that ensued, a few buttons were pressed elsewhere, along with the addition of yet another self-effacing, short-term virus. This ensured that the cooling and venting systems remained offline, while their corresponding monitors displayed false data.

When power was restored, the false readings gave the illusion that everything was as it should be.

The energy released by the radioactive materials kept in storage, dissociating as they were within unvented containers, had been building up to unsafe levels. Soon, this would trigger the security fail-safes, which would ensure the response of those so-called "Guardians."

Thus distracted, the second phase of his plan would go ahead.

A non-lethal gas would render the test scientists and observation teams unconscious for over thirty minutes, preventing them from destroying the missiles in flight. The new ground penetrating missiles, commandeered in mid-test, would be sent to their new co-ordinates where the old year would end with the bang he wanted.

The most satisfying aspect to this part of the plan was the fact that the U.S. Military, always paranoid about secrecy, had not released details of either the co-ordinates or range over which the missiles would be tested, nor the estimated flight times.

Delightful!

Pre-occupied as he was with the imminent execution of his plan, he'd been unaware of the extent of the storm tearing its way through Texas and Oklahoma. It wasn't until one of his cousins called, not ten minutes ago, to inform him of the loss of over five million dollars worth of counterfeit sports goods and clothing from a barn just outside Chattanooga, Oklahoma, that he'd tuned in via the many satellite TVs he had in his office to see for himself.

The goods had been in storage, en route from Mexico, when the town was evacuated by Guardian operatives. They had simply scooped up his workers with some kind of beam, before they could attempt to dispatch any of the merchandise.

The subsequent arrival of the storm ensured the total loss of all products, with no hope of recovery, and again he was faced with the prospect of being unable to live up to his promises.

Initial frustration at the Guardians interference quickly passed, when the screens started flicking across to the emerging situation in Carlsbad, New Mexico. Luigi realized this was a golden opportunity not to be missed.

*They're heavily committed, severely distracted, and I won't get a chance like this again. I guess today is my lucky day after all!* He thought.

Removing an untraceable and modified mobile phone from his desk, he began entering the encrypted codes that would ensure the day would be remembered for all the wrong reasons.

# 13

# Hold The Front Page!

Opinion was divided amongst the news crews who had descended on Lawton—who were now crawling down Route 36, west of Geronimo—as to what to record first. They had a choice between the approaching storm, grinding toward them about sixteen miles southwest of their location, or the six Guardian ships that had just arrived over Geronimo. This was the very first time the public had seen them; their matt black hulls, inverted 'T' shapes, and almost silent approach above the raging wind only added to the ominous overtone.

As they got out of their vehicles, two of the ships immediately began to move silently away over the outskirts of the town itself. Beams of light washed across each and every building, like searchlights hunting down escaped prisoners. Every so often those beams would pause, and a pulse of light would be seen moving from the ground upward, causing much speculation amongst the news crews as to what they were.

"Just picking up stragglers," a voice announced out of the blue.

Jumping, they turned to see a striking Arabic woman dressed in Guardian robes standing in their midst. The wind caused her cloak to flap about in every direction, exposing the two silvers bands about her left sleeve, a stark contrast to the darkness of her uniform, skin, and luxuriant hair.

"Sorry, what?" began one of the reporters nearest to her.

The Guardian indicated the ships. "We're just taking precautions in case we don't stop the tornado in time. Those lights you see are transportation beams. When they locate someone, we scoop them up into the ship to take them out of harm's way."

That same reporter narrowed his eyes, studying the ships with a longing look. It was an expression repeated by every news crew in attendance who yearned to be on board. Hunger!

Everyone ducked slightly as a ship came from behind them and swooped silently overhead.

The Guardian laughed. "Oh, don't worry about the ships. If you get in the way, you'll find yourselves inside one faster than you can think up a lying misquote."

Her winning smile was somewhat clouded by the steely cast to her glowing eyes. She fixed each one of them momentarily with a pointed glance.

Nodding in satisfaction, she continued, "I am Grand Master Anatt Yasin, Commander on scene for the Guardians at this incident. Please do your best not to get in the way, or endanger yourselves or others. If you have a question, just feel free to ask. Okay?"

Stephen McDonald, a veteran reporter for CNN laughed out loud at her directness. He decided he liked the straight-forward Guardian commander. Stepping forward, he whispered in a conspiratorial tone, "Seeing as you like getting right to the point, may I ask a direct question?"

She paused for a moment. Her eyes seemed to bore straight into the depths of his soul, causing a cold "icicle sensation" to pass along his spine. A mischievous light brightened her face in a smile.

Comprehension dawned. "You've just read my mind! Well? If we stayed out of the way and just televised the incident from the ship, would that be in order? There'll be plenty of reports from down here, so ours will show something from a different perspective. Obviously, we won't record anything confidential."

"Oh, I know you won't, Stephen." After glancing upward for a moment, she pointed at one of the ships. "Yes, the Captain of the Falcon has given his permission for you to board his ship. You will be taken to an observation room and allowed to report on things from a very unique vantage point.

Don't mess this up and you may find it's the beginning of a beautiful relationship."

Stephen was about to reply when a familiar beam descended from one of the four ships overhead. It washed over them momentarily before concentrating on Stephen and his two colleagues, whereupon it intensified and their outlines faded from view, being replaced by three glowing balls of light. The lights pulsed and ran along the beam back to the ship. The beam cut off, and the ship continued its course, heading directly into the tornado.

The remaining three ships had been fanning out rapidly, seemingly unaffected by the increasingly battering winds and lightning strikes to the four points of the compass. Once in their formation they began heading towards the approaching tornado.

The remaining news crews appeared annoyed at being out-maneuvered by their colleague, much to the amusement of Grand Master Yasin. She couldn't help rubbing it in: "Well, if you'd had the balls to ask, you could have been up there right now getting some pretty unique shots yourselves. My, my, are they going to see some sights. Probably make the front page, too."

She walked off shaking her head toward some colleagues of hers who had just materialized from one of the other ships. The news reporters threw dirty glances at each other, perturbed by their own timidity.

\* \* \*

*Guardian Observation Station 2*

Naomi had just returned from a break and was strapping herself into the armored scanning module, when her mind, still attuned to the enhanced "psi-optics" of the sensor array, alerted her to possible problems.

Almost instantly she brought her full focus onto the highlighted alert, boosting the Scan Enhancer Psi-optics to lock on to and verify the buildup of heat and radiation at the U.S Waste Isolation Plant in New Mexico.

Why hadn't their security measures prevented such a build up?

*Alert identified, scanning!* She mentally registered on the psi-log, while simultaneously placing her thumb over the DNA reader, thereby taking responsibility for the call with a correlating seal.

She went through the drill like an automaton, having already completed the routine numerous times in the past. She couldn't help but give a little smile as a few seconds later the ultra-sensitive alarms of the station activated.

*Beat you again.* She boosted her astral senses, zoomed into the Carlsbad area of New Mexico, and focused with intricate precision on the facility itself.

The Waste Isolation Plant at Carlsbad, New Mexico is the third largest radioactive waste repository in the world, and was opened in 1999 as a waste repository for all U.S. nuclear Defense Ordinance emitting alpha radiation with a half-life of over twenty years. Materials are kept two-thousand, one-hundred and fifty feet below ground within a three-thousand foot thick salt formation that has enjoyed stable plate tectonics for over thirty-five million years—a must for any viable site.

Within those underground rooms are large containers in which materials are stored using a limited amount of coolant liquid and circulated air. They must be kept vented and cooled to prevent the energy released by radioactive materials dissociating the water into hydrogen and oxygen, and thereby creating a potentially explosive element.

Naomi was relieved to see the plants sophisticated defensive response systems were active and already alerting Emergency Teams within the plant itself. HAZCHEM units from Carlsbad were being dispatched. But why had they taken so long? Usually the safety measures at such facilities were top notch, and protected by tiered cascade backups, so the energy increase should never have reached such proportions.

Her mind silently screamed at her that "something wasn't right."

Enhancing her senses even further, she employed a hardwire piggy-back routine via a cerebral reader, so the automated station systems would record what she thought, saw, and heard. This was a habit Commander Yasin had insisted she adopt.

Naomi listened for a few moments, and became puzzled. Employing a triple awareness band, her superlative cognitive awareness kicked into overdrive, and within a few seconds she had notified the Commander aboard Station Six.

The mental voice of Grand Master Owen suddenly cut into her mind.

*What's up, Guardian Cruiz?*

Although from another station, Grand Master Owen had nevertheless done his homework and knew all the Scan Teams well. He had discovered the prudence of listening to Naomi's concerns very quickly.

Digesting the data displayed in mid-air before him, the Commander couldn't help but be impressed by the concise compartmentalized information presented to him.

Mentally, he responded. *Good call, Naomi.*

He initiated a Response Alert, mentally updating the duty Alpha Response Team Leader on board his own station, whilst simultaneously preparing a Briefing Pod of constructed psychic data for the Delta Teams not already tied up with the tornado.

Finishing this took a whole twelve seconds, after which he returned his attention to Naomi. *Right, run this by me so I can update the guys on the ground.*

Although maintaining observations with one part of her consciousness, and continuing to sweep the target area with enhanced scans, Naomi was nevertheless able to converse quite freely.

*Boss, this place has state of the art protection. All security and protection systems have triple backups and redundancies that are more than capable of recognizing and responding to virtually any scenario you could think of, short of a nuclear strike.*

*So what's got you bugged?*

*This has to be deliberate. If normal systems had failed, backups would kick in and secondary safety protocols would have established themselves, and they would have been electronically logged with a direct order for staff to take a look, or at least run diagnostic checks, yes?*

He replied. *Go on.*

*Well, I've just checked the logs electronically and using enhanced Psi-Scan and it appears there was a power outage about three hours ago. During the outage, all backup generators were showing green lights across the board, and diagnostics reveal all backup solar batteries were fully charged. Despite this, the tiered safety redundancies didn't kick in, although instruments indicated they did, and a subsequent diagnostic by the plant's own main computer is indicating the backups responded normally.*

The Commander responded. *So you're thinking sabotage?*

She thought for a moment, checked her results, then replied.

*Definitely, because while this could have happened by accident or because of some glitch in the system, I don't like the fact the same glitch also affected their entire security mainframe AND all the backups at the same time.*

As he listened, Commander Owen began preparing another briefing Pod, and selected two ultra-sensitive scanning nodes to concentrate on the plant itself. Another was set to interrogate defense department computers to check listings of all scheduled activities for that day, and for the rest of the month in the local and surrounding areas.

Naomi continued. *Now what I don't like is that the Main Frame is indicating the primary line, backups, and redundancies were all working perfectly and that they responded normally, when this is obviously not the case. For a single circuit to display false information is one thing. For the backups and redundancies to do the same, at the same time, is another thing, especially when you factor in the same glitch on the security systems, which also coincidentally occurred at the exact same time.*

The Commander reached the same conclusion. *So you're saying the power outage hid something else?*

*Exactly! The coolant and venting systems to the containers work on completely different and isolated lines, and with good reason. This simply couldn't have happened by accident. While the power was down, the security systems were corrupted. This gave whoever was responsible the opportunity to corrupt the venting system. This obviously happened because they continued to read as normal until the energy buildup became too much to remain hidden.*

*And you're sure it's not some weird affect from this storm?*

*No boss, not a chance.*

*But why?* He wondered. *People know we're alert to such dangers and will respond.*

Suddenly, alarm bells began ringing in Naomi's mind.

*Or that's what they're counting on!* She thought.

Without hesitating, she activated the Standby Alert, notifying her own station's Bravo team to prepare.

A fast scan revealed her Alpha Team was still groundside with teams from Stations One and Three and the American Sectors' duty Delta Team. They were all busy, dealing with evacuations and associated problems caused by the storm.

This new problem was now tying up even more resources from the other stations, and they had to rely on headquarters for backup.

Whatever had caused the glitch at Carlsbad had allowed too much energy to build up in the containers. It was now a major hazard beyond the capabilities of the plant's emergency teams to handle safely and efficiently. It would keep the Guardian Emergency Response Teams busy.

Naomi spoke. *Boss, I've got a nasty feeling something bad is about to happen. Please alert all teams attending to elevate safety protocols and all six orbital stations to initiate level two sweeps immediately. I need an update, yesterday, regarding any planned military or civilian exercises, convoys, tests, anything like that which are scheduled or even underway involving anything hazardous or potentially vulnerable, especially anything involving classified tests. I've a feeling this incident may be a deliberate diversion to stretch us even further. Our sector is the priority, but go wider—you never know. Oh, and get one of the teams to get a tech-head to go over the plant's electronic systems, there's bound to be footprints of tampering somewhere in the system.*

Becoming more impressed by the second, the Commander followed directions immediately.

He was distracted for a moment by a request from Ground Commander Tavares for additional personnel to assist in evacuation of nearby towns close to the plant. A Decontamination Unit was requested to sanitize the irradiated area and prevent further nuclear contamination.

Realizing they didn't have sufficient manpower, Owen sent a call to the Canadian and South American ground sectors for assistance, with additional standby requests being sent to Observation Stations Four and Five.

A few minutes later, the computer began listing all scheduled military, civilian, and contractor tests, displaying them in prioritized groups, and concentrating as Naomi had requested upon those affecting their sector first.

Of these, she went straight to the classified lists.

*There!*

Three items were of particular interest, classified long-range missile tests, orbital satellite platform exercises, and a new stealth submarine war game.

She began running multiple scenarios in her head, assessing which posed the greatest threat.

The Commander queried. *What have we got so far?*

Naomi targeted each option with the station's scanners, requesting backup scans from the sister stations both electronically and mentally before replying.

*The missile tests are underway, evidently with new Ground Penetrating dual warheads. Looks like they're designed to penetrate installations and deliver a low yield short-term lethal blast of gravity and radiation. It has varying yields and can either totally destroy underground bunkers or leave them useable from what I can see.*

*The military appear to have kept to their schedule despite the storm, as these things have new shielded guidance and arming chips. They've used the storm as a good excuse to see if they do what they're supposed to.*

*Then we have new laser satellite platforms. They appear to be testing their Multiple Target Recognition Systems at the moment, but nothing hot is registering.*

*That leaves the war games . . . aah, there we go. They are currently testing new stealth technology on their latest Damocles Class attack sub from the Gulf of Mexico out into the*

*Atlantic. Again, no weapons, just testing the new Aqua Drives and seeing how close they can get to specified targets before detection.*

The Commander asked her a pointed question. *So, in your opinion, should we be looking at any of these as an option or widen our search?*

Naomi scrutinized the information in front of her again, this time widening the search criteria to include both the Northern and Southern American continent. She added a three-thousand mile radius.

She replied. *If I had to make a choice now, I think we should concentrate on the missile tests. They are already in flight, and we still haven't had confirmation of the pre-selected flight plans. They seem to be spread over a very wide area with no range data provided.*

She concentrated some of the station's sensors onto the four missile pods now skimming along the edge of earth's atmosphere high above the mid Atlantic. As she did so, the pods shed their outer skins, and from each pod, three independent tactical nuclear missiles emerged. Engines engaged, taking them out of atmosphere.

The missiles arced outwards in expanding fans. Naomi hoped they were already on a set course. She began computing trajectories, whilst simultaneously bringing up direct line telephone numbers at the mission control centre, which was being listed as Knoxville, Tennessee.

As a precaution, she said, *Sir, we don't appear to be making any progress regarding the Land Busters, may I suggest we get a team to their facilities and make a point in person?*

He replied, *I'm already on it, Naomi. Actually, we're being assisted by an Inquisitor Team from Washington. They are just about to teleport to target and see what's going on there, and they're also sending a team to New Mexico.*

She fine-tuned the sensors again, and discovered all the missiles appeared to be registering radioactive signatures.

Naomi warned the Commander. *Please tell them to get a move on, those missiles are showing live gravity/nuclear warheads and are beginning their descents. At current speeds, we have about five minutes before it's too late. Call it four to be safe.*

For another thirty seconds, the missiles continued on their set courses when suddenly, strangely, the engines stuttered. They re-engaged and burst away from each other onto new trajectories at over twice the speed of sound.

Immediately, Naomi exerted her far-senses and initiated computations to assess the newly projected landfall co-ordinates.

The mental hail of Master Inquisitor Darien Carmichael caught their attention.

*Heads up, you two, this will confirm your suspicions, if nothing else!*

A scene was projected into their minds of a high security stand-alone underground control room accessed by a three-tiered security airlock. The control room itself was littered with unconscious bodies slumped at their positions or on the floor with no obvious signs of injury.

The Inquisitor teams were beginning their sweep, and Naomi couldn't help thinking that they would probably find the scientists had been incapacitated by some form of aerosol to prevent them from intervening in what was about to take place.

*This is connected. We ought to take those missiles out and look at them more closely. I bet we find evidence of tampering.*

Owen sensed her mood. *Naomi?*

She replied. *I suggest we take the missiles out. There's too much going on for all this to be a coincidence.*

*Won't that cause fallout?*

*Not if we target the engines or vaporize them. I believe I'm correct in assuming usual military protocol on live missiles is that the signal to arm is not initiated until just before target.*

The Master Inquisitor agreed. *That would appear to be the case, Naomi. Their computers are indicating what you've just surmised.*

*Well, in that case, it won't matter if they fall to ground. The only danger would be an accidental signal to arm, or if the plutonium casing is damaged on impact. If you want to play it safe, I'd definitely recommend we target and vaporize any of the missiles heading toward populated areas, and that we do it now.*

*A very short mental conversation took place between Commander Owen and their head of active operations, the Lord Evaluator, Anil Suresh.*

Naomi became aware of the Commander's physical presence materializing behind her.

A few seconds later, he was by her side. He entered his command codes into her console, giving her alpha control of the station's impressive weapons array, and auto control of the other five orbital stations.

He whispered quietly in her ear. "Your call, Naomi. Show us what you can do."

\* \* \*

Back at the scene of the approaching tornado, two of the three ships had disappeared from view, accelerating into the whirling dust cloud. Their shields sparked where the larger chunks of debris struck home. The other, nearer ship, also shrank rapidly in size as it receded into the distance.

Grand Master Yasin strode over to the Guardians, preparing to face the storm.

She spoke mentally. *Is everything ready?*

"Yes, this should be interesting," Guardian Ben Williams affirmed. Ben was the scientist behind the experiment they were about to undertake. He was so new to his position that, even after a year as a fully-fledged Guardian, he was still very shy. He was in total awe of his Commander, who was known to speak her mind and whose tongue could take the skin off those who displeased her at twenty paces.

Not only was he a PhD in combined astrophysics, quantum mechanics, and advanced mathematics, but the blue and gold bar on his lapel revealed to his colleagues that his telepathic and elemental abilities, especially in generating vortexes and energy fields in the quantum and upsilon ranges, were his specialty. His abilities would mature in several years within the Master Class range.

He continued. "Once the ships are in place, I will use their barriers to negate the full effects of the targeted microwaves and the quasi-singularities we're going to create, and basically, draw off the energy the storm is being fed by."

As he communicated, he displayed the steps to his plan in their minds in overlapping stages, highlighting the points under discussion.

*Are you sure this is safe, Ben?* Commander Yasin asked. *I know you're the genius when it comes to things like this, but opening singularities here, inter-atmosphere must be dangerous. We're talking about black holes, no matter how small they may. Wouldn't it be safer to use a displacement vortex?*

Managing to smile without feeling like a complete idiot, he explained. "A displacement vortex won't work here. Simply put, the vortex would still be governed by certain rules of physics, which might add to the power of the storm. Storms are powered by opposing high speed winds, or meso-cyclones, of different temperatures."

Yasin nodded her understanding, and Ben continued. "Well, if we were to attempt a vortex of sufficient size to try and siphon off its power, the speed of the process may generate an even more powerful meso-cyclone. This would create a leviathan of a storm that we would struggle to control. We would be working against ourselves. So, if we use quasi-singularities along with the microwaves, we literally shred the tornado and its energy to pieces, as theoretically, a singularity doesn't allow the laws of physics to operate constantly."

*What will the residual vacuum be like?* Yasin asked, showing a sound grasp of physics much to her subordinate's delight.

"Manageable, if we proceed as planned. We can gradually change the course of the storm toward a less populated area. All we have to hope for is that we don't get a strong gamma ray burst as the process takes place, or even an outbreak of them."

*Why's that?*

"Because of the anti-matter radiation it would release. This storm is the most powerful one on record. If we get an outbreak of gamma bursts, even sun factor million wouldn't be enough to protect us."

*And the likelihood of that happening is?* She stressed.

"The chances of that are billions to one. It would have to happen at the exact moment and in the exact location that a quasi-singularity was initially created."

Yasin slapped him soundly on the back. *That's good enough for me, Ben. Fortunately, I'm already blessed with the most extraordinary set of testicles you will ever see on a woman, and they, together with my shockingly strong spine, say it's safe enough! The sooner we get on with this the sooner I can get back to my knitting.*

Everyone laughed at the thought she projected into their minds: they saw an image of her in a comfy chair, feet up, slippers on, in front of a roaring fire knitting a bright pink cardigan.

Still looking unhappy, the young Guardian's mind expressed discomfort. *I just wish we could hurry up and implement the advanced education system we've proposed for them. Once they learn the principles for harmonic repulsor and mitigator waves, and learn to manufacture their own force fields, storms like this will be less of a hassle.*

Yasin nodded in agreement, and put a reassuring hand on his shoulder. *Very true, Ben. We could put in a call to The Overlord and ask him to do it for us. I'm sure he wouldn't mind being interrupted. Whatever it is he's doing can't be all that important.*

The young Guardian shook his head, completely missing the jest. She continued. *Okay then, so it's up to you to play duty hero and go do your stuff. The ships look like they're in position, so let's see how your plan goes, eh?*

They all turned to look at the ships, automatically using their far-sight abilities to give themselves a clearer view of the two closest ships. They could also see the ships on the other side of the tornado that had just reached their designated positions, six hundred yards above ground. They gently rotated inward, so that they were all facing each other, and paused for a few seconds.

A sparkling blue light rolled out from each ship, forming a square shaped shimmering blue curtain, reaching down to ground level.

Once the curtain was fully formed, a pulse was sent out from each ship that strengthened the barrier and turned it a deeper shade of blue.

Ben initiated a mechanical shield around the location, and studied the barrier with his instruments and ultra-senses for a full minute before mentally affirming. *Barrier initiated and fully phased, harmonizing with shield generator.*

He studied it for a few seconds more before speaking to the Grand Master. "This thing would restrain a ten Megaton atomic blast; we're good to go."

Out loud, she replied, "Well, go on then, it's your baby."

Taking a deep breath, he mentally signaled to each ship. *Captains, please focus on the centre of the tornado . . . Now!*

Instantly, four crimson laser beams shot out from each ship, meeting at the exact centre of the maelstrom. Each ship was now locked in position to the center of the storm, and with each other, to ensure the barrier remained at full strength as they drifted in unison with its movements.

*Can you assess the exact position and density of the storms fluctuating downdraft?* Ben inquired.

Four mental confirmations came back, and again beams flashed out from the ships. They were blue and white, wider like arc lights, waving to and fro over an invisible Front Point within the storm. Once they had determined the fluctuating position of that front, each ship took a quadrant, and maintained their beams in one segment only.

The captains signaled their readiness for the next stage.

*Okay, now I want the Falcon and the Argent to target their microwave emitters on their side of the storm. We need to turn the tornado to the left, as it were. We're aiming for the area between Cache and Lawton, which is less populated than the surrounding area. Once we see it beginning to work, I want the Trident to support the Falcon, and the Rapier to support the Argent, so we get a big initial swing to avoid Geronimo and Lawton as much as possible on the way in. Affirm?*

A few seconds later, the Falcon and the Argent began firing their microwave emitters at their respective targets. Golden sparks could be seen fluttering to the right side of the storm in front of the tornado's vortex.

Nothing happened for a few minutes, but gradually a deviation in the tornado's projected course became apparent. Ponderously, the leviathan began to grudgingly snarl its way onto a new course.

Ben breathed a sigh of relief as he saw his plan unfolding. *Excellent, Trident and Rapier, you can begin assisting . . . Now.*

The golden sparks intensified on the right. Soon, the tornado was making a much sharper deviation to the left. It was only fourteen miles away, almost on top of Geronimo, and they could feel the ground vibrating beneath their feet even at this distance.

*How long do we have?* Grand Master Yasin asked calmly, assessing the distances from the tornado to Lawton and Cache.

Although under pressure, Ben did not rush his calculations, and after a few seconds replied with confidence. *The tornado is now travelling close to one hundred and twenty miles an hour groundspeed. Absolutely incredible! We have diverted its path to a point midway between Cache and Lawton, giving us about six minutes to stop it. It's now just over thirteen miles away, and . . . .*

A purple flash accompanied by lightning interrupted his train of thought.

He frowned in concentration, then hailed the ships telepathically. *Captains, we're starting to get stronger gamma bursts. Fire your microwaves in one steady stream along the entire downdraft for your particular quadrant . . . Now!*

In unison the golden sparks intensified in the air over a particularly huge area within the barrier.

Ben monitored the barrage for a good thirty seconds as the monster bore down on them at alarming speed. *This is good; the temperature is now starting to rise.*

*Prepare your singularity emitters. I want random and coordinated fire upon the vortex on my mark.*

There was another purple flash along with a huge prolonged lightning strike, demonstrated the storm's clear intention to fight back.

Ben checked instruments, anxiety beginning to leak through his mental barrier. *Captains, please fire on my mark . . . Now.*

The news crews were feeling decidedly unnerved. The tornado seemed to be rapidly filling the horizon with each passing second, and they felt that at any moment it would bend toward them and chew them up.

The sudden appearance of a million tiny explosions caused two of the crews from ABC and Fox to completely lose their nerve. The explosions were generating massive gravity fluctuations, making it virtually impossible to stand.

They made a dash for their vans, ignoring the warning from the Guardian Commander that they would never drive fast enough to get away, and threw their equipment inside. The engines were started before the doors were even closed.

They hadn't gone two hundred yards before they were plucked off the ground by a beam from one of the patrolling Guardian ships, much to the amusement of the Commander, who looked pointedly at the remaining CBS news crew.

"Care to join them?" she shouted.

Megan Bronson, the weather reporter for CBS, Oklahoma, looked nervously at her cameraman for the day, Eduardo Rafael. Even though they were both frightened, they were even more petrified at the thought of failing. They both shook their heads in unison, before glaring in terror at the flashing, whirling monster looming before them.

Even though they were both finding it difficult to stand, they seemed determined to stick it out. This earned them a nod of respect from the Guardian Commander, who extended her personal shield to encase them.

As it turned out, that saved their lives.

Seeing the two reporters were a little more settled, Grand Master Yasin was about to return her attention to the matter in hand, when she noticed a number of aircraft in the sky a few miles north of Geronimo.

Zooming in on them with her far-sight, she identified several independent paparazzi crews out to make their fortunes by risking their lives to get the most sensational shot of their careers. The storm was only eight miles out. She was about to instruct the Captains of the rescue ships to scoop them up for their own safety, when she noticed two distinct prolonged brilliant purple flashes in the vortex of the tornado. The flashes were shadowed by large lightning bursts, laced with a strange yellow color that seemed to hover for a moment before disappearing.

*Ben?* Notifying Command and Headquarters about the danger, she unconsciously strengthened her shield, and instructed the ship captains and Guardians on site to do the same.

*Ben?* She repeated.

The young Guardian was looking incredulously into the storm. His mind was racing, checking instruments. His mind shouted. *Wait a moment!*

Two more purple and yellow flashes announced their blinding presence, arcing between two of the quasi black holes with a thrumming sound that seemed to make the air throb with mounting power.

It happened again before Ben threw himself to the floor, mind screaming. *ANTIMATTER SHIELDS!*

Reflexes took over as an almighty concussion rocked the earth, and a sizzling sound filled the air, eerily audible above the sound of the storm.

A prolonged burst of hybrid lightning, supercharged and accelerated to almost the speed of light by a singularity, containing over five trillion watts and measuring a staggering one hundred thousand degrees centigrade—over fifteen times hotter than the surface of the sun—arced over the top of the protective curtain, and began hammering down on their shields.

The Class One mechanical shield generator lasted a heroic four seconds beyond capacity before overloading. The Guardians had reflexively raised their own mentally generated shields, which then caught the end of the deadly discharge.

As a Guardian with over thirty years command experience, Grand Master Yasin had already prepared a Reflex or Lifesaver Shield, storing the mental program in her subconscious, to be activated instinctively should the need arise.

Fortunately, she had selected a three-tiered Succubus Shield. Each tier was designed to attract and absorb energy and then disintegrate, draining the overall potential of the strike with each successive collapse. She had extended her shield around herself, her colleagues, and the remaining news crew. The outer level lasted only a second before it was shredded. The middle layer was likewise destroyed only moments later.

This exposed some of the Guardian scientists closest to her who did not possess her shielding ability. Four were incinerated where they stood, exploding from the inside out in the fraction of a second it took for the bolt to travel through them and into the earth.

Half a second after that, the Commander's inner shield was breached. There was no time to teleport away, dodge or even flinch.

Reacting with inhuman speed, she spun a shield around her brain before she was hammered down over twenty inches into the ground. Horrifically, her clothes and teeth exploded from her body, her hair and eyeballs vaporized, and her dermal layer crisped instantly from head to toe in the nano-second the charge took to shoot along her spinal column, ruining organs, muscle, and sinew.

Her blackened plasma staff, blades somehow deployed arced away through the air to embed itself in the ground some two hundred yards away.

As Megan Bronson and Eduardo Rafael got back to their feet with the supersonic boom still reverberating in the air, they were stunned to see the other Guardians had been blasted to the floor fifty feet from them. Only one had managed to remain conscious and he was obviously stunned, while the others were shredded, either burnt to varying degrees, or dead.

"What the hell was that?" Eduardo shouted.

Megan screamed, pointing to a crater, in the middle of which was a smoking, ruined heap of charred flesh.

"Eduardo, is that who I think it is?"

Eduardo clutched his stomach and swallowed down bile. "Just do your job, Megan, this is what we're here for, now report it."

"I know, I know . . . ." She lifted the microphone. It was difficult to stand; they were no longer protected by the Guardians' shields. It felt like something was tugging her forward.

"What's that?" she shouted, pointing toward the tornado. Megan stared in wide-eyed horror at an expanding area of nothingness, the size of a golf ball, then a baseball, then a soccer ball, surrounded by a sizzling sickly yellow halo. It was still within the protective curtain generated by the ships, but growing rapidly, and making its presence felt.

"Run to the ships while you can," a voice suddenly shouted above the wind.

Turning, they saw the young Guardian scientist staggering toward them, fighting the pull of the terror behind him and trying to assist the only one of his colleagues still left alive.

He shouted again. "Run, a black hole is forming! The storm is so strong it created an antimatter nucleus at the exact point of the lightning strike. It's feeding the black hole. In a few moments it will be fully anchored and there'll be nothing I can do to help.

"RUN! I can't teleport, and my friends are dead or hurt, and the ships are too far away."

As they ran for their lives, Megan couldn't help but think that it was a pity she would never live to see the headlines this incident would create.

*At least I was part of it,* she thought.

# 14

# The Burdens of Command

Taking a deep breath, Naomi completed one last check of the current flight paths of the missiles together with their latest co-ordinates and set her priorities. All were on their final attack phase and were locked on target.

Projecting along those flight paths, she saw that the main targets appeared to be cities in Europe, Africa, and both the North and Southern American continents.

However, not all appeared to be locked onto valid targets.

Deciding that civilian casualties were first on the agenda, she initiated a hot response and the targeting scanners of all six stations at her command locked onto the seven missiles she had selected. A split second later, those with the clearest firing resolution fired their pulse lasers.

Seven scarlet beams sliced out of the heavens onto their corresponding missiles, vaporizing them instantly in a brief flash of crimson and white light.

Turning her attention to the final five missiles, Naomi re-checked their targets. One appeared to be heading toward a location just south of La Palma, the most northwesterly of the Canary Islands.

Puzzled, she zoomed in on that location, and discovered a large vessel sailing serenely toward the southern tip of the island. She instantly ordered close range scans of the last five co-ordinates while there was still time.

Commander Owen sensed the agitation in her mind. "Something wrong, Naomi?"

"Just checking something strange about these last missiles—hang on."

Moments later the results were displayed before her, and she broadcasted them simultaneously to her Commander and to the Inquisitor who was listening in.

The Royal Yacht of Great Britain, HMS Queen Elizabeth III, on her maiden voyage with the future King and Queen of the United Kingdom and the Commonwealth on board, sailed sedately towards the southwest corner of La Palma at twenty-five knots. It was only two miles off the coast. The crew was completely unaware that the yacht was the intended target of one of the most sophisticated missiles on the planet.

Naomi brought up the other results. The remaining Land Busters also appeared to be locked on to equally bizarre targets. The first was heading toward the International Space Station parked in low earth orbit. Two more appeared to be aimed at Pearl Harbor, Hawaii, and the Gulf of Mexico, respectively. The final missile was heading for Port Tawfick at the southern end of the Suez Canal.

Mentally, Naomi spoke. *We've only got fifty-five seconds left before impact, but these specific missiles appear different in some way. Look at their selected targets. I think we ought to take a look at them.*

Commander Owen replied. *What are you suggesting?*

*Take out the engines, then retrieval of the missile itself. We've definitely got to take a closer look at the circuitry. I'm betting there's evidence of sabotage in there somewhere.*

The loud mental voice of the Inquisitor cut in. *DO IT! I'd love my teams to take a closer look as well. Good call, Naomi.*

Naomi glanced briefly at the Commander who merely raised an eyebrow and gave an almost imperceptible nod.

She adjusted the focus and wattage of the lasers still actively tracking each missile. A few seconds later, her adjustments completed, she gave the command to fire.

This time, the crimson beams pulsed with a static discharge, which enveloped each missile in a crawling web of purple lightning. Almost instantly, the web of energy rendered the systems inert. After flaring briefly, the engines cut out, and each missile made a nose-dive toward the sea, rapidly decelerating as they cut through the water. The one that had been aimed at International Space Station plunged back toward earth at over fifteen hundred miles an hour.

"Something's still bugging you, Naomi," Commander Owen noted

"I don't know what it is, Sir. Those missiles were obviously different in some way, and I'm just concerned there's more to it."

"Explain?"

"Well, if it was just a glitch in the systems, the missiles had the whole planet for a playground. But instead, they zeroed in on some very precise targets. Not just areas like Pearl Harbor, Port Tawfik, and the Gulf of Mexico, but look at this!"

She projected the very precise co-ordinates of HMS Queen Elizabeth III, and the International Space Station.

"Now, stationary cities are one thing," she continued, "especially when you remember that's what the missiles seem designed for. Cities are a viable target. But The Queen Elizabeth and the Space Station are moving targets."

"It doesn't add up!" Commander Owen interrupted.

"Precisely. I think it might be prudent to either encase them in force field . . . ."

They were interrupted by a low altitude explosion and an expanding halo of blinding intensity. The disabled missile that had been heading towards the space station somehow detonated in free fall.

*How? It was inert?* Naomi thought. She entered her command codes again, and the lasers still targeted on the remaining missiles fired at each one in rapid turn.

Her reactions saved many lives. The missiles lying on the sea beds just off Hawaii and in the Gulf of Mexico were instantly vaporized, the only evidence of their existence being the sharp hissing sound and huge volumes of steam produced by the rapidly heated sea water as the lasers did their work.

The missiles in the Red Sea just off Port Tawfik, and off the southern coast of La Palma, however, had begun their detonation sequence. Before their special combined nuclear warheads were fully armed, they were obliterated.

"GO, GO, GO!" She screamed mentally and verbally to the respective Alpha Response Teams already alerted and waiting on the other Stations.

As an added precaution, she alerted all Bravo Teams to stand by as well.

Within three seconds the teams were there.

Station Five Teams were sent to port Tawfik, where the power of the compression matrix, although never reaching critical mass, had triggered the creation of an irradiated vacuum ball one hundred and fifty feet in diameter. They arrived as the water rushed back in to fill the void, spitting a radioactive plume over two hundred feet into the air and creating an immensely powerful shockwave. A mini tsunami was generated within the confines of the port and bay.

The tremors caused by the shockwave had the strength of a force six earthquake, and several buildings in the port area partially collapsed. All of the cargo cranes around the dock tumbled to the ground or into the water.

Radiological readings and thermal injuries were low, and the electromagnetic pulse only fried equipment within a two mile radius, due mainly to the fact the missile had been destroyed prior to full detonation. The teams were quickly able to establish control of the incident while awaiting a response frigate.

Teams from Stations Four and Six arrived at La Palma to discover the missile had embedded itself into the sea bed less than a mile offshore. As the compression burst initiated, it caused another vacuum ball, but this one generated a higher release of kinetic energy. It vaporized volcanic rock, sediment and seawater, which transmitted the force spherically away from the hypocenter through the water like a whip.

The Queen Elizabeth III never had an opportunity to change course, and took both the shockwave and following bow wave full on portside before the Response Teams could fully deploy.

Despite its latest state of the art stabilizing technology, the ship didn't stand a chance and capsized.

The teams managed to teleport to safety over seven hundred of the one thousand three hundred souls on board as the ship went over, including the Royal Party.

As the rescue mission continued, two guardian frigates arrived to assist in scooping up survivors and treating the injured, as well as assisting people caught along the southern beaches of La Palma itself by the ensuing tidal wave.

Looking on, Naomi was shocked at the rising death toll, and absolutely numbed by what the consequences could have been had she not been so sharp.

*Who would do such an appalling thing?* She thought.

"That's what I aim to find out!"

Naomi startled to find the mysterious Ultra Class Guardian, Victoria, behind her. Somehow she had managed to teleport onto the station without revealing her presence.

Commander Owen was clearly surprised too, as it was believed both Victoria and Andrew were off-world again with the Overlord, doing goodness knows what.

Victoria had been a Guardian for longer than almost anyone else she knew, even the Lord Marshall. Both she and the equally reclusive Andrew had refused promotions repeatedly and kept to themselves when off duty.

Anil Suresh manifested on the deck a moment later. His face was a blank mask of concentration.

It was getting crowded, and the Lord Evaluator, Anil, immediately took Commander Owen to one side and began conversing telepathically.

"Fill me in on everything, Naomi," Victoria said.

Naomi opened her mind and began relaying information to her senior colleague.

Victoria's mind acknowledged the transmission. *Handy skill you have there, Naomi. Well done, that was a smart call and saved a lot of lives. We could use you in the future.*

Naomi was just about to ask who "we" were and what "they" could possibly want from her in the future, when she suddenly jumped.

She gasped out loud. "Oh my God!"

All heads turned to her in shock, as Naomi displayed the terrible results of the hybrid gamma/lightning strike, and the fully formed black hole that had just anchored before the ground team in Oklahoma.

"Order the ships to initiate the safety protocol now!" the Lord Evaluator snapped.

A mental voice thundered, *WAIT!*

Everyone turned to look at Victoria, whose eyes had a semi-vacant stare.

A few seconds later, her intense grey eyes came back into focus and she said, "Sorry about that Anil, but it was necessary.

"Would you be so kind as to oversee the mopping up operations from this missile fiasco while I go down and take charge of the Inquisitors groundside? After absorbing Naomi's briefing, I want to make sure nothing is missed during the investigation. The quicker the bastards responsible for this debacle are brought to justice the better."

The Lord Evaluator, technically the next in command of the Guardians after the Lord Marshall, narrowed his eyes and replied. "Certainly, Victoria, but if you don't mind my asking, why did you counter my command to destroy the black hole?"

"Like I said, sorry, Anil, but you and I both know that would obliterate hundreds of square miles of real estate, and I want to avoid that if at all possible. Besides, I've just notified the Overlord of the incident in Oklahoma and he's on the way."

One of the sharpest minds they had, the Lord Evaluator was nevertheless puzzled. "He's on the way? How? I thought he was on another star search in an adjoining galaxy."

"He was. I contacted him. Now he's on the way. I'll shoulder the consequences!"

The look she gave him said to let the matter drop.

Nodding, he replied, "Let's get on with it then."

Both Ultra Guardians teleported from the station to undertake their respective tasks, leaving behind two very confused colleagues who were wondering what had just taken place.

# 15

# Living Legend

No matter how hard they tried, after just ten yards they found it almost impossible to move forward.

Megan was screaming down her microphone, trying to be heard over the increasing roar of the wind and storm.

Eduardo kept his camera trained backward over his shoulder, glancing at the pivotal LCD screen from time to time to ensure he was still recording the black hole growing behind them. It was now the size of a truck, and with a weird rotating halo along its outer edge.

*At least they'll be getting this digitally,* he thought, being thankful he'd opted for a Bluetooth and digital live link up to the satellite and studio.

He calmly prepared for the inevitable.

Ben clung to his injured colleague, determined to hang on for the vital fifteen to twenty seconds it would take for their ships to reach them safely, knowing it was probably hopeless.

He could hear ideas being thrown about telepathically between the ships' Captains and High Master Thaleton at the control centre. He knew that if nothing concrete was decided fast, the failsafe protocol would be initiated, and they would be sacrificed for the sake of safety.

Then a tingling sensation traveling down his spine made him stop dead in his tracks. Looking around in surprise, Ben couldn't help but laugh in spite of the danger.

The others turned to stare at him with questioning eyes.

Ben was a paradox in Guardian circles. He seemed to be able to detect and manipulate energy at the quantum level, and this should have guaranteed his ability to teleport.

Unfortunately, his teleporting functionality lay dormant within his psychic complex, forcing him to use a transporter. As if in compensation, his ability to detect incoming vortexes was a rare and highly prized gift.

Only five Guardians were known to have this gift, and Ben was one of them.

If someone were teleporting over a short distance, say, within a thousand miles, the jump would be almost instantaneous and provide very little warning.

If someone were teleporting around the planet, they would have to send out a strong leader signal to ensure a safe jump. A planetary jump could be completed in about a second from time of focus to completion. Travel would still be almost instantaneous, but it would give plenty of time for an alert detector to pinpoint the point of materialization.

Ben had detected the unbelievable power of a leader signal being projected. A signal that had begun focusing almost ten seconds ago. And it was still focusing and blooming, indicating that a traveler was now in transit along the quantum pathway.

He knew of only one person with the power required for a single jump of this magnitude. It was a leap of unimaginable proportions, over a distance of many hundreds of thousands of light years in just ten seconds. It would have been beyond the capacity of anyone else, even without the vast distortion of a black hole right on top of the materialization site.

Dropping his colleague, Ben slumped to the floor in relief, laughing out loud again and drawing a gasp of utter disbelief from the young reporter beside him.

"What are you laughing at? Don't you realize we're going to die?" she shrieked in horror.

He shook his head and pointed to a spot about twenty yards in front of them. "We're not going to die. Just point your camera over there and you'll see why in about three seconds from now."

Two seconds later, they got their answer as they were bowled over by the arrival of a being radiating such incredible power, that the tornado and its storm were a mere exhaled gasp in comparison.

One moment there was just an open field with long grass bending crazily in the air, and then a brilliant silver light bloomed out of nowhere, encompassing a grey void of nothingness. The living legend himself stepped casually out of thin air. He was surrounded by a huge psychic halo of blinding intensity, his silver radiance intertwined by gold and royal blue coruscating bands of untapped energy.

As he walked forward, his cape billowing behind him, he gradually suppressed his aura with each step. By the time he reached them, only his eyes retained the shining silver cast for a few seconds longer before fading.

He raised his left hand indicating they should wait a moment, and casually extended the fingers of his other hand toward the crater behind them where the hybrid bolt had struck, vaporizing the Guardian Commander.

Looking back, they saw a green and gold cocoon spring to life around the charred remains of Grand Master Yasin, followed by multiple rotating vermillion and gold bands of light.

Once they started rotating, it was difficult to focus on them. A gasp from Megan's side caught her attention. Ben, his eyes bright with interest, had managed to overcome the awe they all felt. "Sir, is that what I think it is, a 'Time Well'?" he asked his supervisor.

The Overlord, the most powerful Guardian ever to exist, replied casually. "You are quite correct, Ben. Commander Yasin managed to protect part of her brain within a shield, so I've altered time around her, and phase shifted her, until I have the opportunity to take a look at the damage properly. Can you imagine how testy she'd get if she was late for work tomorrow?"

Ben laughed to himself at the truth of the Overlord's observation. He was sure Commander Yasin was just the type to vent her displeasure, even on the Overlord himself if the opportunity arose.

His amusement dwindled as he realized what the Overlord had just implied.

*How can she be alive, there was hardly anything left,* he thought.

The Overlord extended his mind and Commander Yasin's plasma staff extinguished itself and came hurtling through the air and into his outstretched hand.

Megan still couldn't believe what was happening, and she turned a full circle in amazement. When she glanced back, a pair of intense grey eyes, hooded by winged eyebrows, peered down on her. A calm voice spoke. "Are you all right, Megan?"

It occurred to her that the storm had stopped roaring. There was no wind attempting to hurl them into the air, no lightning threatening to incinerate them where they stood, and no irresistible pull from a hell hole trying to swallow them out of existence. She could hear him quite clearly, and after staring wildly about for a few moments, just nodded numbly as he knelt on the grass next to the badly burned Guardians.

Only a moment before, she thought she was going to die. A second later, she was sitting on the grass next to someone who, from what the media had been able to ascertain from the Guardians themselves, was a reclusive living legend.

She looked him up and down, hardly daring to breathe. She fixated on the confirmation of his office, a thick purple band, edged on both sides in gold on each sleeve.

He appeared to be about forty years old. Perhaps older, or younger—it was so hard to tell. A shaved head, thick eyebrows, and slightly pointed ears gave him a look that would have been entirely at home in a fantasy novel, were it not for the bulk of his six foot frame. His body was so powerfully muscled that he looked as if he bench pressed small continents for fun.

Despite this, he moved in a gracefully fluid way. He seemed to flow across the ground from person to person, checking their injuries with almost liquid ease.

Even though he had suppressed his visible aura, power radiated from every pore of his body like a star going supernova, causing Megan's sinuses and teeth to throb.

He was still looking at her as he checked his two colleagues. Once he was satisfied, and they had regained full awareness, he nodded to her left.

She turned and saw a glittering opaque golden dome surrounding them. Inside was utter tranquility and calm, a safe haven from the hellish scene outside. That was why everything had become so serene.

He stood up, removed his hooded cape, and handing it to Megan. "Look after that for me, will you, Megan? I have an urgent matter to attend to." He turned to Eduardo. "You might like to ensure you get this, I don't often get to work with an audience."

He stepped out of the protective golden sphere and into the holocaust in front of them, seemingly unaffected by the hurricane force winds, and lethal flying debris.

By now, the black hole was firmly anchored in space, and was busy devouring anything within reach of its active sphere of influence. The tornado had been swallowed in moments, along with the protective curtain the Guardians had generated to contain it, and the rest of the storm would soon follow. The ground beneath the singularity seemed to fall away as if a void had been opened beneath it, and thousands of tons of earth were being swallowed every second.

A nearby copse was shedding trees like wheat submitting to a scythe, and even the air appeared to be bending close to the apparition in an ever increasing warp, as if reality were about to tear in two.

About a mile above, four heavily shielded Guardian Dreadnaughts were now in position, obviously about to initiate the failsafe protocol that would destroy a huge chunk of both Texas and Oklahoma, but nevertheless stop the situation from becoming lethal to the planet.

The Guardian Overlord raised his hand, issuing a stunning mental command at the same time to stall them. Then he opened his arms as if assuming a near crucifix position, palms open and cupped upwards, and began gathering energy into himself so fast it made the air ripple toward him.

Whatever he was doing seemed to initiate more of the terrible anti-matter bursts, and twin forks of purple and yellow death thundered down out of the swirling maelstrom, striking his cupped hands. It seemed he was catching and intensifying the potency of the strikes. It was almost as if he was absorbing the energy of the remaining storm into his own incredible potential, creating a blinding nimbus of power.

He stomped forward, simultaneously making an over and under handed gesture, as if holding an invisible football that he was trying to twist open by brute force.

A golden halo of sizzling power instantly appeared around the singularity and began building in potency. As it intensified, the halo began to shrink in size, and the effects of its horrendous pull lessened by the second.

Upon meeting the edge of the singularity, it halted, battling against the monumental effects of warped physics and gravity.

The Overlord's body began to shine with intense inner silver light. Stepping forward, he began squeezing his hands together, closer and closer, the muscles of his body clearly bunching and rippling beneath the fabric of his black uniform.

His herculean effort was being resisted by the black hole, so he squeezed again.

As he did so, the halo intensified, flickering with royal blue and white bands of overwhelming power, and began crushing the singularity.

Megan heard Ben marveling out loud to himself, eyes fixated on his founder. "But that should be impossible, how is he both countering and restricting the tidal shearing forces of the gravity well?"

Ben suddenly went pale as comprehension dawned on him. "My God, he's going to manifest!" he exclaimed.

Megan felt the shock triggered in the Guardians by those words, injured as they were, who were now transfixed on what was about to take place in front of them.

"He's going to what?" she asked, intrigued by their reaction.

"He's going to manifest. I've heard of it among the most powerful Guardians, but never actually seen it done. This will be amazing," Ben replied.

"What do you mean?" Megan was totally baffled by the awe in Ben's face. The expression was echoed in the face of the older Guardian next to him.

Without dragging his eyes away from the intensifying vision before them, he inclined his head fractionally toward her. "You know how everyone is different as far as how much their bodies can handle, yes? You get to a certain point, and no amount of training and preparation can get you past a certain limit. It's just inhumanely impossible to pass that mark." Ben turned to face her with wonder in his eyes. "There's only so far you can go, a limit to how powerful you can be, before it becomes too much for the human body. You pass a certain point and you explode."

Megan looked back toward the Overlord, who was now radiating so brightly it was impossible to look at him. "So are you saying he's going to explode?"

"Some do when they become that powerful. We've found the cut off mark appears to be at the High Grand Master level of abilities. Beyond that they go Ultra . . . if they're lucky."

"What, like a superhuman?"

"Ultra is the threshold of psychic human existence. The doorway to something else." His voice was so quiet, she was unsure she had heard him correctly.

The lights seemed to be folding back in on themselves, becoming a swirling mass of thrumming vibrant power, with royal blue and golden bursts of light. Multicolored bursts of energy erupted over its surface as the potential swelled ever higher.

Ben shielded his eyes. "For many years, anyone who went Ultra died in the process. But lately, we've had more and more candidates with an ability that enables them to survive the transition. They transcend to another level of existence."

"What level?" Megan gasped, now totally captivated.

"*That* level." Ben pointed.

Megan looked across and her jaw dropped along with the microphone. In the place of a human being was a vision of utter power incarnate, both terrible and wonderful to behold.

She hardly heard Ben continue. "Those of us who transcend become beings of pure thought and energy. He is the oldest and strongest of us, the first to transcend, and this is the first time anyone has seen him manifest into his natural form in over a century."

"What do you mean 'natural form'? Are you saying he's not human?"

"No, he's just very different to us. He's still human, I think, but a different kind of human."

"But he looks more like an angel than anything else! No wonder we call you Guardian Angels."

Ben was too mesmerized to reply.

"Are you getting this?" Megan demanded of the camera man as she bent to pick up her microphone.

"Oh, yes," Eduardo gasped.

Turning to glance at each other, they couldn't help but whisper "Fuck me!" in unison.

*　*　*

The entity pulsed like an electrum of silver and gold fire, with white, blue and golden plumes of power throbbing throughout. It was over twelve feet high, and roughly man shaped, although it was hard to tell exactly because the bands and tendrils of its form kept flowing through and around itself so much. The lights faded in and out of reality, as if the entity existed in more than one plane of reality at a time.

The angel was floating serenely ten feet off the ground in front of the monstrosity that was still intent on wreaking havoc, both on the apparition and the surrounding vicinity.

Around the entity, a nebulae of rainbow colors swirled, all orbiting the electrum in graceful arcs, some sparkling into invisibility, only to reappear and flare again more powerfully.

The singularity, now only scant yards from it, had somehow been compressed down to the size of a basketball, and seemed to be doing its furious best to cling on to existence.

Strange purple and yellow static discharges of furious anti-matter, like full sized lightning bolts and balls of plasma were now punching out from the edge of the singularity like possessed demons.

Bolt after bolt hammered out of the dark monstrosity against the angel daring to oppose it, with increasing ferocity.

Without realizing it, the bystanders had been walking toward the conflict, hardly daring to breathe. Even the hovering ships seemed to move in to get a better view of something only ever whispered about in Guardian circles.

Further out, the terrified paparazzi who had not crash landed were cursing their luck. Here before them were the pickings of the century, and they couldn't get close enough for fear of becoming part of the news themselves.

Suddenly, the silver mass began to swirl in on itself faster and faster, swiftly becoming a confluence of countering gravity. The influence of the singularity shifted, and was now directed toward the constrained black hole.

The swirling accelerated, and the pulsing silver core became brighter and brighter, swirling out to the edges of the restraining barrier around the black hole, before beginning to draw it irresistibly toward its own spinning maelstrom of light.

Ben gasped. "He's going to subsume it! I don't believe it; he's actually going to subsume a singularity *into* himself. My god, how powerful is he?"

"He's going to do what?" Megan asked, conscious of the fact she'd said that an awful lot today and cursed herself for it.

"He's going to draw the black hole toward himself and then he's going to try and absorb it," said the other injured Guardian standing next to her. The shredded bronze bands on the remains of his sleeve revealed him to be a Master Class Guardian.

She looked at the man, surprised by the straightforward answer.

"More understandable isn't it, when you don't have, 'I'm a scientist so have to use big words', replying to you?" he joked.

They all squinted, watching the scene unfold.

One moment, the singularity was still there, and then with a shrieking roar, it disappeared, fully absorbed into his complexus, as if it had never existed.

The Guardians both stared at each other, clearly shocked, no doubt talking mentally.

"Hey, no fair!" shouted Eduardo, looking at each of them and nodding to his camera.

"Oh, sorry. You didn't really miss much," Ben assured him. "We were just agreeing how awesome that was. Up until now, we've never seen anything like that, even with our advanced technology."

Both Megan and Eduardo looked puzzled. The burnt Guardian Master tried to clarify. "What he means is, we've had the technology for some time now to protect ourselves against the actual pull of a black hole. We shield our ships and bases with special anchors to prevent a black hole pulling us in. But to actually see a black hole being swallowed by something with a stronger pull, now *that's* impressive."

"That's what I just said!" Ben complained.

Shaking his head and punching the younger one gently on his shoulder, (and wincing for his efforts), the older Master replied, "Do you know, when we get back, I'm going to break into your scientist school and steal your special dictionary. You know, it's the one with all the big words in you all obviously go to great lengths to swallow down in its entirety."

He turned to Megan and Eduardo. "I swear there's no word in it less than twelve letters long."

They all laughed at the gentle jest aimed at Ben, then abruptly went silent as they realized the Overlord was rematerializing his human body near to the edge of a huge perfectly spherical crater in the ground.

The silver light was now reduced in size and intensity, no longer swirling. It was condensing back in concentric waves into a man's size and shape, and floating toward them over the crater gouged out by the black hole.

Once at the edge, it abruptly dimmed, revealing a human being once more.

The Overlord stepped calmly onto the grass. "May I have my cloak, Megan? I'm going to need it shortly."

She nodded and reluctantly handed back the dark keepsake she was hoping he'd forgotten about.

He walked over to the remains of the Guardian team, silently standing by each one for a moment before moving to the next. The only sign of any emotion was a narrowing of his eyes or a tightening of his lips.

Sighing, he waved a hand toward them and their ruined bodies crumbled to dust, dissipating into the air within moments until all that remained were darkened stains on the ground to mark where they had lain.

Finally, he strode over to where the pitifully charred and blackened remains of Grand Master Yasin still lay within the Time Well. He studied his construct for a moment as if attuning to it, made a small gesture that caused the rotating rings to expand and encompass him, and disappeared from view.

Megan turned to look to the Guardians for an explanation as to what had happened.

"That's just the effects of the Time Well," Ben said. "They're both still there, but we can't see them as they are out of phase with our normal flow of time. The Grand Master was also suspended in a single moment of time, to prevent her impending death. She was so badly injured, that if the Overlord had left her as she was, she'd have died. That's why he put her inside the dual construct, to freeze her in a single moment. Now he can take his time to do whatever's necessary to give her the best chance of recovery. To us, it will seem like he only went in a few seconds ago."

Megan looked worried for a moment, so the Guardian Master offered to translate.

She smiled wanly. "No need—I'm just shocked because I actually understood what he said."

Eduardo nodded toward the Time Well. "Do you think she has a chance?"

"I really can't say," Ben admitted. "There was hardly anything left. I know he said she'd managed to spin some kind of shield around her brain, but this? I've heard of his capacities, which you've seen with your own eyes, but I don't know if there'll be enough of her to work with."

Moments later, there was a flash of light as the dual green and vermillion construct flared out of existence, and two people stood on the grass. The Overlord was holding a barefoot woman, clothed in his hooded cowl to cover her nakedness.

There was a sharp intake of breath, even from the Guardians, as without question it was Grand Master Yasin, looking tired and a little pale. She looked bewildered, but without a doubt, she was healthy, whole, and without a mark on her.

She looked repeatedly from hands to feet, legs to arms, prodding herself as if to check she was really there.

As one, they all walked forward to greet her, and were met by a gentle but firm barrier generated by the Overlord, keeping them at arm's length.

"I think Anatt has had quite enough excitement for one day, don't you?" he said.

Turning to give the regenerated Grand Master a gentle hug, he said to her, "One minute you're getting vaporized, and the next thing you know, you wake up and the boss is looking at you, naked! People have nightmares about that, you know."

She smiled, obviously well enough to appreciate the dig, but still shocked to discover where she was. She stood next to the living legend himself, and his arm was around her! She blushed, very conscious of the fact she was naked beneath the cloak.

She turned and looked into his eyes, feeling tears well to the surface. She whispered gently, "Thank you, Sir."

"Anatt, there's no need to thank me at all. After all, you and your team provided the highest example of service that anyone could expect from a Guardian; you willingly sacrificed yourselves for others. Oh, and you get to call me Adam . . . For today, anyway."

"Thank you . . . Adam," she whispered.

Squeezing her gently on the shoulder, he replied, "The Lord Healer herself will be looking after you for the next month or so as we ramp your abilities gradually back up to full strength. Take it easy, give your regenerated tissue time to settle and mesh with your psyche, and you'll find I've added a nice little surprise to your psi-well to avoid having to do this again."

She nodded, intrigued, and the Overlord glanced upward at one of the ships.

A teleportation beam washed over the group before it narrowed to focus on the Grand Master herself.

The Overlord continued. "Give Corrine my regards, and ask Captain Hunter to send my cloak back down once you've finished with it. Take your time, okay?"

Before she could reply, the beams had taken her up into the safety of the ship.

The Overlord stared upward for a few seconds before thinking out loud. "Brave girl, it took guts to do that."

He walked back to the edge of the crater, which was over a mile across, and surveyed the damage caused by the black hole. He could see the remains of the ruined fields and, after exerting his far-sight, the leveled towns further south and west became visible.

Extending his sight even further, he watched how hard his people were working to reduce the impact of the cowardly strike inflicted upon the public during the missile attack.

He ruminated for some minutes. Suddenly, a transporter beam illuminated him momentarily, before depositing his cloak over his shoulder, and this appeared to snap him out of his reverie. Turning, he strode back over to the group, and for the sake of the CBS News Crew, spoke out loud.

"I've just finished speaking with our Commander of the American Sector, and the Lord Concilliator. We will appoint a representative to liaise with your President and State Governors to help discuss the options for the revitalization of this area, as well as discuss the impact of other events that have occurred while we were busy here.

"We came too close to a catastrophe today, and if anything, this is a healthy reminder to the world that while we are here to serve and protect, we are neither omnipotent nor omniscient, and as you saw today, we are certainly not infallible.

"You need to learn to look after yourselves in certain areas, so I would strongly suggest you heed the advice of our representative in initiating our accelerated educational programs within your society. This will free us from spreading our very limited resources too thinly, and allow us to focus on other issues."

He began to turn away from the camera, and then appeared to remember something. Turning back, he gestured to the huge crater. "If I may be so bold, perhaps this area might benefit from a suitable memorial. It will remind everyone of what occurred today, and how we all need to learn from it."

Turning to Megan, he held out his cloak. "I believe you wanted this memento?"

Freezing with embarrassment, she couldn't reply.

"I have more than enough of these, I assure you. After all, I do own the company." When she still didn't reply, he placed the cloak into her arms and said, "I tell you what, just look after it for me and when you get fed up with it, just throw it away or give it back, okay?"

And with that, he stepped back, waved, and vanished.

They all looked upward to see another Guardian vessel had materialized above the field. Immediately a blue protective curtain fluttered down over the crater from one of the emitters, ensuring no one would be able to stumble into the deep hole.

The Guardian Master's eyes got that faraway look for a moment. "Evidently, we're hitching a lift with the Argent. Sorry, guys, but I'm not a teleporter and that damned hybrid strike shorted out my transporter ring."

"Mine too," Ben affirmed. "Hey, Megan, do you need a lift? I noticed your van was swallowed."

"Thanks," she said gratefully. "Oklahoma City is a long way for us normal people to go with all this equipment." Looking back at the crater and surrounding devastation caused a chill to run down her spine.

"What's wrong?" Ben asked, noticing her discomfort.

She shook her head. "I was just thinking how easily that could have been us, gone, swallowed whole. If the Overlord hadn't turned up, we wouldn't be here now."

"I see your point, but would you like to know something that will help put things in perspective?"

"Go on then."

"Well, you could say the Overlord swallowed everything the black hole had swallowed. Hard as it may seem to grasp, you could technically say he's walking around now with a whole load of Oklahoma and your van inside him. How weird is that!"

Stunned by the logic of his argument, she couldn't help but giggle. "I didn't think of it like that."

"Damned good way to end your report, though," Eduardo noted, totally serious.

She had to agree; both men had valid points.

# 16

# What Was He Thinking?

It was inevitable that the day's events would completely overshadow the televised release of the captive test subjects from their prisons around the world earlier that week.

The world was still incensed by the fact that people had been abused in such a disgusting way.

But these new events presented a paradox that shouldn't exist.

Just as the euphoria was sinking in, the world had turned upside down, and their saviors were exposed as fallible; everyone was suddenly drawn into a quagmire of disappointment.

And really, could you blame them?

The revelation that their Supreme Commander appeared to be an angelic super being with seemingly limitless power, had caused pandemonium.

What he had done was astonishing.

But if a man could have such vast power, why hadn't he been able to protect the three hundred and twenty-three souls that died when the missiles exploded?

How were the Guardians so easily caught off guard, as to allow four hundred and fifty-eight of the survivors to get so badly injured?

In contrast, once televised footage of the tornado incident was aired, the female Guardian Commander who had hopelessly sacrificed herself to save others became immortalized forever.

To see her incinerated in such a terrifying way, only to be miraculously reprieved at the moment of death, captured the hearts of all who witnessed her brave attempt.

People were on the edge of their seats when her "resurrection" was revealed.

But that presented an unacceptable conundrum.

Were mankind being watched over by genuine Guardian Angels or not?

Were they really there to help everyone or just the ones they wanted?

Is that why no one else was resurrected that day? Were they not important enough?

It didn't add up, and some were quick to make their feelings heard, causing a backlash. Some were critical of the Guardians, and others felt they could do no wrong.

One line of thought did become predominant around the world.

Whether they loved him or hated him, many wanted to know why the Overlord had revealed himself in such a way. Now that the world knew his kind existed, expectations would only get higher.

And sure enough, the avalanche of media inquiries into the Lord Concilliator's Office following the incident was as expected as it was inevitable.

\* \* \*

*December 6th*

The following morning, a certain young lady had been called into the offices of her supposedly stricken superior, Henry Gould, at the BBC offices in Washington.

Gould was still ill with pneumonia and should have been at home in bed, but had made his feeble way into work to be there to break some startling news to his protégé and witness the shock on her face when he told her.

And he hadn't been disappointed!

Although a rising star within the BBC, Cathy had been relatively unknown to the public at large, until unexpected circumstances had thrust her into the limelight as the live correspondent present at the freeing of the hostages from the CIA headquarters at Langley.

To say that she had held her own on such an important debut performance would have been an understatement.

She had absolutely nailed it, seeming to be at ease among the Guardians, and remaining thoroughly professional.

It would seem her efforts had now marked her as a Guardian Correspondent by "The Powers That Be." The Editor in Chief of the BBC in the United States, Harold Bennett, had asked for her personally after being approached by representatives of the Lord Concilliator's Office of the Guardians that morning, wishing to arrange a special interview regarding the shocking events in the USA, Canaries, and Egypt the previous day.

That conversation made it clear the BBC would be favored with such interviews in the future. The co-operation of both CNN and CBS, who were on scene at the tornado, as well as a number of other international agencies from Egypt, Spain, and France, would be approached by the Guardians to facilitate as thorough a report as possible.

To be presented with the opportunity to deliver such an expose would be a dream come true. It was also a daunting task.

She faced the ordeal of a lonely studio, echoing to the voices of just her guest and herself.

Talk about being thrown in at the deep end!

Although Cathy relished the opportunity, she was fully aware of her lack of experience in this area, and a certain thought had been running through her mind since then.

*What was he thinking?*

The conference room of the Guardian Headquarters within the grounds of the Training Academy had been unusually full that morning.

All Lords and their deputies had been required to attend, along with the Academy's Heads and Chief Instructors. The agenda had been a foregone conclusion.

The recent jailbreaks, as they jokingly referred to them, were still a topic of much deliberation. Their initial elation over the success of that venture had been somewhat tempered by the "other" event.

Although they had never boasted about their calling, it had been gratifying to receive some recognition for their efforts. So, to think that someone had set out to deliberately expose their flaws and weaknesses was both deeply upsetting and frustrating, especially as lives had been lost.

It had been an important wakeup call for some of the younger and less experienced Guardians. They now realized they were imperfect and made mistakes. While this was only human, the Council of Lords reminded them that when Guardians made mistakes people died!

The world was waking up to this fact, and the reputation of their service was tarnished. In response, academy instructors were reminded to emphasize the true nature of their calling.

To raise everyone's spirits, the Council of Lords announced that inquiries currently underway to hunt down those responsible for the despicable attack had already produced results.

The new Lord Inquisitor would now take charge of the investigation, to ensure that justice was served.

They announced that should the world still be open to the idea of the Guardians working closely with their emergency services and legal systems in the future, they would put forward a groundbreaking proposal. That offer would contain the framework for new legislation to recognize and utilize psychic abilities.

The second half of the meeting went on to include the bombshell of the Overlord's manifestation. They all wanted to know what he had been thinking, especially as the world now knew of the existence of transcended individuals.

The Lord Marshall, Earl Foster, had gone to great lengths to reassure his staff that there would be no foreseeable problems in that regard. The new proposals contained specific guarantees to ensure the rights and privacy of all Guardians.

The conference room was clearing now, leaving the Lords to conclude their meeting in private.

As the last ones left, Earl activated the privacy shield around the room. As an added precaution, he phased in a temporal scrambler to ensure the utmost confidentiality without possibility of interruption.

"Expecting eavesdroppers?" asked the Lord Procurator, Jade Heung.

"Just being careful, Jade," he replied. "You never know with some of our wilder talents how ingeniously creative they can get when they want to be nosey."

Jade appreciated the Lord Marshall's caution. "So what's first on the agenda?" she asked.

Earl looked across to Corrine, the Lord Healer, and inclined his head toward her. "Would you like to start us off, Corrine? How are our new guests settling in?"

A rosy flash of excitement bloomed around her.

She stood up to pace habitually. "They're settling in very well, Earl. They have a wide range of talent, and really our only problem seems to be the candidates from China and Russia. They're used to an institutionalized way of doing things that we have to constantly remind them to relax.

"We've shown them various classes from different years and emphasized that although the training will be tough, it's still something they can enjoy. Hopefully that will sink in the longer they're with us.

"Even that aggressive young man Jose Calderon has surprised us, as his talents will make him a first class Inquisitor if he successfully completes training."

Earl looked somewhat dubious at that remark, so Jade was quick to support her colleague. "She's right! We've given him something he's always craved, a healthy sense of pride and self-worth. He's the kind of person we're after! If we can channel his energies in the right direction, it makes all this worthwhile."

Earl conceded. "What about Robin?"

"Robin's going to take a lot of work," Corrine replied. "It will take about five to six months to completely undo the effects of years and years of loneliness and neglect, and of course his initial aversion to his abilities, but after that we can begin bringing him into the program. He'll be a welcome addition to the family once we help him overcome his personal demons."

The Lord Marshall nodded. "Speaking of overcoming demons. How is little Becky coping? The loss of her mother can't have sunk in yet."

Corrine stopped pacing and stifled an excited outburst of psychic energy. "No, she hasn't been able to deal with the loss yet. The deep psychic wound is plain as day, but she's coping remarkable well for one so young. No doubt that's been helped by the fact we found living relatives."

Anil had been listening quietly until now. "I thought Alexander said there were none alive?" he asked, pleasantly surprised.

"That was only his preliminary report based on CIA records. It's something we should have expected when US authorities deal with Canadian nationals," Corrine explained. "Becky's Grandmother, on her mother's side, Valerie, had an older sister back in Canada. Although that older sister died, she had a daughter in later life, Valerie, who is alive and well. Valerie is only a few years younger than Karen, Becky's mother."

"Where is she now?" Anil asked.

Jade, who was finding it difficult to suppress her excitement, suddenly blurted out, "As of two days ago, here at the academy!"

*WHAT!* Exclaimed both Earl and Anil mentally.

Vladimir Arihkin, the Lord Concilliator merely raised his eyebrows in surprise.

"She's here!" Corrine exclaimed. "It turns out psi abilities run strong in the family. As you know, Karen, Becky's mother, was offered a place on one of our admin teams in the States. She wasn't strong enough to undergo the Guardian training program, but was capable enough to serve in a supportive role.

"We took in Valerie just over eight years ago, after Karen left. After graduating three years ago, she served aboard Observation Station One, and since then she's been on the Canadian Sector's Response Teams for just under a year. She's about to be inaugurated as a Master Class Far-Scanner, Empathic and Telekinetic in the New Year."

"Why didn't I know this?" demanded Earl.

Jade gave him a steady but sarcastic look. "Probably because you still haven't read my report. Forgive me for being blunt, but had you read it, you would already know. You would also know that her husband will be joining her at the end of the month. He's a Guardian Master, specializing in combat training. It's taking a little longer to work out a replacement for him, but he'll be an asset here at the Academy for sure.

"On top of that, they have a baby girl, Emile, whose only three years old! She's an up and coming Ultrasensor and Compulsive. The children are already getting along famously. Even better—Valerie is going to be appointed Becky's legal guardian. Even with what's been going on, a few strings have been pulled by our new Lord Concilliator."She paused to smile at Vladimir, who remained a silent observer. "The State authorities in the U.S and Canada have been very keen to cooperate with us, especially as Becky's such a tender age."

Earl sighed. "I stand corrected!"

Corrine took over. "Not really, Earl, because we've saved the best for last. We tested her psi range, and we confirmed she's an Ultra candidate. From what we can see, she's got extremely high potential with her telekinetic and elemental abilities, although not all her abilities have manifested."

The men looked at each other in bewilderment, stunned to silence.

Anil was uncharacteristically lost for words. Eventually, he mumbled, "But she's only five and completely untrained."

"This is where it gets interesting," Jade said. "When her mother was with us, she assisted in the development of the fledgling compressor program that accelerates the learning process. So, even after she left, Karen must have remembered enough about the new techniques to actually apply them to Becky while in the womb. We can say that for a fact because Becky's mind shows signs of early stimulus that resulted in her incredible psychic development."

Jade displayed the results of what Karen's input had done for her daughter's abilities.

Anil's eyes glazed over slightly, a sure sign he was computing data in his mind. A few seconds later, he gasped. "My God, look at this!"

He displayed the results of his calculations in the air before them.

Earl's eyes narrowed as he studied the results. "So, if she continues to grow and mature as she should, she's going to be stronger than any of us?"

"And one of her strongest abilities is going to be healing!" Corrine added triumphantly.

"I wouldn't be too smug about that if I were you, Corrine," Vladimir said. "Twenty or thirty years from now, that little girl will be after your job."

"Sorry to burst your bubble, Vladimir, but we don't foresee any problems," Corrine countered.

Earl interrupted. "Do any of you think it strange we're finding people like this, now, when 'His Nibs' suddenly upped the tempo?"

"You know we shouldn't try to second guess our illustrious leader," Anil chided. "All I can say is that it would be very unwise to think that absolutely nothing is going on."

They all agreed. It wouldn't be surprising to find that all these coincidences were linked in some way to the Overlord's plans.

As they chewed things over, Anil suddenly piped in. "Talking of Adam's manipulations, how is Grand Master Yasin coming along, Corrine?"

Corrine shook her head. "I've been a healer now for nearly two hundred years, the Lord Healer for a hundred and ten of them. I've never seen healing of this magnitude in all my time."

As she spoke, the other Lords became totally silent. Although they shared a friendly informality amongst themselves when alone, they also shared the deepest respect for each other's strengths. They knew that when it came to matters of healing, Corrine knew more than anyone present.

She continued. "As you know, Anatt had time to spin an instinctive defensive shield around her brain before the hybrid antimatter bolt hit her. That shield prevented her brain from being instantly vaporized, although she still suffered a total of ninety-nine percent damage to her frontal lobe.

"She's very lucky. Even full body regeneration takes over six months. This is the regeneration of almost a complete brain along with its personality, cognitive processes, autonomic nervous system, and neural linkage. It's impossible, but she's recovering, and her psi abilities are not only intact—they're *more* than energized."

"What are you implying, Corrine?" Vladimir asked.

"As you all know, we have yearly checkups as part of our regimen, including calibration of our psi range and strength.

"Anatt's elemental and telepathic abilities came up in her check-ups. She also had a latent well of self-regenerative and healing ability which never manifested—until now."

Earl sat bolt upright in his chair. "What? Are you saying she has somehow re-energized further abilities?"

Jade interrupted. "Anatt is one of my staff, and she's very good, Earl. She commands the respect of her people under High Grand Master Thaleton. She is, or should I say was, fully aware of her limitations and constantly pushed her boundaries. Well, now her boundaries have shifted. When the Overlord regenerated her, he mentioned he was so impressed with her that he added a 'surprise' to her psi-well to ensure she didn't have to go through this again. We've all see the footage and studied the report. Corrine and I have been checking her every hour since then."

"So what's happening to her?" Anil inquired, thoroughly fascinated.

"She's growing again," Jade explained. "Not only has her complexus begun to swell beyond its previous threshold, her latencies have been boosted. The mental synergy we're seeing is stunning."

"I'm the Lord Healer. I'm supposed to be top dog in this field," Corrine said, equally impressed. "I don't have a clue how he did it, but it's beautiful to watch. The scans and the Compilator show her psyche is fully intact, and her long established abilities are growing again, while her psi-well has expanded to incorporate her latencies. We think those abilities will mature at Ultra level."

"I'm sure I don't need to ask this," Vladimir began. "But would I be right in guessing that her abilities will become so strong that she's virtually guaranteed to survive the transcension process?"

He was already nodding, answering his own question.

"Bingo!" Corrine exclaimed. "Whatever the Overlord has done, it's big, huge!"

They all looked at each other for a moment, both excited and aghast at the same time. Earl had known the Overlord for many centuries, far longer than anyone else present. He was suddenly disturbed at how little he knew about his oldest friend. "Does she know yet?" he asked.

Corrine shook her head. "No, she's been through enough as it is without us adding to it. Even the ramping program he implemented is the most wonderful piece of work I've ever seen. It's gradually siphoning through her abilities at a rate that corresponds to her recovery. I'm not certain at this stage, but it also looks as if it will allow her to achieve Ultra level without actually triggering the change. She'll have time to adapt."

They all nodded their heads in wonder at the images she projected into their minds. The mental program that was working its magic on Anatt was a majestic construct of immense intricacy that revealed ever deeper and more profound levels of complexity the longer you looked at it.

Vladimir's eyebrows rose and he exclaimed, "Of course, but it's so simple! As I was studying the Overlords program, I couldn't help but think of Robin. Since we know the Overlord is capable of such regenerative marvels, why don't we simply ask for his help?"

The simplicity of the possible solution for the troubled young man had been in front of them all the time.

"Aha, but who would ask him, and anyway, I thought he went off world again?" Jade wondered.

*NO NEED TO ASK.* A monstrously loud mental voice boomed in their minds, causing them all to jump in surprise.

*My apologies,* the Overlord added. *I was listening in and didn't realize I would cut through the shield so easily. Earl, we really need to re-calibrate them to a more secure level.*

They all glanced at each other, awestruck by the ease with which the supposedly psychically impenetrable shield had been pierced, and dumbfounded at the possibility of approaching any level he might find 'secure'.

*Of course, Sir, I'll be sure to get on it right away,* Earl assured him.

The Overlord continued. *I will be finished on this assignment in a couple of days, after which I will brief Andrew on what needs to be done, and he can take over. That will leave me free to spend some time with you, Corrine, and your department heads, training you in the use of some new regenerative techniques.*

*Thank you, Sir.* She beamed.

*Earl, have you made the new appointments yet?* The Overlord inquired.

*We're just about to. Andrew and Victoria are waiting for us outside.* Earl paused. *I take it there will be a new position available in a few years' time for when Anatt is ready?*

Everyone present tried to stifle their surprise. A deep echoing laughter throbbed in the ether. *Aah, it's about time you started anticipated my ways, old friend. She's perfect for something I have in mind, tailor made you might say, and she'll be a solid addition to your team.*

*Tailor made?* A tingle went down Earl's spine at the implications of that thought. *I thought so. Any clues as to what you're up to now?*

*Andrew will fill you in after the appointments. Oh, and Earl—don't give him a hard time, he's acting on my specific instructions, okay?*

Putting his hand in the air, the Lord Marshall replied. *No problems from me, Sir, I assure you.*

And suddenly the presence was gone, leaving them all totally flummoxed, apart from Corrine. She was in raptures at the help Robin was going to receive, and the opportunity she would have to personally witness the Overlord at work in her hospital wing.

Anil was looking intently at his superior, obviously weighing something in his mind.

"Anil?" Earl said.

Smiling, the Lord Evaluator replied. "My friends, earlier on, many of us were wondering what the Overlord was thinking, revealing himself like that in front of the public. We were so sure there couldn't possibly be a rational explanation for his actions, but as we're seeing, none of the things he does are without reason. We may not understand them, but I think we're getting a glimpse of what's to come.

"We've been discussing expansion, and have forgotten to look inside ourselves. An expansion of range, ability, and power appears to be occurring right now. I think we'll all find this was exactly the right time for the public to find out that Guardian Angels are literally walking among them."

The Lord Marshall couldn't argue with his friend's logic. "Let's hope the public will want us around long enough to find out!"

And with that, he cut power to the shields, and extended a mental invitation to the new Lords to enter and officially receive their commissions.

# 17

# The Deep End

That day found Lei Yeung reflecting on those same events, but for very different reasons.

Those within The Council gifted with remote viewing skills had provided some startling details of what had actually happened, and he was still chewing those facts over.

He had no doubt that Member Espasito was responsible for the attacks. He also had no doubt that the fool didn't realize what he'd done.

The Guardians response to the containment threat in New Mexico had been impressive. They were all over the place within minutes of the doctored alarms eventual activation. It was a huge operation in response to a genuine threat. Despite the scope of that commitment, they'd been able to recognize it for what it truly was, just a diversion, and a piece in larger puzzle.

Within minutes of discovering the subterfuge, they had managed to zero in on the sabotaged missile tests, which were already underway.

What Yeung found fascinating was the tiered level response system they had employed to react as quickly as possible.

Espasito's plan meant the missiles should have remained undetected. But they didn't!

They had destroyed all those missiles heading toward populated areas. Realizing something was different about five of them, they had attempted to retrieve them safely to analyze them for evidence.

Whoever was responsible for the Guardians response levels could have been forgiven for getting complacent at this stage, as they were obviously unaware they had been rigged to explode if anything interrupted the preprogrammed flight plan.

Moments after the first surprise detonation, the others were instantly targeted and the command given for their destruction. Two instantly destroyed and the remaining two vaporized as they began their detonation sequence. Unbelievable!

Yes, three hundred and twenty-three people had died, and over four hundred and fifty had been badly injured, but it could have been much worse.

And he wasn't naïve enough to imagine for one instant that their incredible operating procedures wouldn't be tightened even more now, making it virtually impossible to try anything like this in the future!

It was impossible to tell what the Inquisitors would discover from any micro-fragments they managed to recover, or what forensic evidence would be found at the mission control site, or even from the minds of those they interrogated.

The news had been silent on the results of investigations so far, but that didn't mean they weren't making progress. However, this wasn't what worried Yeung the most.

He was concerned about their Overlord and any others that may be like him. How could anyone fight beings of unknown potential?

How would the Overlord direct his Inquisitors to respond?

Yeung was relieved this lunacy did not have the backing of The Council and that the person responsible for pushing Espasito's buttons had now been dealt with. He was sure that had he not exercised appropriate caution this could have been the end of them.

It would certainly be the end of Member Espasito.

He shook his head sadly. *Jumped in off the deep end this time didn't you? Pity you forgot to remove your concrete boots first.*

* * *

The new Lords eventually made their way out from the conference room of the Training Academy by the midafternoon, leaving behind a speechless group of people.

"That went better than I expected." Andrew was the new Lord of Shadow Operations, or the Dark Lord as Jade had jokingly referred to him as. He'd had to draw the line at letting her call him Darth Vader; otherwise it would have been around the Academy before he got back to his room. Truth be told where Andrew was concerned, the total opposite would have been more appropriate given his almost unique heritage.

Victoria, his newly promoted colleague and the new Lord Inquisitor, smiled to herself as they walked along. "Remember, they've had to absorb a lot in a short space of time and it can't be easy. The world is changing and they've got to keep up. At least they know which direction things will go if we manage to ride the storm and get over this latest hic-cup, and the Unification Process goes ahead as foreseen. We've waited a long time for the probability lattices to coalesce at last, so everyone needs to be ready for anything."

Chuckling as they walked, Andrew fine-tuned his thoughts to an ultra-secure mode to prevent any chance of eavesdroppers. *True, but can you imagine their reaction in the future when they eventually find out who we really are?*

Victoria initiated a security pulse, just in case, to ensure no one was trying to catch the thoughts of the newly promoted Lords.

She stopped. Looking her colleague in the eye, she clenched his mind in a compulsive grip for a split second, causing him to almost wince out loud. *Shut up, dickhead. Don't even think thoughts like that. Especially now they're beginning to forge through the transcension barrier. You never know who's strong and talented enough to pick up your thoughts!*

He held up his hands and backed away from her. *Okay, okay, I'm sorry, jeesh, it's not like I'm threatening to turn anyone to the Dark Side or anything.*

She turned to face him fully. *Just be careful. Do anything to screw this up, and you'll risk him losing his temper. Remember what happened last time?*

Andrew sobered. *Yes, you're right. The last time was such a long time ago I tend to forget what happened. Sunk without a trace just doesn't describe it, eh?*

He suddenly brightened. "At least he's got you jumping in off the deep end. Phew! First day on the job and you've already got one hell of a major investigation to solve! No pressure, the future of our continued relations with the whole world may rely on it.

"And a New Psychic Law and Order Bill to push through, too. Just think of the reaction that's going to bring, when people realize that our Inquisitors will be able to lawfully mind probe apprehended suspects, or mind snoop suspects to illegal activities. Ouch! Where's he going to find the sucker to head that little operation?"

Suddenly stopping to make a dramatic gesture, he pointed to her and said, "Oh yeah, I forgot, you're standing right next to me. Ha!"

Victoria punched him on the arm. "I'm not afraid to step up when it's required. At least Vladimir and I will have something constructive to do. To be honest, I was more concerned at Jade and Anil's reactions, as they were a bit put out I got the job over them."

Andrew reverted to mind speech. *That's because they think you're a lot younger than they are, and less experienced. They think it should go to someone older and more, what was she thinking . . . aah, 'tested in the field?'*

"If you think about it, he's thrown me in at the deep end in more ways than one, eh?" Victoria said out loud.

Grinning like a Siamese cat, Andrew patted her on the back and nodded.

After a moment, the new Lord Inquisitor's eyes narrowed. "At least I'm not the only one. The look on their faces when you told them Adam's been off world again, already looking for viable planetary colonization candidates, and that you'll be taking on that assignment full time until further notice . . . priceless."

Andrew looked thoughtful for a moment. "Yes. He does like to plan ahead, doesn't he? But at least they know why we've been absent so much lately. There's a lot of Space out there to check, even when we can limit our initial scans to stars in the early F, G, and mid K spectral range. Then, once we've narrowed the candidates, a far-scan takes a lot of concentration to find available planets. You know the hassles as well as I do. And that's even before the teleportation hyper-jump we have to go through to get there to check them out in person!"

Nodding in agreement, Victoria adopted a statuesque pose and recited "The Drill" for him. "Bio-diversity, geo-chemistry, constancy of planetary rotation, stability of habitable zone, availability of liquid water with an absence of tidal locking and acceptable atmospheric dynamics for sustained bio-development."

"And clean underwear!" they said together, bursting into laughter, and drawing the attention of passersby as they entered the main corridor of the Academy which was still full from the earlier meeting.

Upon seeing who it was, the passersby, both students and instructors began to bow in respect.

In painful resignation, Andrew whispered, "Aah crap! The word's already out?"

They bowed respectfully back to their colleagues. "It would appear so. Shall we take the plunge together?" Victoria asked.

Andrew sighed. He linked his arm through hers as they moved out into the corridor. He caught sight of their sleeves. "Better get these tailored—everyone will catch on were not properly dressed. Got to set the right example now that we're official, eh?"

She smiled in reply, still nodding to passers-by when she suddenly had a thought. "Hey, talking of taking a plunge, how about doing that literally? That dolphin pod is back."

"What, the ones who try to swim along close to us when we go supersonic?"

"Yup, those are the ones. It will be nice to mind talk with some intelligent creatures for a while before I deal with the lowlife again tomorrow."

"Oh, speaking of which, how would you like to do a spot of undercover work for me before you go floating off among the stars?"

"Love to, why?"

"There's someone I want you to impersonate for me, just for a morning or afternoon here and there. It will facilitate an arrest I'm hoping to make within the next week or two if the latest intelligence I'm getting from my investigators is correct."

"What, another breakthrough already?"

"Thank God, yes. We need this now more than ever, but I don't want to go rushing in until I've conducted a mind ream or two personally." She looked him in the eye and winked. "You know how I love to delve into the minds of scumbags, eh?"

He nodded, ignoring the joke at his expense. "I think you have yourself a date. Let's stroll down to the beach right now, but slowly. We don't want to deny the gawkers a good long look, do we?"

They casually strolled along the academy corridors, letting everyone get a good eyeful of the latest source of gossip.

* * *

Those who walked the corridors that day were struck by something they had never really noticed before.

As the two new Lords strolled, looking relaxed and comfortable in the limelight, it was noted that they appeared almost identical in their temperaments, mannerisms, and bearing.

Those closer to them noticed something else coincidental.

They had the most amazing grey eyes. Eyes like liquid magnets that, once they had captured your gaze, were difficult to tear yourself away from.

# 18

# The Honeymoon is Over

*December 10th*

Earl stared across his desk at the man opposite him.

Vladimir was wading through the sheaf of newspapers, poll results, and the incident report relating to the missile attacks of the week before.

Earl was glad that he wasn't the one who had to figure out how to minimize the media's hostile reaction to the situation.

Initial news reports following the attacks streamed in, each over-estimating the number of casualties. They also exaggerated the damage to the environment. A very negative view had been projected of the Guardians and how they had handled the matter.

The fact that the Guardian Commanders on the ground had initially been more focused on saving lives and dealing with the emergencies at hand, and had declined to comment or guess as to the source of the attacks or extent of the devastation, only added fuel to the fire. Many news agencies were quick to seize on this lack of response by accusing the Guardians of hiding something and failing in their duty.

This triggered an aggressively focused internet poll, which due to its subtle wording and slogans, went viral in less than twenty-four hours.

Since the day following what the media had dubbed the Guardian Buster incident, headlines dominating most of the front pages displayed similar sentiments. "Guardians Standing on Shaky Ground, Fallen Angels, Bombed Out!, Nuke kids On the Block Crash and Burn," and "Will They Be Able to Handle the Fallout?" were just a few examples.

The influence was also evident at a number of emergencies the Guardians had attended over the last few days, where demonstrators had actually interrupted relief efforts. Needless to say, they weren't happy at being kept out of harm's way by the Guardians as they went about the task of helping the trapped or injured.

After an age of silence, Earl spoke up. "Vladimir, what do you think, is there any ray of sunshine in there?"

"To be bluntly honest, Earl, we did exactly what we were meant to do. This negative reaction is just a frightened response to a cowardly deliberate attack."

"Yes, I appreciate that, but have you seen the polls they're forcing through? Especially that global one they're pushing for in the New Year? It's already had over two billion replies, and those frightened people you refer to may stir up too much negative feeling against us and end the Unification Plan before it's even begun. The way Adam is, he won't force change. They've got to want it."

The Lord Concilliator raised a placating hand toward his friend. "Earl, relax, let me do the job Adam chose me for and we can worry about them telling us to go to hell later, okay?"

"So how do you propose we deal with this?"

"Well, we're planning to hold a news address later today at the BBC in London to offer our official response to the attack."

"Who's going to handle that, you or your deputy?"

"I think this is the perfect time for the public to meet Deputy Concilliator Joseph West, don't you? He's not transcended, and a fully human representative will remind them that as powerful as we are, we make mistakes like anyone else.

"Oh, and don't worry, it will be a straight forward statement, the interviews can come later if we survive the first round and start to win back their confidence. Joseph will deliver that initial statement and will emphasize our role. I will stress to him how vital it is that he re-clarifies our role, because the public needs reminding that we are there to protect them to the best of our ability."

"I'm sure they don't feel all that protected at the moment."

"Aah, but that's just the point, Earl. We have to point out the full facts to them. Otherwise, no! They won't appreciate just how alert we were!"

"Alert! You think they'll agree we we're alert to the danger?"

"By the time Joseph has finished, oh yes. I'll be briefing him to reveal quite a few details they are not yet aware of. For example, forensic Inquisitors have now established beyond doubt that the specific signals to activate the ghost protocols within their systems were not sent by Espasito until things began getting out of control in Oklahoma. He must have been watching the events on TV, and timed his attack to catch us with our pants down.

"Once the world realizes how well those responsible hid their actions until the last minute, I do think they will agree that we were as alert as we could have been.

"A lot of planning went into the events that day, Earl. People need to know that the attack was a diversion that could have rendered Central America uninhabitable for thousands of years, and caused hundreds of thousands of people to become susceptible to all sorts of cancers and genetic deformities."

Earl had to concede; it was a good point. "Will that be enough?"

The Lord Concilliator shook his head. "On its own, probably not. That's why Joseph will also be emphasizing how the perpetrators infiltrated a secure military facility, stole the chips, had them doctored by experts from Japan and China, and then returned without detection."

"Anything with that yet?" asked the Marshall, referring to the apprehension of the persons responsible for that phase of the attack.

"Victoria tells me we should have all eighteen of them by the end of today, tomorrow at the latest. We already have the idiots responsible for sabotaging the missile control test center in Tennessee. Well, all but one that is."

Earl was clearly surprised. "Are you saying someone actually got away from us?"

"Technically, yes. He was a Major in the U.S. Air Force Science Division who owed the mob a lot of money. He helped a mob team from Chicago gain entrance to the facility to doctor the ventilation system the week before the test flights. When the Inquisitor team arrived, he'd already downed almost a full bottle of bourbon and just said 'I'm sorry!' and bit down on a capsule in his mouth."

"I'll be damned! I take it no healers in the group then?"

"Not top tier, no. One of the team, Guardian David Williams, is a top notch forensic reader, and was able to telepathically skim the full sordid details regarding his part in the matter before brain activity ceased. His testimony has been verified by the new Wave Reader which we have allowed Federal Agents to test, and they are more than satisfied in the authenticity of his reading."

"How did they take to our version of a lie detector?"

"Oh, they love it, at least we've made friend with the law enforcement agencies. The sooner they go into mass production the better—if they still want us around, that is!

"Anyway, that gave us the breakthrough we needed with the mob connection, and it pointed us in another direction which has proven very fruitful in more ways than one."

Earl nodded and sat back in his chair, eyes still locked on his friend. "Have we established a link with the one Victoria warned off?"

"Not directly. It looks as if he may walk in the same circles, but from what the Inquisitors have uncovered so far, he was in this alone. If he does belong to the same organization, this was completely unsanctioned, and we've seen clear signs they have distanced themselves from him as much as possible."

"Do you think they're sending us a message?"

Vladimir shook his head. "Hard to say, but no doubt we shall see."

"So, when do we let on the mastermind behind this blatant act of terrorism was psychically gifted, and that we have virtually all his cronies?"

"That will be my job when I take to the stage next week. Victoria tells me she will have completed her investigations by then, as Andrew is helping her in some way before he starts his next assignment. Her plan is to have Espasito in custody the day before my interview.

"Just as well, as although it's being chaired by the new Guardian Correspondent, Cathy, who is on our side, she's determined that no one accuse her of bias. She's planning to be very direct, so I expect the sparks will fly. Thankfully I'm well prepared for it, and let's just say that when they find out that the missiles were doctored by psychic criminals, this information should prove to be our trump card. What with that, and the results of the new Wave Reader proving their indisputable guilt, we should weather the storm quite comfortably. I hope!"

Looking a little more relaxed, Earl said, "So they're all accepting Victoria's testimony regarding the international links and Espasito's connection before she brings him in?"

"Certainly, the Wave Reader confirmed the truth of her testimony, satisfying their Codes of Criminal Procedure. The FBI is more than happy to accept the findings. They've all given her their blessing to haul him in, and are keen to waive his rights to anonymity so the world gets to see who the real enemy is.

"Both the Supreme Public Prosecutors Office in Japan and the Supreme People's Court in China were also very supportive, especially as she also submitted to a number of tests under the supervision of their experts. They seem really taken with the Wave Reader and can't wait to get their own."

"Let's hope the public reacts in a similar way after the interview, so we can start to undo some of the damage these polls are causing," Earl replied.

The Lord Concilliator stood and leaned over so his fists were on the desk. "Let's be honest about this, Earl. You know as well as I do that this day was going to come. Not if, but when. There was no avoiding it. Doing what we do means that people will expect the impossible from us. It was only a matter of time before someone tried something like this. The honeymoon's over and reality sucks. But when it comes to handling flack, we've got broad shoulders."

"We both know that anti-brigade isn't going to like it, no matter what we say or do," Earl reminded him, indicating the newspapers.

"I know, Earl, I know. But this needs to be addressed. The touchy feely relationship may be over, but that's a good thing. We're beginning to impact the law. We can't be seen to be overly soft and friendly all the time when we'll soon be putting away some very nasty individuals. Especially if the Espasito fellow is the tip of the iceberg regarding psychic criminals."

He quietly exited the Lord Marshall's office, leaving behind a very worried man who was wishing he could take a long relaxing vacation until it was all over.

* * *

*December 14th*

Luigi Espasito sat quietly in his study at the family estates in Brolo, Sicily, transfixed by the bank of TV screens before him. He was both disappointed and delighted with the results of his handiwork.

His initial outburst of anger at discovering most of his missiles had been destroyed had quickly been replaced with a deep sense of relief when the news reports began rolling in, and he'd discovered the extent of the carnage.

The new royal yacht, Queen Elizabeth III, sunk. (If only there had been a higher loss of life!) But at least he had the consolation of knowing that La Palma would be quarantined while the asshole Guardians assessed the damage to the local strata and coastline off the southern tip of the island.

Port Tawfik, although having been saved from the full effects of the detonation, would be closed to shipping while further safety and radiological checks were made. This was causing mayhem to one of the most important trade routes on the planet.

All in all, not a bad days work! He couldn't believe there wasn't a higher loss of life, but at least those who had died would be a major cause of embarrassment to those idiots who had put themselves on a pedestal. The collateral damage caused to the environment, trade, and commerce would keep the knife twisting in their guts for a long time to come.

And talking of twisting the knife, look at their plunging popularity in the polls!

Oh, he was going to have so much fun ramming this down the throats of the Council members at the New Year's meeting.

Luigi decided to toast himself and his accomplishments again. Finding his glass empty, he rang the bell for a top up, and continued to gloat, firmly believing he was beyond accountability.

When the door to the study opened a few minutes later and Gianni, the housekeeper, came in with his favorite Black Pearl Louis XIII cognac on a silver tray, he insisted the old servant stay with him and drink to his success. "Come, Gianni, stay, celebrate with me. Good times should be shared with trusted friends."

The gesture wasn't missed by Gianni. At fifty-five thousand dollars a bottle, the cognac was one of the most expensive in the world, and he quickly poured a generous helping into two glasses. As he handed one to his boss, he paused momentarily to savor the bouquet of the blended flowers, fruits, spices, and the deep amber color of the aromatic liquid. "You're looking particularly pleased with yourself today, young Sir. Good news?"

"It's the very best of news, Gianni, and one that appears to be maturing with age." He replied without looking away from the screens.

The old housekeeper tossed down his drink in one and shuffled to stand deferentially behind his employer. He listened as yet more reports of the suffering caused by the missile detonations were announced. "That mess doesn't look like there's much to be happy about, Sir. Surely that doesn't please you, does it?"

"Aah, Gianni, sometimes, when you need to make a point, you have to catch your enemy's attention," Luigi replied. "You have to ensure they not only respect you, but fear you. I'm pleased because I've done just that. Wouldn't you agree, my old friend?"

When no reply was forthcoming, Luigi naturally assumed the old housekeeper must have been unable to hear his question. Turning in his seat, he felt a peculiar throbbing, tingling sensation in his teeth and sinuses. "I said 'wouldn't you agr . . . .'"

Luigi's voice choked off in his throat as he caught sight of Gianni's eyes. The distinctive, familiar, lazy old eyes of his longtime employee seemed to be undergoing some kind of metamorphosis. Gone was the semi-vacant, un-focused faraway look he always seemed to display as he pottered about. Instead, Luigi was looking into the hardest, most piercing eyes he had ever seen, eyes that seemed to glow with an inner furnace to match the cold look of rage chiseled onto his face.

The shock made him drop his glass onto the carpet, spilling about three thousand dollars worth of the deep amber nectar.

Transfixed he watched as Gianni's body straightened, grew, and bulked out. As the years fell away from his face, he realized without a doubt that he was going to fully shoulder the burdens his choices had wrought.

Before him stood his own personal living nightmare made flesh, dressed from head to toe in black. Instantly he felt the fire rising within him, straining for release.

The Guardian stepped forward, making the barest of gestures with his finger as he did so, and Luigi found himself lifted into the air by some unseen force. He was held motionless, helpless as a puppet awaiting the commands of his master.

Nodding at the screens, the Guardian spoke. "Allow me to introduce myself. I am Andrew, Guardian Lord of Shadow Operations. Did you seriously think you'd get away with something like this?"

Luigi stared defiantly back, fighting to overcome his shock at the Guardian's presence, and surprised at the lack of access to his ability. "Do what you want, asshole, at least the world sees you as the frauds I knew you were!" he hissed.

"Do what I want? I'd love to, but unfortunately my boss won't let me."

Luigi stared impotently back at his nemesis as he strolled closer. Once he was standing in front of him, the Shadow Lord said, "As for exposing us as frauds? Well, I really don't know why you would think that. We never said or intimated we could be everywhere at once. The world's a sad enough place as it is without you adding to it. All we are doing is trying to help people avoid as much heartbreak as possible."

Andrew pointed to the repeat bulletins on the screens. "So, once the world finds out that all this was the deliberate act of some sick and twisted psycho who didn't care how many suffered, just so long as he could score some points, how do you think they'll react to you, Luigi?"

The point struck home. Luigi struggled in an attempt to slap the Guardian across the face, to do something to help vent the building fury inside him.

Helpless, he continued stewing as the Guardian moved so close he was able to whisper in his ear. "And when they find out about your abilities, can you even begin to imagine how they'll react to that? You worthless, spineless, pathetic little man. I really wish they'd let me play with you before we throw you to the wolves."

"Fuck off, asshole, you don't scare me."

"Scare you?" Andrew smiled wickedly. "Oh no, Luigi, that's not my job. That's hers!"

The Guardian gestured behind Luigi at the same moment he let go with his telekinesis. Although Luigi only dropped about a foot, he crumpled to the floor, becoming acutely aware that the strange throbbing in his teeth was even more pronounced than before.

Turning, Luigi was met with a vision of such barely contained power and fury that he immediately soiled his pants.

Andrew squatted beside him. "Allow me to introduce you to the head of our investigations branch. This is Victoria, our Lord Inquisitor, and she's very pleased to meet you after all the suffering you've caused."

Victoria stood in front of the TV screens, wreathed in a visible static discharge that blew the circuits of all the electrical equipment in the office and made the hairs on Luigi's arms and head stand on end. Her eyes, so similar to those of the Shadow Lord, intensified in luminosity and turned from grey to white hot. Luigi shielded his eyes and cowered on the floor in his own excrement.

*What a fool I am.* He thought.

In reply to his thoughts, the Shadow Lord said, "Yes Luigi, what a murderous, cowardly fool of a man you are. I think the whole world will agree when they find out, eh?"

Luigi had to agree. He had not only made a fool of himself, but of the Council, too. If anything was ever traced back to them, he knew the consequences for him and his family. He had only one option left.

Deep within his skull, at the point where the brain stem flows into the spinal cord was his own personal ticket to oblivion, an ingeniously crafted piece of nano-technology. Called a "Lazarus Shell", it was designed to prevent any of the Apostles ever betraying the Council by immolation of their minds.

The Shadow Lord gestured towards the Lord Inquisitor. "No, Luigi, as angry as I am, you have no reason to be scared of me. Pity I can't say that about her."

And with that he vanished, leaving a panic stricken victim scrambling on the floor as the Lord Inquisitor walked slowly toward him, the icy cold talons of her immensely powerful mind already sinking into his skull, ready to peel him open like a ripe fruit.

Closing his eyes, he decided to welcome death instead of shame. He activated the Lazarus Shell and whispered, "Fuck you!"

* * *

Excerpt from UK Edition of the global periodical "Weekly Observer", December 20th

*Make your vote count!*

*By: Current Affairs Editor, Sally Franks.*

With only thirteen days to go until the results of the poll that could change your lives forever, I would urge all normal people, everywhere, to make sure you don't forget to vote. We make up the majority of society and must ensure our voice is heard.

Using the basis of friendship, the Guardians have attempted to insinuate their way into society by employing an age old con— that of a Trojan Horse. All along, they've been intimating we need their help and guidance for "a better future." Wheedling their way into our hearts and minds, they've fooled us into thinking that, without the changes they propose, we have no hope!

However, recent events have shown us that not all of them and especially not the more powerful of them are even human. So, what's the real reason behind this "iron fist in velvet glove" approach to the hand of friendship?

Why would those who are clearly not human want to help us when they can so easily dominate us?

That's food for thought isn't it? Is that what they have in mind when they offer all these gradual changes for the future? A subjugated world farm full of willing sheep, ready to do their masters' bidding?

If you have any doubts about this just ask yourselves these simple questions. Why is it that a group of individuals who can swallow down a black hole—the most destructive force known to exist—without breaking into a sweat, be unable to stop a few missiles?

Don't they flit about, teleporting in the blink of an eye all over the world? So why couldn't they get to more than several places at the same time?

Are some people not as important to them as others, and if so why?

We all saw the interview earlier this week where they attempted to justify their criminal lapse of care with all sorts of excuses designed to divert our attention. So the persons they say are responsible for the crime are now in custody. All that is, except for the psychic criminal mastermind behind the affair who "conveniently" committed suicide!

Doesn't it strike you as suspicious that these Guardian Angels suddenly became very competent when they felt it necessary to protect their name? Yes, when it suits them, they can be very capable and extremely resourceful. When they can't be bothered, we die!

Thank goodness providence has smiled upon us and exposed them for what they might be before it was too late. A deadly cancer!

January 2nd 2016 is only thirteen short days away. Your elected representatives and governments need to know how you, their electorate, their people, feel while there's still time. So get out and make YOUR vote count too.

\* \* \*

Excerpt from the UK National Newspaper "The Daily Chronicle", December 23rd

*Does This Mean the Honeymoon is Over?*

*By: International Affairs Correspondent, Julian Forbes.*

*"Time and unforeseen occurrence befalls us all." (Ecclesiastes 9:11)*

Amid the furor and backlash following the tornado and attacks of December 4th, I find myself questioning the integrity of all those would be "do-gooders" who say they speak for the ordinary person, and who shout loudly that we should be apportioning blame and laying it squarely at the feet of the Guardians. The simple truth of the matter is, notwithstanding the awful and tragic events of the day in which three hundred and twenty-nine persons lost their lives, they were not to blame. We were!

In their opening televised interview, watched by millions of viewers worldwide, the Guardians plainly stated they were under "No Illusions" about their limitations or being hailed as godlike saviors. They specifically asked for our patience and understanding while they stretched their resources to the limit to offer a full global service of a better standard of protection against emergencies and natural disaster. And sure enough, that protection was afforded us in a number of very practical and sometimes startling ways. And yet, every day we continued to lose loved ones to old age, disease, accident, and sheer bad luck. Why? The answer was revealed to us when a wise man was once inspired to write, "Time and unforeseen occurrence befalls us all."

That simple fact continues to unite us in grief thousands of years later, despite the addition of technology, advances in medicine, and new friends with seemingly limitless powers.

And yet, during this honeymoon period, not once did we seek to lay the blame for these continued tragedies of everyday life at the door of our new friends. Why? Because we were happy to become complacent!

Why did it take the events of December 4th to make us realize that life is still a fragile, tenuous thing? The fact of the matter is, that day was the culmination of the bitter hatred of a twisted man now known to be one Luigi Espasito. Espasito was a newly appointed Mafia Crime Boss from Sicily, who unfortunately for us, was not only gifted with psychic powers of his own, but also blessed with the time, resources, and influence to set in motion a series of events that, had he been successful, would have resulted in the deaths of millions of people. Not content to simply launch a surprise terrorist attack on some of the world's most crucial economic, social, and military targets, Espasito went to a great deal of trouble to arrange the perfect diversion. A meltdown that had become almost unstoppable prior to the intervention of the Guardians, whose prompt actions not only saved the lives of millions more, but who also averted an ecological disaster of biblical proportions.

I'm sure I am not the only one who is glad they were there that day despite the tragic outcome. Even the most powerful being can't be in two places at once, so why are we expecting the impossible from those who were clearly doing their best?

So, does this mean that the honeymoon is over?

There are those who say it is, and they are extremely vocal in their protestations. They say we should send the Guardian Angels packing and ask that we make this clear by our voting in the global poll they've instigated, a poll in which nearly five billion have expressed their views so far.

I ask you, do we really want that? Are we seriously considering the possibility of a world without them? Have we already forgotten the events of December 1$^{st}$ that brought universal praise for their actions?

Only the results of January 2$^{nd}$ will say for sure.

I know how I'll be voting! If anything, this incident has highlighted our very real need for our new friends as they strive to shepherd us along a difficult path towards a greater understanding of science, medicine, our environment, and ourselves. We should all be very grateful that they are willing to take the next step to a closer relationship with us, by implementing the proposed "Psychic Law and Order Bill."

That our continued security would be safeguarded by this legislation, and supportive technology to be made available to law enforcement agencies worldwide, is beyond doubt. The skillful ease with which the cowards responsible for this disgusting crime were brought into custody is testimony to this fact.

It is my sincere hope that all countries involved unite, to bring speedy justice to those responsible, and show overwhelming support to our philanthropic new friends who continue to put our wellbeing beyond their own.

# 19

# Preparations

Andrew completed the mental report of his latest and perhaps most gratifying discovery with a great deal of satisfaction.

He'd discovered this planetary body within a small solar system on the very edge of the Pegasus Dwarf Galaxy the year before, but only now was he taking the time to complete a detailed survey.

Fortunately, Pegasus was part of a local group of galaxies centered on the Milky Way and Andromeda Galaxies. Pegasus was a satellite of Andromeda itself.

This planet, about half as big as Earth, and fourth from its sun, was ideally placed in a solar system positioned at the very edge of the galaxy. It was free from the lethal radiation often found closer to galactic hubs.

Its parent star, a bluish white sub giant, with one point seven times the mass of the sun, had initially put further investigation to the bottom of the pile. It had six times the luminosity of Earth's sun.

However, always the stickler for thoroughness, (a trait inherited from his father), Andrew had returned a year later to investigate the planet more thoroughly.

The planet itself was twelve and a half thousand miles in diameter, with a land mass that accounted for forty-one percent of its surface area. It had an axial tilt of seventeen degrees, and an orbital eccentricity of zero point zero two, ensuring habitable seasonal variation. Its vast oceans were comprised of drinkable water, albeit full of trace minerals and elements, but nothing proper filtration methods couldn't handle.

The atmosphere was comprised of seventy-four percent Nitrogen, twenty-two percent oxygen, with the rest made up of Carbon Dioxide, Argon, Helium, Hydrogen, and Ammonia, along with other trace elements. Although this resulted in a distinctive tang in the air, it would easily be addressed by atmosphere processors.

Two moons meant there was a high tidal variation, but tectonic stability of the land masses meant this would pose no problem. Neither would the fact that it had one point three times the gravity of earth, and days that were thirty-nine hours long. People would adapt, and this would be a wonderful place to start again!

The huge bio diversity evident on all three continents was a delight, having only a handful of dangerous predators. The high concentration of water vapor in the atmosphere negated the otherwise harmful effects of the sun. The atmosphere generated a very dense ozone level, and also filtered out all harmful radiation.

This also ensured there were no desert areas, and much of the lush, rampant vegetation was more than suitable as a highly nutritious food source.

Mineral and ore deposits were plentiful, and would delight any scientist or geologist studying them for many years to come.

*All in all, an absolute gem*, Andrew mused. With a bit of tinkering, this would ensure the Overlord's plans stayed on schedule if public opinion could be swayed. And if not, at least there were enough of them now to start a viable self-sustaining colony.

*At least I'll be on time for the meeting later tonight. I can't wait to find out what else has been cooked up while I've been off playing astronaut!*

Finalizing the details of the report in his head, he paused one last time to savor the beauty of the planet and its tranquil mood. *Mmmmh, she's a beauty all right.*

He smiled to himself as he realized that would be a good name for her.

Running the term through his head in different languages, he experienced a poignant memory from the past. *Kalliste! That will do nicely, and hopefully we'll do better here than we did before.*

Filing away the report within his vast psyche, he began spinning the hyper spatial translation matrix that would take him home in two vast leaps.

He took one final look, and then he was gone, leaving the beautiful world below spinning in silent majesty awaiting the changes to come.

\* \* \*

*Old District Tokyo*

Lei Yeung went through the proposed minutes of the New Year's meeting for the third time, anxious to ensure he hadn't overlooked anything.

Never one to miss an opportunity, he had used the existence of the anti-Guardian movement to ensure that everyone under the influence of The Council had obeyed the direction to vote against the Guardians in the poll. Every vote would count for something, and while mud might not stick against their whitewashed facade, it would get stained if you threw enough!

However, he wasn't so naive as to think that unless they reviewed their key goals and aspirations they would survive the coming year.

They had drawn attention to themselves, and Espasito's monumental failure would only ensure the Guardians' response to any perceived threat would be swift and decisive.

So, for the time being they had to back off, exercise prudence and gather their resources.

The latest trends showed a high likelihood that the Guardians would be rejected soon enough, so it would be a course of wisdom to allow public opinion to do most of the Council's work for them.

\* \* \*

Waiting for the axe to fall seemed unbearable for some of the Lords.

Corrine was pacing up and down, drinking endless cups of coffee. Every so often she would stop and speak to no one in particular. "People aren't stupid, it will be all right."

Jade and Vladimir were deep in discussion, debating the legality of some of the recent activities of their opponents, and formulating a few ideas as to what they could do to minimize the rash behavior they had witnessed by demonstrators at several of the incidents they had attended.

Anil kept scanning through the freshest updates of the latest tracking poll, revising his estimates as to how the world leaders may react, and how they themselves would fare.

He had to admit, their opponents had used a very clever strategy.

Using the momentum generated by the negative response of the media, their benchmark poll via the internet on the day following the missile attack had targeted a narrow but specific cross section of the public. This ensured a "reactive" response from the most volatile and disruptive elements of the populace.

The viral reaction this created a strong response bias around the world and attracted the attention of opinion strategists everywhere.

By the time a follow up poll was initiated a few days later, they had adjusted their target audience to cover a wider demographic of the population, but had also employed some very subtle and subliminally worded adverts to maintain a continuing bias among the general public.

"Liberty", the new survey specialists, came on board and offered to run a global poll.

They had hit the mark beautifully, impacting the attitudes of the general public, and had triggered the global poll the following day. It had drawn the attention of over five billion "concerned" readers.

Poignantly, those same polls revealed the almost overwhelming support of the world's emergency services for the Guardian Angels. They could relate to a life spent in the service of others while facing constant criticism.

It was a pity there were not a lot more of them, because current estimates were indicating the results would definitely lead to a worldwide referendum.

The only other ray of sunshine to break through the heavy clouds of negativity was the almost unanimous approval being voiced for a Memorial statue at Lawton.

People's hearts had gone out to Grand Master Yasin and the sacrifice she had made, and that of her team who had given their lives in fighting the tornado. Strangely, despite the poll, popular demand had been calling for a statue of the Grand Master herself to be erected, plasma staff in hand, brandished at the heavens.

However, her polite request to have a simpler, more dignified monument erected had been grudgingly acknowledged. Preparations were now underway for the erection of a statue of a male and female Guardian, standing either side of a family, and displaying the simple declaration, "In Honor of All Who Protect Us."

The Lord Concilliator's office had been assured that the erection of the monument was set in stone, and would go ahead even if the poll went against the Guardians.

Andrew was discussing some of their options with Earl, the Lord Marshall.

"Earl, you know as well as I do that if they tell us to pack our bags and leave we can't simply do that. It's going to take time to lift and shift everything, so I was wondering if you wouldn't mind if I made a suggestion or two."

"Will I like these suggestions?" Earl asked cautiously.

"I don't see why not, I'd just recommend we don't abandon everything, that's all."

Earl was intrigued, as were a few of the other Lords who began listening in. "What do you mean?"

"Well, for one thing, almost all of our Command Centers are accessible only by teleportation. With their current levels of technology, they don't have anything that could breach our security anyway, so we only need to reduce power and run a skeleton staff, in most cases behind encoded mitigator shields."

"What do you mean skeleton staff? You think we'd leave someone here?"

"Of course we will! We'll need to keep an eye on this planet and its people even if we depart en-masse. You know their future potential as well as I do. More and more gifted ones are being born with access to high powers, but they're suspicious of us now, so we have to be careful. We'll need one or two places on the ground to keep a closer eye on them, and especially on this other lot who seem intent on carving out a little empire for themselves. They do have people capable of teleportation, and we don't want to run the risk of them gaining access to our technology."

Earl nodded in agreement. "I like your thinking. Anything else?"

"Yes, I think it would be prudent to jump gate most of the orbital stations away. Kalliste is an option if we have to, or we could just park them in moon orbit. They're beginning to realize we have this capacity now. By moving the stations we can ensure they won't cause any unnecessary accidents if and when they come snooping. If we leave a few here, in variable high orbit, cloaked and silent, that will give us plenty of scope to accurately assess new candidates and detect when the mood changes toward us in the future. If we need support at short notice, we'd have the bases on the Moon, Mars, and Titan to provide cover until backup arrived from Kalliste."

Earl was intrigued. "So, who would you suggest should stay?"

Victoria, who had been listening in on the conversation, looked intently at Andrew. A silent communication flowed between them for a few moments.

She shook her head at one suggestion, so Andrew shrugged and turned back to the Lord Marshall. "Victoria's just reminded me, we'd need specialist teams for this. The normal training regimen can continue uninterrupted. If you let me begin choosing my Shadow Operations staff now, I can have enough people with the right skills to keep things ticking over nicely while the rest of you are away.

"Victoria's offered the help of some of her specialists, and we can operate out of the older, cloaked surface installations still here, keeping them manned and ready to go while the Academy relocates to Moon Base."

"Moon Base?" everyone gasped in unison, the surprise evident on their faces.

Glancing toward each other again, Victoria and Andrew engaged in another lightning fast mental exchange.

"As you know, Andrew and I have been used on numerous occasions over the years by the Overlord on quite a few confidential assignments. One of those assignments was the enlargement of our biggest off-world facility so far, Moon Base," Victoria explained. "The current base only accounts for seventeen percent of the total facility, which was enlarged to manage future operations. You know how sensitive Adam's precognitive ability is, so he may have foreseen the need for re-location to that site in the future. It's also subterranean, so they can't scan it with their current levels of technology. Not even the new lunar satellites will pick it up, but it's still near enough to ensure the proper development of Earth's emerging mind."

Her statement was met with stunned silence by everyone else in the room.

"How come I never knew about this?" Earl demanded.

Warmly grasping his colleague's shoulder, Andrew replied. "Sorry, old friend, you know what he's like about the secrecy of certain operations. He sealed the extended facilities behind temporal barriers himself and entrusted us with its maintenance."

"What will he do now you've revealed its existence?" Corrine wondered.

Thinking for a moment, Andrew scratched his chin. "Hell, I don't know, Corrine. It can't get any worse than it is, so hopefully he'll appreciate it has given us something to focus on. I don't know."

Another mental exchange took place between Andrew and Victoria. Andrew nodded and said, "Okay, so he'll probably kick my ass, but it will be worth it."

Suddenly businesslike, Earl replied, "Yes, it will be worth it! We might as well be prepared for what's coming. As you say, at least it will keep us busy."

Turning to the others, he began issuing orders to ensure each department was ready for a full scale mobilization of staff and resources at short notice, while ensuring emergency cover was not compromised in the meantime.

Andrew wandered off toward the TV area to await the list from which he would choose his staff.

Suddenly Earl turned to Victoria. "Victoria, you always seem to know where he is and how to contact him. I need Adam's permission if we're actually going to go ahead and do this. Where is he?"

She turned and got a faraway look in her eyes for a moment. "Sorry, he's busy. He said he'll be back after his appearance tomorrow and you can discuss things then."

Vladimir cut in. "You mean he's going ahead with that media circus event in the UK despite what the polls are saying? Is that wise?"

Victoria merely shrugged her shoulders before going to join Andrew over by the TVs.

As she sat down, she discovered Andrew was watching an Italian operatic production of "Cavalleria Rusticana." It was causing him to repeatedly shake his head and laugh quietly to himself.

"What's so funny?" Victoria asked, bemused.

He snorted. "You know how in action films, when they're fighting against overwhelming odds and everyone gives up except for one bright spark who says, 'It ain't over until the fat lady sings?'"

"Yeah, so what?"

Andrew nodded at the screen.

Victoria looked, and saw the image of a very fat lady kneeling beside an ex-lover, obviously dead, singing her heart out to a packed theater.

Andrew leaned in to whisper. "I just hope this tragic ending isn't symbolic of the results of Saturday's vote for us."

# Epilogue

*New Year's Day 2016*

"Once upon a time" is a common way for most fairy tales to begin.

Tales where the life journey of the main character is invariably depicted by the endless struggles they face and the grief they have to cope with, all packaged in a heart rending spiral of torment.

And just when you think it can't possibly get any worse, they end up facing an even greater catastrophe from which there seems to be no hope of salvation.

No hope that is, except for the intervention of a guardian angel, that special someone who steps in at the last moment to perform an act of kindness that protects the main character and allows them to live happily ever after.

Samantha Drake, although still exasperated by the antics of her son, was a firm believer in fairy tales.

She was awoken at dawn on New Year's Day by Joshua, while he used his bed as a trampoline. She lay listening to his unending energy, channeled into its usual boisterous outlet.

*Noise, noise, and more noise!*

She smiled to herself and reflected on that day, now months ago, when her dynamo of a little boy was almost taken from her. He wouldn't be alive today if it weren't for the intervention of a real life guardian angel.

As a mother, she couldn't care less that Joshua had been the first to be publicly rescued by the Guardians.

It wasn't important to her that subsequent inquiries by British officials to the Lord Concilliator's office had proved the mysterious benefactor to be none other than their Overlord himself.

*The Overlord!*

She was very relieved that someone had been there to save her boy. Although she had to admit, if the Overlord had the power to make him be quiet for a change, well, she would be even more impressed.

Samantha found the planned events for this New Year's Day a little daunting. Instead of the quiet day she had wanted with her family, recovering from the celebrations of the night before, she would be party to a major media event.

At noon later that day, she and her son would be the focus of the world's cameras when they would meet the man himself, the mysterious Adam. They would stand before all sorts of dignitaries and other important people who were determined to put Exeter on the map the very day before the biggest poll in history.

She wasn't happy about that, as she was aware they would probably have to run the gauntlet of Anti-Guardian protesters, and it would make her anxiety at being in the public eye even more acute than it was.

Fortunately, the new BBC correspondent she liked, Cathy West, would also be there. She was interviewing them both about the rescue, so it would hopefully remove some of the pressure she felt and give her someone to chat with afterward.

But waiting for it to actually happen? *Aaargh!*

Burying her head under the pillow, she wished fervently that she could skip a day so that it was all over. Being in the limelight was definitely not her scene.

*Goodness only knows what Joshua will do in front of the cameras*, she thought, *unless he's heavily sedated, gagged, and tied in a sack of course?*

Now that was a serious thought!

She let her mind go blank for a moment, wishing the day would just go away, when she suddenly realized Joshua was unusually quiet.

*Strange!*

Getting out of bed, she went to investigate.

She paused for a moment outside the door, checking for any indications of movement or sound, and thought she heard two people laughing quietly.

Opening the door, she was surprised to find Joshua sitting alone on his bed, holding what looked like a glass orb in his little fingers. He was fixated on the blooms of light in a myriad of rainbow colors that curled in spirals in and out of the orb. When they touched his hands, arms, even his face, he giggled quietly to himself as if the lights gave him pleasure.

Some of the tendrils flowed toward and around the top of his head where they flared into silver white suns of blinding intensity, surrounded by halos of gold and royal blue.

"What have you got there, Joshua?" she asked tentatively.

"It's my present for being a good boy and being very special," he announced proudly without even looking up.

"Special? Present? Who gave it to you, Joshua?"

Still fixated and giggling at the lights, Joshua replied, "My friend. He said I can have another one if I'm good today."

"What friend?"

Looking up at his mother as if she were unusually stupid, Joshua let go of the orb and it floated gently down onto his bedside cabinet.

"He's gone now, silly, but we'll see him again later. I like him, he has shiny eyes."

And with that, he got back into bed and fell almost instantly asleep. *Miracle!*

Samantha was too stunned to say or do anything, and just stood there for a few minutes looking backward and forward between the orb and her soundly sleeping son, as if she expected one of them to move again.

Then she glanced at the bottom of the bed, and clearly saw the imprint of where someone much larger had been sitting.

A tingle went down her spine. "Aah, I see. I hope his new friend can arrange for this every morning, I could do with sleeping in like a normal person for a change."

A voice echoed in her mind. *No promises, Samantha, but I'll see what I can do!*

The hairs on the back of her neck sprang to instant attention as she received the impression of luminous grey eyes set within a smiling face.

"No way!" she gasped, looking quickly about.

Picking up the orb, she placed it next to her blissfully sleeping child, whereupon it bloomed to life again, the tendrils bringing a smile to his little face.

Backing carefully and quietly out of the room, she stood there wondering what to do next, when she was brought back down to earth with a resounding *thump*. It was the sound of her hung-over boyfriend stirring in the next room, demanding his usual morning mug of tea.

*I knew it wouldn't last!*

Plodding downstairs to get the tea-kettle on, Samantha looked out of the kitchen window at the frost covered yard and the sky above. Billowing dark clouds were beginning to form overhead, blotting out the sun and causing an unexpected chill to pervade the entire house.

Shivering at the eerie silence it brought, she thought, *Knowing my luck, it'll probably all go downhill from here!*

# About the Author

Andrew P. Weston was born in the city of Birmingham, UK and grew up in the towns of Bearwood and Edgbaston, eventually attending Holly Lodge Grammar School for Boys where he was School Captain and Head Boy.

He was an active sportsperson and enjoyed rugby, martial arts, swimming, and was a member of athletics teams throughout the city.

On graduation in 1977, he joined the Royal Marines fulfilling a number of roles both in the UK and abroad.

In 1985, he became a police officer with the Devon & Cornwall Constabulary, and served in a variety of uniformed and plain clothed departments until his retirement in 2008.

Over those years, he wrote and illustrated a selection of private books for his children regarding the life of a tiny kitten, called *The Adventures of Willy Whiskers* and gained further qualifications in Law and Religious Studies. He was an active member of Mensa and continued to be an active sportsperson, providing lessons free of charge to local communities.

An unfortunate accident received on duty meant Andrew had to retire early from the police force, but after moving to the sunny Greek island of Kos to speed up his recuperation, he was at last able to devote time to the "Guardian Concept" he had developed over his years in the military and police.

When not writing, Andrew enjoys Greek dancing and language lessons, being told what to do by his wife, Annette, and hunting shadows in the dark.

...ion can be obtained at www.ICGtesting.com
...A
...012
...002B/4/P